The Dark
Rites
Of Cthulhu

Edited by

Brian M. Sammons

An April Moon Books Publication
Published in arrangement with the authors

Edited by Brian M. Sammons

For Jamie D. Jenkins
Not even with a whole bunch of words could I express
everything you mean to me, so I'll just use three: I love you. *Brian*

For my mum, my wife and my children.
None of whom should really be reading this book. *Neil*

UNMENTIONABLE RITES FOR NAMELESS HORRORS
By Brian M. Sammons

"He must meet the Black Man, and go with them all to the throne of Azathoth at the centre of ultimate Chaos. That was what she said. He must sign in his own blood the book of Azathoth and take a new secret name now that his independent delvings had gone so far. What kept him from going with her and Brown Jenkin and the other to the throne of Chaos where the thin flutes pipe mindlessly was the fact that he had seen the name "Azathoth" in the Necronomicon, and knew it stood for a primal evil too horrible for description."
H.P. Lovecraft, "The Dreams in the Witch House"

Sorcery, witchcraft, the occult, rituals, and black magic have all been a part of H.P. Lovecraft's weird world of horror, oftentimes collectively referred to as the Cthulhu Mythos, from the start. While many think of ancient, alien, god-like horrors when the topic of H.P. Lovecraft's stories are brought up, magic has always been at the heart of the Mythos. Whether it's the bloodthirsty cults who commit indescribable atrocities in the name of eldritch horrors they worship, or the ancient tomes penned by madmen, full of knowledge and rituals man was not meant to know, magic has always been there, promising unimaginable power, often delivering unbelievable torment

In some cases, vile thaumaturgy was what a Lovecraft story was all about. From "The Terrible Old Man" and his collection of strange bottles, to the horrifying secret behind "The Thing on the Doorstep." The magical melodies of "The Music of Erich Zann" brought only madness and worse, and "The Dreams in the Witch House" were never pleasant. Even Lovecraft's epic tale, "The Case of Charles Dexter Ward" was about forbidden sorcery and the price one inquisitive soul pays for meddling with it. In Lovecraft's world, magic is very real, and very dangerous. It doesn't heal the sick, mend broken glasses, or make brooms come alive to clean your house. It allows mankind to talk to the Great Old Ones, or worse, lets them bring the exiled horrors forth. It could smite a foe, or steal everything away from them, including their very body. While it could be used to cheat death, it could also inflict a horrible existence upon the unwary where death would be a sweat release. There were no Gandalfs or Dumbledores in Lovecraft's stories, only madmen with the desire to risk it all for the chance to play with power that should have always remained beyond their reach.

In that tradition of mankind meddling with forces beyond their control, here you will find 16 all new tales of Mythos tainted magic. The stories span time and space and explore all facets of the Black Arts. From cults full of true believers engaging in well-rehearsed ceremonies, to the lone practitioner following his own twisted plan. Here detectives will investigate ritualistic slaughter, and professors will try to keep arcane secrets out of the hands of those that would use them to their own selfish, and destructive, ends. Those with the talent for sorcery will pay a high price for their craft, and those seeking occult knowledge may soon regret their lifelong quest. Would be wizards will play with the very building blocks of reality, with damnation, madness, and death awaiting those that slip up even the slightest bit. This is where great power and greater danger walk hand in hand. These are The Dark Rites of Cthulhu.

Brian M. Sammons
February 12th, 2014

The Keeper of the Gate

William Meikle

THE KEEPER OF THE GATE
By William Meikle

We almost went off the road twice, lights flashing and sirens blaring, doing forty on the bends despite the snow. *Shots fired* was the message. We were too late to stop any bullets hitting their targets—and far too late to catch the shooter. Two bodies—two children—lay in the driveway, half-naked and already freezing, single gunshot wounds to the back of the head. The father sat in the hall just inside the door—shot in the left eye with an exit wound that had taken off the back of his skull and decorated the wall in Jackson Pollock red.

"Where's the mother?" Jake Rogers asked me, but I didn't have an answer.

We searched the house and did a tour around the outside. Ours were the only footprints in the snow, and there were none around the dead girls' bodies. No tire tracks either.

"Did the father do it, then do himself?" Jake asked.

"If so, where's the weapon?" I replied.

That had us both stumped.

We had a wait ahead of us—the forensics boys were tied up on another shooting downtown—Saturday night in the city this close to Christmas brought out more crazies than normal, and tonight was no exception. Jake and I were used to seeing shooting victims—just not out here in the 'burbs on the coast, and not pre-teen girls lying half-naked in snowy driveways. I'll admit I was more than a bit twitchy as we stood in the relative warmth of the hallway waiting for the cavalry to show up.

Matters didn't improve any when the chanting started up in the cellar.

"Didn't you check down there?" I whispered.

Jake had his gun out already.

"I thought you did."

The chanting got louder—there were at least three voices, maybe more.

Jake reached for the door handle. As soon as his fingers touched it the chanting stopped, like a needle taken off a vinyl record. Everything went quiet again.

"Cover me," Jake whispered, and pulled the door open.

There seemed to be nothing but darkness beyond, but Jake wasn't to be deterred. I followed him, gingerly, down the cellar steps.

"I don't think so," Jake replied, and pointed into the left-hand corner of the room.

At first it was just a darker shadow that seemed to suck the light away, leaving only bitter cold behind. My eyes strained to make out detail as the chanting rang in my ears and the room vibrated in sympathy. The light fitting swung lazily in time. My whole body shook, vibrating with the rhythm. My head swam, and it seemed as if the walls of the cellar melted and ran. The light receded into a great distance until it was little more than a pinpoint in a blanket of darkness, and I was alone, in a cathedral of emptiness where nothing existed, save the dark and the pounding chant.

I saw stars—vast swathes of gold and blue and silver, all dancing in great purple and red clouds that spun webs of grandeur across unending vistas. Shapes moved in and among the nebulae; dark, wispy shadows casting a pallor over whole galaxies at a time, shadows that capered and whirled as the dance grew ever more frenetic. I was buffeted, as if by a strong, surging tide, but as the beat grew ever stronger I cared little. I gave myself to it, lost in the dance, lost in the stars.

I don't know how long I wandered in the space between. I forgot myself, forgot Jake, dancing in the vastness where only rhythm mattered.

After a while I dreamed. I dreamed a funeral—an open coffin where Jake's pale face stared up at me, a face I could barely see through my tears. I stretched out a hand to touch his cheek.

A gunshot brought me back—reeled in like a hooked fish, tugged reluctantly through a too tight opening and emerging into the blazing light of a cold cellar.

Jake stood in a firing crouch, emptying a clip into the corner. I drew my own gun and joined in, despite not being able to see anything but darker shadow. My ears rang, almost deafened by the shots in the close confinement. All too quickly my trigger pulled on empty. The echoes died away leaving dead silence behind.

Jake and I stood in a quiet, empty cellar that suddenly felt warm and stifling. We took one look at each other and headed for the steps at a run. He beat me to it, just, but I was level by the time we barrelled through the hallway and stumbled, almost fell, out into the driveway. A blanket of cold stars mocked us from on high as we drove off, leaving a squeal of tires in our wake.

"What the fuck just happened?"

O'Hara's bar again, and more of the black stuff, helped down with whiskey. Jake hadn't spoken since we left the cellar, but at least his hands stopped shaking as we headed into the second pint of Guinness.

"Magician's tricks and fucking hocus-pocus," he said. "That's what fucking happened. I told you there was something hinky going on, I fucking told you."

What I'd seen—and felt—back in the cellar was a bit more than *hinky*, but I knew when to keep my mouth shut, if nothing else.

"We're onto something," Jake said. "Somebody just tried to warn us off."

"Actually, I think they succeeded," I said, and got more of the Guinness inside me, trying to make a warm spot in a body that still held too much memory of dancing a cold empty vastness.

Jake took out the small notebook—I'd forgotten all about it, but he'd had it in his pocket the whole time.

"This is it," he said. "This is the thing that will crack the case open for us."

I wasn't sure where he was getting his certainty, but I trusted his instincts. He started to rifle through the pages.

"Maybe we should just leave it alone?" I said. "I saw something back there. I…"

"I don't want to know," Jake replied. It wasn't fear in his eyes this time—it was pleading. "Whatever we saw, it was just a trick. What else could it be?"

That was a question I asked myself all the way home. I fell into bed, but sleep was a long time in coming. When I finally drifted off, I fell into dreams of dancing galaxies, naked women lying on crudely carved circles, and Jake's dead eyes staring up at me through my tears.

I didn't feel rested on wakening, and when I got to work we caught a drive-by shooting that took us most of the morning to wrap up. When we finally got a quiet minute back at the precinct, Jake pulled me aside next to the coffee machine.

"I showed Kaspervitch the notebook. He says it's a simple substitution cipher. He's working on it now. We should get the gen in an hour or so."

"And then what?" I asked. I was weary. I couldn't see an end on Jake's current path that I liked, and I kept seeing that last dream, of him in the coffin. I started to get a real bad feeling, and what I wanted more than anything else was to just lose myself in the daily grind and forget all about the Mitchell case. But Jake was my partner, and that bought him a lot of slack. I decided to back his play—for the time being at least.

He hadn't noticed my reticence.

"I told you—we'll crack this case wide open. We're onto something. I feel it in my water."

All I felt in mine was cold, a deep chill that even copious amounts of black coffee wouldn't shift. Jake whispered something as we went back to our desks. I didn't quite catch it, and didn't know how important it would prove.

"I've seen it."

"It's a diary," Kaspervitch said, dropping the notebook on Jake's desk and making Jake's fifty disappear into an inside pocket. "Dates and places, I'm guessing of some kind of business meetings, for a lot of the names in his email contacts turn up in there too. But if they are business meetings, the times and places are off—unless I've made a mistake, all these meetings take place in quiet spots, in the middle of the night."

Jake looked up at me and smiled.

"See—I told you it was hinky."

He turned to Kaspervitch.

"So when's the next one penciled in?"

"Two days' time—but he won't be there, will he?" Kaspervitch said.

"He won't. But we will," Jake replied. He had his game face on and the bit between his teeth. Nothing I could say now was going to make any difference. All I could do was tag along, and hope I could prevent the coffin dream from ever coming to pass.

The Thursday meeting was due for two in the morning in a disused warehouse in the docks. Jake and I got there early, around midnight. We parked well away from the place and walked in through the alleyways of derelict offices and factories. Both our fathers had worked here, way back when, and as kids we'd run together through these same docks, filled then with workmen and noise and vitality. Now they were as dead as the cellar beneath the Mitchell house, and damned near as cold. We took up a spot in the girders that made up what was left of the rafters of the warehouse, and tried to make ourselves comfortable for what might prove to be a lengthy stakeout.

Jake was quiet, scarily so, for I've rarely met a more voluble man, but he seemed content to sit and watch. He wouldn't allow any discussion of the events in the cellar. I couldn't really blame him for that—but I also couldn't help but wonder whether he had seen a dream of his own—and whether he might have been looking down at me in a coffin in his version.

My butt was starting to get numb from the cold seeping up through the girders when we finally saw some action. We were alerted firstly by the slam of car doors—two followed by a third a minute later. After a delay, three men, dressed in long, hooded robes that might have been comical in another situation, walked into the warehouse from the west-end and immediately started drawing diagrams and circles on the floor. The end result was all too familiar—it seemed to perfectly match the one that had been etched beneath Mrs. Mitchell's dead body.

I realized I was holding my breath, waiting for something—distant chanting maybe, or another vision of the cold depths of space. What I didn't expect was for one of the three figures to stand in the center of the diagram, turn, and look straight up at our position. "You can come down now," a deep male voice said. "The show's about to begin and you'll get a better view from here."

Jake didn't seem in the slightest surprised by the turn of events, leading me to wonder again what it was that he had seen in our time in the cellar. I was still wondering as we clambered down through a tangle of metal and girders to the floor of the warehouse.

The tall robed man was so polite it was almost surreal.

"Welcome, gentlemen," he said. "We've been expecting you."

"You saw it in advance, didn't you?" Jake said. "That's what you do—you use some kind of new trick to see what's going to happen."

"Oh, it's not a trick, I assure you," the robed man said. "And it's not new either—the Gatekeeper has been showing people the way since time began. You'll see for yourselves soon enough."

"I've got no intention of seeing any more," Jake said. He drew his gun and aimed it directly at the robed figure's chest. The other two—neither of whom had yet said a word, stood several paces further back, but showed no sign of getting involved.

"Jake," I whispered. "We can't do anything here. We've no proof of anything."

Jake waved his pistol towards the tall man.

"He did it—I know he did—he killed the Mitchell family."

The tall man laughed.

"Is that what this is about? I'm afraid you have it all wrong. Mitchell saw what needed doing at our last meeting. His wife was going to die—he saw it, and he knew it—that's the way it works. Once something is seen, it cannot be changed. Poor Mitchell couldn't handle it. He snapped—and you saw the results. And of course, his poor wife died anyway—such a shame."

He didn't sound in the slightest bit concerned, either at the death of Mitchell and his family, or by the fact he had a gun pointed at him.

Jake's earlier calm was rapidly being replaced by anger.

"That's not what happened—there's no way Mitchell could have done it—his gun was in the cellar."

"Oh, I did that," the tall man said casually. "I had to, you see—I saw it, so it had to happen. And I think I'm beginning to understand why it had to happen. It brought you here, to this place, this time. It brought you to the Gate. Yog-Sothoth has something for you to see."

We'd just taken a jump—another one—into the Twilight Zone. This wasn't going the way either of us would have predicted. Or rather, not as I would have predicted, for Jake seemed to know exactly what he was doing. He raised his gun.

The robed man drew a knife from up his left sleeve—a long curved thing with writing carved along the length of the blade.

"Put down your weapon, sir," Jake said.

"I assure you, it's purely ceremonial," he said, and raised it above his head.

"Put down the weapon or I'll shoot."

"You'll do what you have to do," the man said sadly. "I've already seen it."

He lifted the knife high, stepped forward and let out a yell.

"Ia!"

Jake put two bullets in him.

The tall man fell to the ground, grunted twice and coughed up blood all over the chalk circle.

Jake stood over the body, eyes glazed as if he was not really sure what he'd just done. I wasn't sure what to do about it—by rights I should have hauled him off downtown, but he was my partner—I trusted him. I just hoped I was going to be able to believe his reasoning.

As it turned out, I didn't have time to think. A colder chill blew through the warehouse, and behind it came the first distant sounds of chanting.

"Step out of the circle," one of the robed figures said. "Please, step out of the circle."

I took a step back—all that was needed to get me beyond the widest extent of the drawing—but Jake stood his ground, standing over the prone robed body.

The chanting got louder, the same dissonant mixture of singing, yips and screams we'd heard in the cellar.

"Jake—I think you should get out of there."

"Don't worry, pal," he said, grimly. "I know what needs doing—I've seen it."

The cold bit at my bones, and the chanting rose to echo and ring all around the warehouse. Something shifted—I can't describe it any better than that, and that's exactly what if felt like—a shifting to somewhere subtly elsewhere—or elsewhen.

It started small; a tear in the fabric of reality, no bigger than a sliver of fingernail, appeared in the center of the circle above Jake's head and hung there. As I watched, it settled into a new configuration, a black oily droplet held quivering in empty air.

The walls of the warehouse throbbed like a heartbeat. The black egg

13

pulsed in time. And now it was more than obvious—it was growing.

It calved, and calved again.

Four eggs hung in a tight group above Jake's head, pulsing in time with the rising cacophony of the chanting. Colors danced and flowed across the sheer black surfaces, blues and greens and shimmering silvers on the eggs.

In the blink of an eye there were eight.

I was vaguely aware of Jake shouting, but I was past caring, lost in contemplation of the beauty before me.

Sixteen now, all perfect, all dancing.

The chanting grew louder still.

Thirty two now, and they had started to fill the warehouse with a dancing aurora of shimmering lights that pulsed and capered in time with the throb of magic and the screams of the chant, everything careening along in a big happy dance.

Sixty-four, each a shimmering pearl of black light.

The colors filled the room, spilled out over the circle, crept around my feet, danced in my eyes, in my head, all though my body. I gave myself to it, willingly. The warehouse filled with stars, and we danced among them.

I strained to turn my head towards the eggs.

A hundred and twenty eight now, and already calving into two hundred and fifty-six.

Jake had tears in his eyes as he looked at me.

"This is how it has to be," he said.

The protective circle enfolded what I guessed to be a thousand and twenty four eggs. Jake lifted his gun and emptied the clip into them.

Several things happened at once. The myriad of bubbles popped, burst and disappeared as if they had never been there at all. Jake screamed—a wail that in itself was enough to set the walls throbbing and quaking. Swirling clouds seem to come from nowhere to fill the room with darkness. Everything went black as a pit of hell, and a thunderous blast rocked the warehouse, driving me down into a place where I dreamed of empty spaces filled with oily, glistening bubbles. They popped and spawned yet more bubbles, then even more, until I swam in a swirling sea of colors.

I drifted.

When I got back—was given back—to what passes for reality, thin daylight lit the floor of the warehouse. There was no sign of the two robed figures—nor of the body of the man that Jake had shot. The chalk circle on the floor, and any blood that had been there, had been scuffed and scraped into the dust so much that any forensics gathering would be almost impossible.

14

Jake lay on his back, dead eyes staring up at me.

I didn't shed a tear in the warehouse, but the funeral is later today. I have to do my best not to cry, but I fear that I will.

This is how it has to be.

Dead Man's
Tongue

Josh Reynolds

DEAD MAN'S TONGUE
By Josh Reynolds

"A man enters a room, carrying a strangely proportioned package. He is not seen again, until his screams alert his fellow tenants in the boarding house as to his distress. The door is busted open, and not one, but two bodies are found. The origin of the first is obvious, but the second—ah, that's the mystery, ain't it, Carter?" Harley Warren said. He rubbed his hands together gleefully and sank down onto his haunches just outside of the room in question.

"A mystery we should perhaps leave to the police, don't you think Warren?" Randolph Carter asked nervously. He and Warren were a study in contrasts. Carter, the tall, thin lantern-jawed expatriate from Massachusetts, and Warren, the short, stocky cat-eyed South Carolinian, made for an odd pair. Carter often found himself wondering how and why he was still in South Carolina, in Charleston, and still trundling in Warren's oft-disturbing wake. Times like these only made such moments of introspection occur more frequently.

"Seeing as the police are the ones who came to me about this here little conundrum, I'm going to go out on a limb and guess that they wouldn't be at all grateful in that regard," Warren drawled. Carter glanced back down the hall, where several uniformed Charleston police officers stood nervously. They'd come knocking sheepishly on Warren's door, and had escorted them to the boarding house where they now stood. Warren had an odd relationship with the local constabulary. For the most part, they were inclined to ignore him. But sometimes, something happened and men would come, seeking quiet consultation or, as in this case, something more active.

Carter had first visited Warren's Charleston residence seeking a consultation of his own. Then, as now, Warren had displayed a level of occult competency that Carter found both comforting and not a little frightening. Carter had sought relief from the night-terrors that flapped and squirmed and tickled his soul with rubbery talons and scorpion tails and Warren, opium-numbed and erratic as he was then, had guided him through the labyrinth of dreams that he had been trapped in. But he had found relief from one nightmare only to be propelled along new avenues of dread in the months since. Warren had set aside the dragon-pipe at Carter's insistence, but remained erratic; indeed, he had become almost predatory since Carter had moved in to the strange house on the Battery.

Warren now hunted the unknown through yellowed pages and across rolls of papyrus and cowhide, looking for any gleanings of old knowledge left behind. He looted tombs-or paid others to do so-and collected the detritus of centuries with compulsive glee. Warren collected the hideous and the beautiful in equal measure, and Carter occasionally suspected that he, too, was a part of his friend's collection, in some odd way. But the purpose of that collection still eluded him. Warren was hunting something, and Carter feared the day that he finally caught it.

Warren cocked his head and looked up at Carter. "If it's a strain on your delicate sensibilities, why don't you just beat feet and go back to scribbling out another penny dreadful for that hack, Wright?"

"Farnsworth is hardly a hack," Carter murmured. "Old Plato is quite a decent editor. And besides, you invited me to accompany you."

"A decision that I already have reason to regret," Warren said loudly. He hunched forward, balancing on his knuckles. "Does he look like he's been throttled to you?"

"Which—ah—which one are you referring to?" Carter asked. He plucked a handkerchief from his coat pocket and pressed it to his mouth and nose as he leaned over Warren and into the room. There were, as Warren had said, two bodies occupying the small square of space, one on the bed, and the other on the floor. The one on the floor was bad enough. He'd seen similar looking examples of mortality in the trenches of France; the dead man's face was twisted in an expression of horror, his eyes bulging and his tongue sticking out of his mouth.

But it was the body on the bed that drew most of Carter's disgust, and not a little worry. It was a shrivelled thing, it's dried and cracked flesh was shrunken tight to its bones and its body was curled into a loose ball. It was nude, so far as Carter could see, and he could tell that it stunk strongly of strange spices and exotic unguents, even from a distance. There were rags and shreds of what looked like brown, decaying linens scattered over the bed and the floor, as well as on the body of the dead man.

For a moment, he fancied that it had moved, ever so slightly, when he leaned in. He heard nothing, saw nothing, but even so, he felt it. And he froze, the way a mouse might freeze, when it feels a snake watching it.

"The one that don't look like jerky," Warren said. "And don't lean too far into the room." He swatted Warren on the shin with his knuckles.

"What? Why?" Carter said, startled from his paralysis. Warren didn't reply. Carter looked down at the body on the floor. It was clear that the man had indeed been throttled by some powerful grip. Even a layman such as himself could tell what those wide, dark bruises indicated. He looked up from the body and let his eyes scan the walls.

Someone, likely the dead man, had covered them in scraps of paper covered in strange markings that he recognized from several books in Warren's library. He had no idea what most of the markings meant, but, familiar or not, they seemed to swim before his eyes, crawling like insects across the badly patched and plastered walls. Shivering, he looked away. Those sigils he did recognize did not bode well.

Warren rose smoothly to his feet and ran his fingers along the door frame. Without entering the room, he reached around and felt the interior frame. "Ha," he said, "There we are."

"What is it?"

"Somebody was whittling," Warren said. He grabbed Carter's hand and forced his startled companion to feel the frame, even as the latter let out a squawk of protest. "See? He had himself a high old time with a buck knife, by the feel of it."

"Yes, I see that, thank you," Carter snapped and jerked his hand out of Warren's grip. "Is that pertinent?" His fingertips felt greasy where they'd touched the wood. His stomach roiled, and his eyes strayed to the leathery thing on the bed. He'd been studiously avoiding looking at it, but now he felt compelled. It was as if reaching into the room had drawn its notice. As before, he felt as if it were staring at him from beneath its brown, wrinkled lids. Between it and the unpleasant symbols stuck to the peeling wallpaper, he was feeling decidedly nervous.

"Ain't you the one who reads all those detective stories? Everything is pertinent," Warren said. He tapped Carter between the eyes with a finger, snapping him out of his reverie. "Clues, Carter," he said.

"Yes, clues, I understand, thank you," Carter said, slapping ineffectually at Warren's hand. He rubbed his fingers together and looked at the doorframe again. "What was that I felt? I—I can remember touching something of similar shape and convolution before, though I can't…I can't seem to recall where."

Warren peered at him for a long moment before replying. Carter had the feeling that he was choosing his words very carefully. "It's the sign of Koth, Carter. You've probably seen it in one of my books, when you were making notes for your little stories."

"I—yes, obviously," Carter said, pushing aside the hazy, half-formed not-quite memories of a certain black tower, standing alone in the twilight vale of his dreams. He shook himself and rubbed his arms. Such dreams were one of the reasons he'd come seeking Warren's help in the first place, and he didn't care to be reminded of them. He blinked as Warren's words sank in and said, "Little stories?"

"Focus, Carter," Warren said and snapped his fingers. He looked back at the room. "Only reason a fellow might want to carve that particular sign on his door, or put them other ones up on the walls, is to keep something out." He frowned, as if something unpleasant had occurred to him and added, "Or in."

Carter wrung his hands nervously. He felt a thrill of fear. He'd seen that look in Warren's eyes more than once in their brief, but eventful, association. It was something more than curiosity; it bordered on obsession. "Warren—Harley—perhaps we should call someone…"

"Carter, I surely do hate to tell you this, but I *am* who people call for something like this," Warren said. He knocked on the doorframe and then, before Carter could stop him, stepped into the room.

Carter held his breath. Warren turned in a slow circle, looking about him. He murmured soft words that Carter didn't quite catch, under his breath. The thing on the bed didn't so much as twitch. Carter wondered why he'd thought it might.

Warren went to the small writing desk opposite the bed and sifted through the papers there. "Shipping receipts," he murmured, "Iceland." He looked back at the bed. "Is that where you're from?"

"They have mummies in Iceland?" Carter asked, still staring at the thing on the bed. "Are those markings on the walls Icelandic as well? Have we stumbled upon some ancient rite from the sagas?" he asked excitedly, forgetting his fear, momentarily, in a rush of curiosity. "Wait until I tell Conrad and Kirowan!"

"They have mummies everywhere, Carter," Warren said. "And no, those markings are not Icelandic. They're Tibetan." He sank down beside the body on the floor. "You don't happen to recognize him, do you?" he asked. "Come on in, get a good look."

"I'd rather not, if it's all the same to you," Carter said.

"Carter--get in here," Warren said.

Carter grimaced and stepped into the room. He watched the thing on the bed as he did so, though he couldn't say why. Surely it was no threat? He looked down at the dead man. He was no threat either. He looked down at the man's death-mottled features and shook his head. "No, I don't know him. Do you?"

"Nope. Pity, I was hoping to learn who it was who thought they were going to perform the rite of *rolang* here in this pleasant little domicile," Warren said.

"The rite of what?" Carter asked. Instinctively, his hand dug for the small moleskin notebook and pencil stub he habitually kept in his coat.

"Don't you dare pull that damn notebook out," Warren snapped. He reached inside his own coat and extracted a heavy, antique revolver from a shoulder holster. The pistol was a LeMat, a Civil War era revolver that Warren had some attachment to, despite its age and unwieldy size. Warren had never shared the origin of that attachment with Carter, despite the latter's numerous attempts to pry it out of him. "You're going to have your hands plenty full with this."

"What?" Carter stepped back, hands raised in protest. "I'm not the sort for guns, Warren."

"Take the pistol, Carter. I need you to hold it for me for a minute," Warren said, flipping the revolver around so that he proffered the butt to Carter. Carter made a face, but took the weapon. It was heavy in his hand, far heavier than the pistol he'd carried in France during the Great War. In its own way, it was as much a relic of ancient times as the thing on the bed.

"Fine," he said. "Now would you mind telling me what you're talking about? What is this--this 'roh-lang' you mentioned?" He hesitated, struck by an unpleasant notion. "It doesn't have anything to do with that business in Arkham last year, does it?" he asked quietly.

"Not quite," Warren said, smiling slightly. "You'll recall I spent some formative time in Tibet?" He pushed himself to his feet and dusted his hands. "I learned a lot in those mountains. Mostly things I'd rather not know, but you can't always pick your lessons or your teachers, if you catch my meaning." He grinned crookedly and Carter felt a shiver pass through him, though he couldn't say why. Warren went to the bed and looked down. "At any rate, there are certain men of power in the hinterlands of Tibet who swear by the rite of the rolang. They spoke of signs and marks like those plastered on the walls, and told me of scenes just like this one here, rolang and all."

"And what, pray tell, is a rolang?" Carter asked.

Warren gestured to the thing on the bed. "That handsome fellow right there.'Rolang' roughly translates as 'corpse who stands up' or some such, depending on the dialect." He scratched his chin and looked down at the brown thing.

"He's--ah--he's not standing up," Carter said. His skin crawled at the thought even as he said it. He had an image in his head, of burying grounds full of crawling, rising corpses, and he clutched himself as a cold chill ran through him.

"You sound disappointed." Warren shoved his hands in his pockets and leaned forward. "This particular rite involves a prepared body, often that of a sorcerer or a lama, and a sealed room. The undertaker of the ritual, whom I'm guessing was the fellow on the floor, and is almost always a wizard, gets on top of the body, repeating a certain formula to awaken the spirit slumbering in the corpse. The corpse gets frisky, tries to escape, and the wizard must hold it down until he can bite off its tongue."

Carter made a sound of disgust. "And if he fails?"

"The rolang kills him. As it will kill any other living thing that it gets its leathery paws on," Warren said serenely as he bent low over the withered features of the thing on the bed. "Nasty thing, a dead sorcerer. Ain't that right, Mr. Rolang?" Warren went on, as if speaking to the thing.

Carter felt a thrill of horror as he saw its eyelids twitch. The LeMat bobbed up in his grip, almost of its own volition. Warren carefully pushed the barrel aside. "Whoa there, not yet Carter," he said.

"It moved!"

"That it did, but that ain't no call to plug it quite yet. Probably wouldn't do any good anyway," Warren said.

"If it can move, why didn't it leave?" Carter demanded.

"I did mention that the room was sealed, didn't I?" Warren said, gesturing to the doorframe.

"It was trapped," Carter said. He felt a sinking sensation in his gut.

"Yep," Warren said, still examining the thing.

"It was trapped and you brought us in here with it?" Carter nearly shrieked. The LeMat came up again, and again Warren gently pushed it aside.

"You're in no danger, Carter, now calm down!"

"Why would you do this?" Carter hissed, backing away from the bed. Warren's hand shot out and snapped closed on his wrist, trapping him. Carter tried to yank his arm free of Warren's grip, but to no avail. Warren was surprisingly strong when he put his mind to it.

He dragged Carter close and snapped, "I said calm down." His eyes flashed weirdly, and he let Carter go. "This thing will be dangerous now that it's been woken up. Sorcerers always are, alive, dead or otherwise. The ritual, once started, must be finished, or the rolang could escape to cause harm to any who cross its path." Warren looked back at the thing on the bed. "Can't have some poor policeman or other getting throttled by our guest here, now can we?"

"What--what are you going to do?"

"Just stay back, Carter. And don't hold that gun like it's a damn snake. It's just a pistol, for God's sake," Warren said.

"What should I do if it gets up?" Carter asked hesitantly.

"Well...shoot it, obviously," Warren said, as he got onto the bed and straddled the corpse. "And try to avoid hitting me, if you can possibly help it."

"But you said that the gun wouldn't work," Carter said.

"No, I said it probably wouldn't do any good. But it couldn't hurt. Not much on this earth can take a face full of sixteen gauge buckshot and keep smiling." Warren smiled crookedly. "At the very least, it'll give you time to get out the room."

"Warren--Harley..." Carter began.

But Warren wasn't listening. As he positioned himself over the corpse, it began to heave and twitch, its limbs flailing flaccidly beneath Warren's own. Warren pinned the corpse to the bed with his weight and held on for dear life. Carter tensed, ready to lend his meagre weight to the fight, regardless of Warren's warning to the contrary.

The corpse heaved, and Warren was nearly thrown from it. It bucked and thrashed, and its spidery limbs uncoiled. Its jaws sagged open, and the air throbbed with a basso hum that made Carter's teeth itch. It sounded as if a hundred voices were speaking at once, and the things they were saying crawled on the air like flies on a screen. Strange shadows grew on the walls, cast by nothing visible to the human eye. The air felt damp and heavy, as if there were a thunderstorm brewing.

Warren cursed as thin fingers stabbed into his arms. The corpse made a sound like a punctured tire, and Warren was shoved up and back as the rolang began to sit up. He grabbed at it, struggling with it. Its fleshless jaws champed mindlessly as its fingers sought his throat. Carter cried out and raised the pistol, but he couldn't get a clear shot. Warren tumbled backwards, the rolang atop him. It had him by the throat. He clawed at its head, fighting to keep its jaws from his face.

"Warren, damn it, get away from it," Carter shouted.

"No," Warren hissed, forcing the rolang's head back. His face was beginning to turn red as the thing's grip on his throat tightened. Carter hesitated, and then lunged forward. He hooked the rolang's neck with his arm and pulled it back, trying to force it to break its grip on Warren. He pounded on its skull with the butt of the LeMat. The dead thing twisted around bonelessly, and far faster than he was prepared for. It released Warren and grabbed for Carter, shoving him back. He staggered away from the bed, and the thing followed with rickety steps, jaws chattering.

"Warren, help me!" Carter yelped.

"I told you to stay back, Carter," Warren shouted, stumbling off of the bed. He wrapped his arm around the rolang's neck and tried to haul it away, to no avail. It forced Carter back against the wall. "Shoot the damn thing!"

Carter twisted his head away and shoved the barrel of the revolver up against the creature's sunken belly. He pulled the trigger and the roar of the pistol was followed by the sound of splintering bone and tearing flesh. Warren gave a triumphant yell and drove his foot up into the thing's back. It bent backwards. Warren jerked his arms and there was another, louder, crack and the thing's head came away in his hands.

The fallen body squirmed like a broken-backed snake, grabbing blindly for Carter's ankles as it slithered after him across the floor. Carter looked to Warren for help, and saw him raise its head in his hands. A black, swollen tongue protruded from between its jaws and Warren caught it between his teeth in a single, sinuous movement. As Carter looked on in horrified wonder, Warren jerked his head and tore the tongue from the rolang's head.

The body stiffened and fell still. Warren dropped the head and took the tongue from his mouth. "There we go," he wheezed, "Easy as pie."

"It almost killed you," Carter said. Then, "It almost killed me!" He looked around the room. The shadows had cleared, and every scrap of paper had fallen from the walls.

"But it didn't," Warren said, weighing the tongue on his palm. "No sir, it did not. And now the ritual is done, and our Mr. Rolang is safely over the River Styx."

They stared down at the body for long moments. Carter fought to catch his breath. He could hear the policemen on the stairs, talking loudly, but apparently making no move to investigate the gunshots.

"You never said what the ritual was for," Carter said, finally.

"Hmm?" Warren said, still examining the tongue. He hadn't taken his eyes off of it since he'd torn it free of the dead thing's head.

"The ritual. Why would someone undergo such a hideous experience?"

Warren held up the withered lump of meat. Carter thought, for a moment, that he might drop it. Instead, he stuffed it into his pocket.

"Why does anyone do anything, Carter?" Warren said, and smiled.

The Dark Horse

John Goodrich

THE DARK HORSE
By John Goodrich

The dry, yellow wind off the Dominion of Manhattan brought a bitter scent to Laura's nose. The building's broken windows and splintered doors moaned in the acrid wind. She'd holed up in this apartment because the door was still on its hinges. Something skittered behind her. Laura whirled, spear at the ready. A filthy raccoon with one pus-filmed eye twice the size of the other glared at her from the doorway. She tensed, ready to pin it to the floor. The coon crouched. They considered each other, the wind's low dirge the only sound for long moments.

Laura reached behind her with one hand, and found a crinkly wrapper by feel. She tore it open with her teeth, and flung it at the coon. She didn't like to waste food, especially something as good as a Twinkie, but she didn't want trouble from the coon, either. With that eye, it wouldn't be good to eat.

The coon sniffed her offering, then tore big bites out of the golden cake. She watched it gulp the yellow thing down, then lick the plastic wrapper clean, manipulating its treasure with humanlike front paws. It glared at her with its good eye, then limped out the doorway.

She ought to follow it, find out if it knew where any food was. But she'd eaten well for days, and wasn't feeling hard up. She could afford a little generosity. The apartment building had been good to her: a safe place to sleep, good forage, and no one else around. Eating from old cans was a lot easier than scrambling after rats and roaches.

Laura threw some wood and paper on the coals of her small fire, and soon the flames leapt high. The night was cold, and the fire would be dead by the time she woke. She should have closed the door to keep the coons, cats, and dogs out. With the fire warming the concrete floor, she threw an old rug over herself and curled into a ball. She hoped she wouldn't dream.

She woke with a start to see a man squatting before her fire. Before she was fully awake, she had rolled into a defensive crouch, spear in hand, ready to kill. He just raised his hands, showing her that he had no weapons.

"I just want a can of your food, some time by your fire, and a little talking."

"I got the clap and AIDS." Her voice was gravelly and rough. She hadn't spoken to anyone for more than a month. "Do me, and your cock'll rot."

His eyes were sad.

"I don't want that."

She'd heard that before. Looking him up and down, he didn't look like the men from the Dominion. She noted a big knife in a belt sheath, and the way he kept his hands away from it. An unkempt mane of white hair cascaded down his shoulders. A long-healed scar ran across his temple, just below the hair line. His skin was dark and weather-beaten, a flowing white beard covered much of his face. The long leather coat was only just more travel-stained than he. A heavy carry-bag was slung across one shoulder.

"What's your name?"

The rumbling undertones in his voice reminded her of her father, kind and strong. But that was no reason to trust him. She adjusted her grip on her spear.

"What kind of food do you want?"

"A can of whatever you're willing to spare." He was still on his haunches, warming his hands over her little fire.

"We'll see. What did you want to talk about?"

"Can I at least know your name? Mine is Travis Dornier, and I've come a long way to see you."

"What do you mean?"

"I want to know your name, so I can be sure you're the right person."

She eyed him warily.

"Sheila."

"That's not it and you know it."

"Mary."

"I'm not going away until I learn your name. It's important."

He didn't seem like a sorcerer. They had people to do things for them. They didn't go wandering around alone. She might not understand magic, she'd never heard that anyone needed your name to cast a spell on you.

That wasn't enough reason to trust him, though. They were playing this stupid game about her name, and she could feel him trying to make her like him. She looked him over again. He was lean, probably stronger than her, but she could outrun him no problem. She didn't want to talk with him, but the need for company welled up in her.

"Laura," she conceded.

"I wondered if it was."

He reached for his bag, and her spear was at the alert again. With one hand, he made a placating gesture.

"I'm not going to hurt you. I would never hurt you."

He took a blue box from his bag. It was glossy and shiny, with a picture of a girl. Laura held her breath. She was beautiful, the way only people from Before could be. She had long yellow hair and fine, pale skin that hadn't seen a lot of sun. And yet, there was something sad and perhaps lonely about her. Inside the box were the mirrored disks that told stories of the Before time.

"What's this?"

"Laura, I've waited more than ten years, and come more than three thousand miles to meet you. I'm so relieved to finally be in your presence."

"Me? You've come to see me?" She tightened her grip on her spear. "What's this about?"

"Do you see the girl on this box? She was the chosen one who would stand against the Masters – "

"Liar. No one knew about the Masters in the Before Time."

He looked down at the fire before he spoke again.

"Some of us did. Some even tried to warn everyone before the Corpse City rose, and the world went mad and the dead were piled as high as buildings."

Laura shuddered. Though years gone, she remembered the nauseous, omnipresent stench of the corpse-piles, some half the size of city blocks. For a moment, there was no sound but the low dirge of the wind.

"Maybe if we'd tried harder . . ." He didn't finish the thought. "We failed. And a lot of people died. But now I have found you, the new chosen one. And you can put this right."

There was a lump in the pit of her stomach.

"Me?"

"You, Laura. If you cannot drive the Masters back under the ocean, no one can."

"What can I do? I'm just me."

"You are more than you know, Laura. The girl on the box, her name was Laura, too. If I could, I would tell you all the stories on these disks. Stories of her bravery, how she did not give up when everyone around her had."

Laura vaguely remembered the big windows that told the stories on the disks. She hadn't thought about them for a long time. She glanced at the broad, dark window in the apartment, but it was just so much junk, like most Before stuff.

"And you are like her, Laura. You are chosen, the one that can, that will, defeat the Masters, drive them back to where they came from, and make the world like it was."

Laura's goals were simple: find untainted food, locate shelter, stay away from the Dominion of Manhattan. Now, there was an unfamiliar feeling inside her, almost a hunger of the soul. She pondered her two-fingered right hand, maimed long ago when some dogs had chased her down. She had other scars, too. A large pucker where a cat had torn a chunk out of her shoulder, three thick lines across her breast where a dog had scratched her. She had a short line across her belly, and two on her left forearm from men with knives.

"It won't be as it was, not for a long time. But if you listen to me, and do as I say, you can kill the Masters, kill them all. And then, peace."

"The Dominion's tower for women?"

"No more tower."

"The Lord of Manhattan?"

"Destroyed utterly."

"Impossible. The Masters are as big as buildings. What can I possibly do against them?"

"Do you know any magic, Laura?" He said it slow and long. She shook her head, resisting his enticing tone.

"Magic is only for the Masters and the people they favor."

"There is more than that. I have a spell that I want to teach you."

The thought thrilled through her. To have that power, to be a sorcerer, like the Lord of Manhattan.

The noises he made were an unintelligible jumble of mixed sounds.

"Repeat it."

She did her best.

"No. Say it again."

She did.

"No. Do it again."

"How will I know?"

"You will know. Say the words again."

She did.

"Did I get it right?"

His sour look did not indicate success. He repeated the words, and then she did. She tried to hear the difference between what they were saying, but she ended up randomly emphasizing this word or that. And then, after ten minutes, a hot spark flew from her mouth, and she tasted tin. Her hands flew to her mouth. Her teeth were hot, her breath scorching. And she saw the triumph in his eyes.

"Now, say the words again."

She did, and got it wrong.

"Again."

The taste of tin returned. Her mouth dried out with the heat of it.

"Once more."

She got it right instantly. Her tongue felt like it had been left in the sun for days.

"You must say it to yourself every morning, and every night before you go to sleep."

"Will it kill the Masters if I say it to them?"

"It's not that kind of spell. But if enough people say it, chanting it at the same time, it will kill all the Masters."

An awe mixed with fear welled up in her.

"How many?"

"It has to be at the right time, said by thousands of people. As many as you can teach. And when the time is right, we will destroy them all." A fire lit in his eyes as he said it.

"How long will I have?" She was disappointed that she wouldn't be able to simply point her finger and destroy the Masters or their servants. In the wake of the ruined fantasy, hope remained.

"Laura, tell nobody that you are the chosen one. If the Masters or their slaves catch wind of it, they will stop at nothing to kill you. For your own safety, say nothing to anyone."

"I won't."

His hand shot out, and he grasped her with painful strength.

"You must promise me. Promise you won't tell anyone." She tried to yank her hand away, but his grip was hard, and his fingers sank into her flesh.

"All right, I promise."

He let her go.

"I didn't want to hurt you. But you have to understand how important it is that no one else knows."

It didn't feel right, but he'd given her the key to the world, shown her who she truly was. He looked away from her, his mouth set in a deep frown, eyes down as if searching for something on the floor. She wanted to say something so he wouldn't feel bad.

"When will the time be right?"

"Not for a while."

"But you'll tell me."

He shook his head.

"I won't be here." She felt a stab of fear. "I have a lot of research and preparation to do."

"You'll be staying at least a little while?" She felt lost. How would she know what to do as the chosen one if he didn't guide her? A part of her wondered how she'd come to need him so much. She regarded him again. Only her small fire held back the darkness. He looked strange and sinister with flickering shadows thrown against his face.

"I cannot. I have spent years finding you, Laura, perhaps too many.

If it isn't too late, I can proceed with the next stage of my plan."

"But what do I do?" She sounded desperate in her own ears.

"Teach. Travel, find other people who have escaped the Masters. Teach them that peace is coming, and that if we all act together, Cthulhu and his spawn will be destroyed."

She shuddered at the dread name.

"When?"

"If I am not with you, I will send green lights into the sky that you will not be able to miss, no matter where you are."

"You can do that?"

For the first time, he smiled. It made his face warm, and she felt herself liking him even more.

"I can do many things. And this . . . this is important. Do me proud, Laura. Say the words every morning after you get up and every night before you sleep. Teach those who are willing. You are the chosen one. If you cannot destroy Masters, no one can."

He reached out and she thought he was going to caress her cheek, but instead he claimed a can of food, which he stowed in his pouch. She sat, silently amazed, as he walked into the darkness. After several minutes of listening to his footsteps recede, she closed the door.

Laura's mind whirled for the rest of the night, thinking about what Dornier had said. It kept echoing through her head; that she was the one person who could eliminate the Masters, possibly even sink the Corpse City back into the ocean.

She did not forget herself so much that she didn't keep an ear out. She woke from sleep to hear a pack of dogs on the ground below, but they passed by without stopping.

In the Before time, dogs had been pets, and people slept safe at night. In the Before time, Mom and Dad had watched over her. Before Mom had been torn apart and eaten. Dad had lasted three more years, until an infected bite had gotten him. She remembered staring in terror at his still form, unable to believe that he would never move again. She stood vigil for two days, not eating, not drinking, waiting for him to get back up. Watching his skin sink and turn grey. She tried to keep the insects away, but there had been too many. Dogs had ended her vigil, chasing her away and reducing her father's carrion to scraps and bone. Laura hadn't remembered that for a long time.

So many people lost, until now she was alone. She remembered friendly people, and smiling faces. She couldn't bring them back. The world hadn't always been this way. Dornier had given her the means to make it better, to make it free from danger. As she thought about it, there was nothing she wouldn't do to get that sense of safety back.

Her fire had faded to embers, and she shivered in the chill darkness.

She whispered the words to herself, and felt the hot spark fly out of her. This was how she would to set things right.

At first, Laura skulked around the fringes of the Dominion of Manhattan. She didn't even try to talk to the men. They were all crazy because their women were locked up in the tower. They feared the Lord of Manhattan more than death. Boys were interested enough to talk with her, and she could outfight or outrun them easily.

None of them remembered the time Before, but she found that if she made promises about the destruction of the Masters, they cooperated. She taught them the spell, and told them when it was for, and they promised to repeat it when they were alone. She seldom saw any of them again. She wondered how many of them would practice like she told them, before going to sleep at night and first thing on waking.

Winter was difficult, as it always was. Laura knew how not to leave tracks for a hunting party to stumble across. If someone armed with a gun found her, that would be the end, chosen one or not. She watched the night sky for any hint of green, but the remote stars were all that stood in the unending black. She wished Dornier would meet her again. She had so many questions.

When summer came, with the hot, humid weather the fish-men didn't like, she decided to take a greater risk than just talking to boys. All the women in Manhattan were kept in an old tower made of ornate stone, about five miles from the Lord of Manhattan's court. It was old, but solid. A fence surrounded it, and above the second floor, the windows were covered with chain-link fencing. Inside this perimeter, fish-men patrolled, rifles in their large, web-fingered hands, their unblinking eyes ever watchful.

Laura found another building like it, several abandoned blocks away, and learned how to climb the outside. At first, her efforts were clumsy and loud, dislodging fragments of stone, dropping them noisily into the street below. Every time she slipped, or raked her fingers bloody on the unforgiving walls, she reminded herself that she was the chosen one. She could do it. At night, when her fingers wouldn't stop throbbing and her muscles ached, the knowledge gave her comfort. After some weeks, she learned to wedge herself quietly into windows, and grip the cracks between stones. She would teach the women in the tower the spell. No one would want to destroy the Masters more.

After a month, she began to climb in the dark. She learned a slow, stealthy pace that didn't disturb the roosting pigeons until she reached up and grabbed them. She ate well. All that was left was to wait for a sweltering day followed by a hot, airless night.

The cruel Manhattan weather did not make her wait long. The Sun dragged across a sky of molten metal, and the air was heavy with the reek of asphalt. Laura spent the day in the shade, her breathing shallow, mind racing at the prospect of the hot night ahead. She was slick with perspiration, and the death of the Sun brought no relief. It was time.

She threaded her way through the piles of discarded and rusting cars, keeping eyes and ears open for fish-men. She hid behind a burned-out hulk of a car, watching the fenced perimeter that surrounded the tower. Enormous hybrids in ill-fitting clothes patrolled the inside of the fence with listless motion, rifles slung across their backs. Laura nearly gave up and sneaked off at the sight of their glassy and unblinking eyes, but she thought of Dornier, and being able to make everything right. When a patrolling sea-devil had shuffled into the omnipresent dark, she ran to the fence, vaulted up with a clatter of metal on metal, sprinted to the building and started to climb.

She was nearly at the second floor before the fish-man came back to the fence, rifle at the ready. Laura froze, barely daring to breathe, and tried to press herself closer to the building's hot stones. How good was their hearing? She was sweating freely, would they be able to smell her with their flat nostrils like cut holes in their faces? Her heart hammered, and she felt her grip slipping, and perspiration seeped into her eyes, stinging like ants. Below her, the fish-man grunted, and was joined by a second one. Their movements were sluggish in the simmering heat. Laura's arms burned as she clung to the side of the building, still as a stone. How good was their hearing? Would they hear if she shifted her hand? They would see her if only they looked up. They were so close. She could have landed on them, but she would never be able to overpower their hideous strength.

Eventually, they moved on, croaking guttural imprecations. Laura didn't know if sweat or tears ran down her face. Her arms were cramped from being locked in one position, but she forced them to work, feeling for grip points and toeholds, hauling herself up.

The third-floor windows were covered with chain-link fence. Laura thanked the Masters for their consideration. With very little room, she gripped the window ledge with her toes, and clung to the fence. She couldn't reach the window, and just as she was wondering how to contact anyone inside, a gaunt face appeared in the window.

They stared at each other. Laura hadn't expected the women in the tower to be pretty, but she hadn't anticipated anyone this haggard. The face that looked at her was so worn that Laura couldn't begin to guess her age. She was frail, with colorless hair surrounding her head like a gossamer halo. Tattered rags barely covered her swollen belly. Seeing Laura, she, pressing one fist to her mouth, reached out with the other.

The window opened only a little, just enough for the stranger to get her hand under the sash and toward the wire fence. Her fist smothered a sob when Laura touched her stick-like fingers. At first, she didn't know what to say, clinging to the side of the building, staring at the weary, desperate woman who clutched at her fingers.

"What's your name?" She whispered it for want of any other question.

She moved her fist and said, "Monica," her voice was tentative and achingly fragile, just within hearing. "You have to get us out of here."

"I don't know how."

Tears glistened in Monica's eyes. Laura looked beyond her, and saw lumped forms lying on the floor, sleeping or shifting uneasily. Cats lived better than this.

"I have something that can destroy the Masters. Get rid of them all."

Hope flared in Monica's eyes, and the realization of how young she was hammered into Laura's gut.

"Can you do it right now?"

"No. I have to teach you. And then we have to wait for the right time."

Monica gestured to her distended belly, tears of frustration streaming down her cheeks.

"I can't wait. I can already feel its claws."

Laura avoided the desperate eyes. What could she tell Monica? She was doomed. The pregnancies of the fish-men ended with screaming and blood. She didn't know when Dornier would turn the sky green. Would it be days? Weeks? Years?

"But you can teach it to the others."

Laura watched as Monica's newfound hope was snuffed out. Her worn, despairing face looked away and then back, seeking any sort of solace. They gripped each other's fingers, as tears ran down the pregnant woman's face.

"We can stop this from happening again," Laura whispered. "If we can kill them, they won't do this to anyone else, ever."

Monica opened her mouth, but nothing came out. Laura could do nothing but hold her fingers as she silently wept. After some time, Laura couldn't tell how long, Monica straightened up and wiped at her tears.

"Teach me."

Laura whispered the spell, her mouth filling with the taste of hot tin. It took a long time for Monica to get it right, with Laura whispering encouragement from the other side of the fence, correcting her pronunciation as best she could. Her arms and legs were shaking with fatigue, but she hung on, desperate for Monica to get it right. Then Monica's frail hands flew to her mouth. Laura had her repeat it twice more, to get her used to the taste, and the exact words.

"Teach the others, but don't let the fish-men know. Whisper it to yourself before you go to sleep, and when you get up in the morning. When the sky turns green, it will be time."

"Make it soon." The pleading in Monica's eyes and voice was almost more than Laura could bear. She gripped Monica's fingers, hoping the frail, imprisoned woman could take strength, or hope, or anything from the contact. Only when her trembling limbs threatened to fail did she let go. She stretched as best she could, and prepared her aching muscles for the descent. Her final glimpse of Monica was of the skinny, pale face nearly lost in shadows. Then Laura was on the ground, over the fence, and running into the darkness before the fish-men could respond.

She spent the next day collecting food, and set off North, across the river, and away from the Dominion of Manhattan.

At first, the country looked much the same, with ruined concrete, steel, and stone towers, but they got shorter as she walked away from Manhattan. After days of walking, the buildings became houses, and twisted, malevolent-looking trees crowded in on her. She touched one and found it wept a goo which burned like a knife cut. Other bloated and quaking plants squished underfoot.

Laura had never been outside the Dominion of Manhattan. Her hunting and escaping skills served her well in this savage green place. Often, she killed only to discover her prey had some sort of rot or grotesque growing out of it. These she abandoned. Only once was she desperate enough to eat a healthy-looking part of a deer whose putrid, blackened skin was peeling away from its ribs. The days of vomiting and chills in the middle of summer were enough to teach her that it was better to go hungry.

In the wilderness, she found small enclaves of humanity that resisted the Masters' grip. Or at least, were too small to be noticed. Most drove her off with gunfire, but a few welcomed her. To these, she taught the spell, always pointing to the sky, waiting for it to turn green. She would stay for a few days, and always leave alone.

Seasons passed. She grew lean and hard, her skin darkened with sun and travel.

After three summers, at the hottest peak of the year, Laura saw a Master. A bloated, flabby, man-like body with a cancerous, tentacled head waded through the trees like a man in a pond. She was paralyzed with horror by the impossible size, and cringed on the ground, driving her teeth into the stubs of her missing fingers to keep from screaming. The ground shook as the colossal aberration shattered trees with its passing, and Laura wept with sick fear hours after it was gone. How could she ever stand against something so mighty? When Dornier spoke of dealing with the Masters, it had seemed like a pretty dream. Confronted with their enormous reality, despair clawed at her. She repeated the spell over and over, letting each hot spark fly up to the sky, each one a wish that the Masters would be destroyed.

The next morning, weak after a night without sleep, she decided to return to Dominion of Manhattan. She wanted to see if the children remembered, and teach them again, if necessary. How large had Dornier's rebellion grown? How many people whispered the spell to themselves at night and the first thing in the morning? She didn't know how many times she had repeated it. The hot spark of success no longer surprised her, and she could taste nothing but hot tin.

The return to Manhattan was long, and every night, Laura looked to the sky, hoping for some hint of green. Monica would be dead, she knew. Even now, the thought saddened her. There would be fewer women left, but she would have to visit the tower again.

On a warm and clear morning, she saw again the familiar broken skyline of the Dominion of Manhattan across the great river. Conflicting emotions roiled in her. She was relieved to be home, even though the memory of Monica and the women in the tower lurked in the back of her mind.

The Lord of Manhattan had changed his ways in her absence, and Laura crept into a trap as she tried to sneak across the great, creaking bridge. Men and sea-devils with guns emerged from wrecked cars and chased her down. She cut three of them before being overwhelmed. They tied her tightly with straps onto a metal frame, and carried her, like a slab of meat, into the Dominion.

The Lord of the island kept his court in the tremendous Central Park, his throne at the bottom of a large depression with seats, his castle a little ways off to one side. The crumbling towers of Manhattan stood silent and stern above it all.

The theater was full of filthy men, who pounded hands on their thighs as she was carried down the steep incline. They grunted an unintelligible monosyllable in time with their fists. When she reached the nadir she was pitched upright, face to face with the grossly fat Lord of Manhattan. Wedged into a leather, bucket-seat throne, at least three times as wide as she, blubbery fat as if he wanted to grow huge like a Master. His face was heavy and drooped like diseased fungus off a tree trunk. Four inhumanly tall fish-men flanked him, guns in their frying pan-sized claws. In front of the massive sea-devils were a pair of young, naked woman, absent-mindedly running their hands through the Lord's hair and touching his greasy skin. Their eyes were deader than those of the fish-men.

"A wild girl, I see." The Lord's deep, forced rasp sent unpleasant chills up her spine. "Let her go."

The straps were undone in a moment, and Laura was unsteadily on her feet. Above her the still sky was white with overhanging clouds. She stared into the Lord of Manhattan's pale-blue eyes, and said, very slowly, "There will be a time when you and your Masters will die."

He laughed, a heartless, fleshy earthquake that left him coughing and wheezing.

"You're one of Dornier's little followers, aren't you?" He moved his face close to hers. Laura turned away from his reeking breath, but someone grabbed a fistful of hair and forced her head back to him.

"Let me guess, he told you that you are the chosen one."

"The what?" She tried to bluff, but her heart quailed. His laugh was cruel.

"Release her." And she could move her head again. "Dornier is just like us, the only difference is that he was stupid and backed the wrong horse. We came to power, and now he's just a beggar, seeking after the scraps left by our lord. He finds gullible children and tells them they're the chosen one, like a fable off TV. He teaches them a useless spell so they think they're something special, then runs off to find another one. We've killed six of his chosen ones this year. I don't know what he thinks he's doing, but he can't stand against the might of Great Cthulhu."

The crowd shuddered at that awful name.

"You see that?" He regarded the cringing throng with open contempt. "That's power. Fear is power. You want to get anywhere, people have to fear you. I've got the power of life and death over everyone here, and your Dornier lives like some sort of shit-eating scavenger. Nobody tells me what to do." He glared at the mob.

"You!" The man he pointed to was pale and wasted-looking, with few teeth left in his head. The crowd backed away, as he fell to his knees, too paralyzed to beg for mercy.

"Tear him apart and feed him to the crowd."

Two of the sea-devils were on the man instantly, his inarticulate screams replaced with wet tearing and the spatter of liquid on concrete. Laura didn't even bother turning away. After they'd ripped the terrified man into raw chunks, they jammed handfuls of human meat and offal into the terrified faces of the crowd. They ate, the blood coursing down their chins. They hated it, and glared in the direction of their Lord, but they ate.

"That's power, little girl. They hate me. They'd kill me if they could. But I've got power, and your precious Dornier doesn't. All he can do is seduce the young and send them out to learn one of Azathoth's idiotic spells."

Azathoth. One of the words of the chant. Laura tried not to show recognition, but the Lord of Manhattan smirked. "Azathoth. Goddamn blind demiurge, the size of a star. The awesome daemon-sultan, that sits and does fuck-all at the center of the universe. Destroys everything he touches, doesn't even know what power is all about. What the hell is your idiot god going to grant anyone? The power to drool and shit themselves? Dornier backed a second-rate loser, not even a contender. Your spell doesn't do anything, you stupid bitch."

Laura concealed a relit spark of hope. The chant did something, even if she didn't know what. And if the Lord of Manhattan didn't know what the spell was, it would take him by surprise. She looked at the sky.

Two fish-men grabbed her and took her away. It didn't do any good to struggle—they had hands like steel. They wrestled her into a cell at the Lord's castle. The door was too strong for her, the walls unforgiving stone.

Now she knew the despair that Monica felt. Tomorrow she would go to the tower, and sometime later, a fish-man baby would tear its way out of her. If she survived the first one, there would certainly be another, and then another until whatever luck or strength had sustained her gave out. Would the spell work if she was dead? She thought about the Lord's jibe about Dornier and the chosen one. He was a liar.

She watched as the clouds slowly broke up, revealing a fine red sunset. Daylight turned to darkness, and no one bothered her, not even to feed her. She paced in the nearly-blind dark, the stars remote and uncaring. Did she have it in her to escape from the fish-men?

She curled into a ball for what might have been hours in the timeless, trackless cell, sick with fear and failure. Almost imperceptibly, darkness gave way to a faint green luminescence. She looked up. Beyond her tiny cell window, the sky was a roiling, inverted pot of boiling green water. She marveled, dumbfounded, before realizing what it meant. The time had come. Dornier was calling for her and everyone who knew the spell. She chanted. Somehow, she had imagined doing so surrounded by many people, the women and children she had taught, their voices joining up into a triumphant, ascending chorus. Instead, she pressed her face against her cell's filthy bars, chanting alone, her words echoing off stone walls. Nothing happened. The hot spark flew up, but that was all. Was that it? She started again.

And then she heard a reply, off from the distance. First one voice, then many. Women's voices, and then more, men now, men angry with the Lord of Manhattan. Laura sang it, stronger now, exulting in the sound of the people around her, all chanting the same spell. After two inconclusive tries, they were suddenly all saying the same words at the same time, clamped together by some force greater than all of them. When the last syllable was said, an invisible hand pulled her tongue out by the root.

Laura collapsed, hands at her mouth. When she moved them, there was no blood. Her tongue was numb, her teeth scorched and blasted. Somewhere deep inside her was a dull ache. The green churning had vanished from the sky, leaving once again the moon, and remote stars. Nothing had changed. She measured time by the painful throb of her body. Laura wept. She hadn't been good enough, or strong enough. Not enough people had chanted, and their single opportunity had been wasted. They were defeated, the Masters had won.

When she glanced up, a strange new light was filtering into her cell. Hope surged, and she pressed herself against the bars of the window. The sky had turned a tainted red. A tremendous new object dominated the horizon, nearly touching the zenith directly overhead, somehow behind the moon.

Laura stared, her mind numb with fear at the sight of the impossible, seething monstrosity of chaos. She saw its inconceivably alive, churning surface, and the thick tentacles like the snouts of blind worms, questing with slow, terrible majesty. She quailed before Azathoth's horrifying size and awful splendor, its utterly alien nature.

Uncountable tentacles groped out blindly. One touched the moon, and then a storm of tentacles swarmed over the surface. Laura watched in sick horror as the thick worms rent the moon asunder with slow grace. In fifteen minutes, all that was left was a coating of light dust on the reddish tentacles. Done with that, they reached out again, inexorable, blindly seeking something new.

Laura scrabbled at a corner of her cell until her fingers were bloody, desperately trying to find something–anything–to put between her and the slow, monstrous tentacles that grew ever larger.

> "Then, crushing what he chanced to mould in play,
> The idiot Chaos blew Earth's dust away."
>   - HP Lovecraft, *The Fungi From Yuggoth*

Changing of
the Guard

Pete Rawlik

CHANGING OF THE GUARD
By Peter Rawlik

From the Files of Detective Robert Peaslee

November 20, 1928

Megan and I walked through the dreary streets of Arkham and made our way over to Miskatonic University for my morning appointment. An icy wind had moved in from the North and turned the air of the city frigid. Morning reports said that there was ice on the river. The year seemed determined to end on a bad note. So much had happened, so much horror had been hinted at, hinted at and more, I doubted that Arkham could endure another year like the one that was nearly over. There was hope that something could be done to bring the current round of horrors to a close. Some had an idea to prevent them from ever happening again. This is why we were on our way to see the library staff. We were to speak to learned men who thought that something could be done, and that they were the ones to do it.

Oddly, to meet with the university library staff, I didn't go to the library. There isn't room for them all there. The Old Marsh Library, what they now call the Tabularium, has its main hall, mostly filled with files, school archives and the like, but it can hold one hundred people easily. My plan was to fill it with the entire staff of librarians, their assistants, the clerks, and those members of the campus police assigned to the library. It was a simple request, and it needed to be. Things needed to change, and the powers of this little empire had nominated me to be the one breaking the news.

Cyrus Llanfer, the Acting Director while Armitage recovered, met me at the steps and escorted both myself and Megan inside. He was a nervous little man who looked at his watch disapprovingly. "You are late, Detective Peaslee." His pace was almost frenetic.

"The cold and wind slowed us down," I lied. "Is everybody here? I don't want to have to go through this again."

Llanfer nodded. "Everyone is waiting, from Armitage all the way down to that annoying little woman down in receiving. What is her name? Stanley." He clucked her name. "Some kind of prodigy: a Law degree at twenty-two, but she ditches that to work in the pit. Who does that?" The inside of the building was warm. The old library had its own furnace and the old thing was still in fine working order.

Megan touched my hand. "I'll wait in the reading room."

Llanfer spoke with a condescending tone. "Thank you Miss Halsey. Be sure not to wander around, there are no clerks or librarians available to help you, and I would hate to see you get lost."

I call out to her, "This will take me an hour, not counting questions." She kisses me on the cheek and I watch as she struts down the hall while Llanfer takes me through the massive double doors of the entrance to what was once the Marsh Library. The room beyond was full of chattering academics. The venerable Doctor Armitage was sitting in a chair off to the side. He looked weak and sad. His actions had thwarted the Dunwich Horror, but while he had been fighting monsters, his wife had fallen ill, and eventually passed away. Her funeral had been just two weeks earlier. Behind Armitage was Harper, the former director, who was a little younger than Armitage, but not nearly as spry. He was supposedly retired, but still maintained an office and did a little research. Occasionally he served as an academic advisor to graduate students, but only to very promising candidates.

As I scanned through the crowd I recognized several of the more troublesome members of the staff, ones who were not going to take kindly to what I had to say, or what was going to have to be done. Anthony Alwyn and David Sandwin were in the back smoking. They were odd birds, younger than most of the others, more talented, more curious, excluding Stanley. Llanfer was right; she was a prodigy, just as talented and curious as any, but quite a bit more cautious. I thought that made her less dangerous, Megan thought the exact opposite.

Llanfer took the makeshift podium and tried to quiet his subordinates, but no matter what he did the uncontrolled conversation continued. It wasn't until Armitage rose and tapped the floor with his cane that the normally quiet caretakers of the Miskatonic University Library ceased their babble and gave me their attention. Llanfer fumbled through an introduction and then sheepishly left me to do the talking.

"Gentlemen, and lady, thank you all for coming. Doctors Armitage and Llanfer have asked me to come speak to you today concerning some changes I've recommended concerning access to some of the library's holdings." A murmur went through the crowd. "I understand that this may be antithetical to your work, to the philosophy behind your profession, but I think most of you might have a clue why these changes are necessary."

There was a voice from the back, "I don't, why don't you stop being all mysterious and explain what is going on. There has been too much rumor and gossip of late. We deserve some explanations." It was Scott David, a junior reference librarian who specialized in geography and genealogy.

"I don't disagree," I responded. "It would take more time than I have to cover things in depth, so I'll just go over the highlights." I took a deep breath. "Back in January, graduate student Walter Gilman and Wilbur Whateley of Dunwich both consulted the Necronomicon, or at least we think they did. In March, Amos Tuttle died, and as part of his bequest to the library, his lawyer dropped off the real Necronomicon. Turns out, the one in the case was a very clever copy. In May, a rat ate out Gilman's heart, and three months later Whateley was killed by one of the library dogs. Dr. Armitage will attest that the events in Dunwich were related to that dread book. Shortly afterwards, Dr. Llanfer informed me that he had discovered that someone had broken in and again stolen the Necronomicon, or at least so they thought. Dr. Armitage had taken certain precautions and replaced the real book with the copy. The fire down at the Tuttle place may have been because the wrong book had been stolen. Also, some of you might remember Seth Bishop of Aylesbury, he visited quite often from 1919 through 1923. Late last month he killed Amos Bowden." There was an overwhelming silence in the room, but I had to drive it home. "Some of you worked with Bryant Hoskins, one of the junior librarians under Dr. Llanfer. He was assigned to work on the Tuttle Bequest. Hoskins was unsupervised and used his access to read portions of the Necronomicon. He stole two books, the R'lyeh Text and the Celeano Fragments. They found him up in his cabin, he's been confined to the county asylum at Sefton. The books he stole have been placed on the restricted shelves. We are going to place more books in that room."

Scott David was outraged. "Why? What gives you the right?"

Dr Cyrus Llanfer rose in defiant response, "There are some things man is not meant to know, and some books man is not meant to read."

A dull roar filled the room, but once again Armitage rose to quell the disruption. This time he spoke and his voice was filled with emotion. "This is not open to debate. Detective Peaslee has outlined a set of procedures and measures that we are going to begin instituting immediately. If you are unhappy with this decision the University will provide you with a month's severance and a letter of recommendation."

As Armitage sat back down the crowd settled and I was finally allowed to begin discussing how I was going to make sure that the collection was more secure both from the public and unauthorized staff. Faculty and student use would be limited, controlled by a committee of four with two members each from the faculty and the senior library staff. Locks would be installed on doors and new cabinets, also with locks, would be used. They would have separate keys, which would be assigned to specific curators. The keys would be of a proprietary design, duplication privileges would be limited to the committee of four. The collection rooms themselves would be redesigned. The books would not be allowed to leave dedicated reading rooms. Books would be viewed by appointment only, and only for limited periods of time. Curating staff would not leave the room while a book was out of a cabinet. The transfer of books from a cabinet to the table and back again would be handled by the curators. No one else was to have access to the storage cabinets. Emergency switches for alarms were to be installed in every room.

It took an hour to go through my designs and recommendations, and to answer a handful of questions. The obligatory handshaking and thanks came from Llanfer and Armitage, as well as Harper. A scowl of disapproval was directed my way from Scott David, and another from Anthony Alwyn. Miss Stanley went out of her way to catch my attention, but then changed her mind and shuffled awkwardly away. By the time I made my way out of the room Megan had been free to do whatever she wanted for more than an hour.

She took my hand and as the hall emptied, expertly helped guide me through the crowd of slightly stunned and annoyed library staff. We said nothing and as the herd left the Tabularium and headed back to the Library we turned the opposite direction and headed off campus. It was only then that my fiancée Megan Halsey began to smile.

"They really are just a hypocritical lot of pompous old fools aren't they?" She pondered out loud. "There are things man was not meant to know. What they mean is they want to be able to control the information. They want access to it, and to keep it away from everyone else. My father would have slapped the man."

"It's what they believe." I told her. "At least it's what Llanfer believes, probably Armitage too. They truly think that they are incorruptible, that their education and position as librarians sets them above everyone else. They've set themselves at the top and by controlling the information they make sure to keep themselves there."

"Until somebody like us sneaks in and takes it away from them."

I smiled back. "How much were you able to destroy?"

"Everything that we were looking for, say what you want about librarians but they are very well organized. Everything was filed exactly where it was supposed to be: West's thesis, the file on the Whateleys, what they found in the ashes of Hartwell's house, your father's papers, Tillinghast's designs, even the journals of the 1902 Hawks Expedition. All of it went into the furnace."

"Well done, you're still comfortable doing this?"

"It has to be done." There was a kind of lament in her voice.

The clock tower chimed and I turned round to look at it. The smoke from the stack above the Tabularium had changed from white to black. I thought about how much we had just destroyed, just a few boxes of papers, and yet so very dangerous. Changes needed to be made. The thought was sobering. Llanfer and Armitage were going to follow my directions. The new security would be put in place. Only a few people would have keys, including myself. Things were going to be different. I would make sure of it. I wouldn't be able to touch the ancient books; they were too high profile, too noticeable. The other things, journals, accounts, notebooks, things that were just piled up waiting to be properly catalogued, these things could be destroyed quite easily.

Let the old men have their black lettered grimoires and illuminated manuscripts full of legends and ridiculous spells which only hint at what might be. It's the more recent documents that actually tell the truth. This is a new age, with new ideas, and a new morality. Someone must make sure that we don't end up destroying ourselves. There are things man was not meant to know, but is it really up to a bunch of old librarians to control? Perhaps not. Perhaps it is time for someone else to take a turn. Why not Detective Robert Peaslee and Megan Halsey? Why not two people who had suffered as a result of that information and those who had used it?

I can think of no one better

.

The Murder at the Motel

Brian M. Sammons

drizzle towar...
...e parking lot and pull...
...d blood and black feat...
...e entrance of the Sunsh...
...e back of his mind the...

THE MURDER AT THE MOTEL
By Brian M. Sammons

Dennis pulled his rusting Ford Ranger into the parking lot and killed the engine. The all-day downpour had, at last, slowed to a sprinkle as evening gave way to night, which was a blessing, as the Ranger's cracked wiper blades had made a streaked mess out of the windshield. The motor in the old pickup truck pinged as it cooled and inside the cab, Dennis – AKA the Amazing Kraygen, AKA the world's biggest loser – sighed and looked out his window. *The Sunshine Harvest Motel*, a flickering neon sign brightly proclaimed. Next to the words was a painting of a dew-beaded orange doubling for a smiling sun, looking down at a grove of orange trees. Below the sign sputtered a flashing word: *Vacancy*. Dennis had driven an extra hour up I-75 looking for a place to stay that he could afford. Sadly, this looked like it.

Come on now, it's not that bad. It's even kind of quaint, a small voice perked up in the back of Dennis' mind. It was the voice that had first gotten him interested in magic as a child. It was the voice that had told him to quit his job as an accountant to become a full-time magician six years ago. And it was the same damn voice that had told him last year to walk away from his home before the bank took it from him and try his act out on the open road. Dennis guessed that the voice was his 'inner child', or whatever shrinks were calling it these days, and that it represented his optimism and wonder at the world.

Whatever it was, Dennis hated that damn voice.

He slid out of his Ranger and stretched, causing joints to pop. He'd driven eighteen hours straight to make it to Miami and this year's MagiCon. Once there, he'd spent two hectic days trying to rub elbows with his peers, make connections, trade hot leads, and perhaps even pick up a new trick or two. All he got for his troubles was two days of cold shoulders, phony smiles, the opportunity to marvel at some overinflated egos, and snickers at his humble credentials. Now, in the middle of a twelve hour drive to his next booked gig, Dennis was in a bitter mood that would not leave him. He was exhausted, both physically and mentally, and sure of only three things at the moment. One, he hated that little voice in his head that kept pushing him along in this magic business. Two, this motel was a cheap sty he was going to hate. Three, all magicians were assholes, and this went double for himself.

Pulling his tattered leather suitcase from the passenger seat, he began to trudge through the cold night drizzle toward the motel's office, so lost in self-loathing that he didn't even notice the black Mercedes gliding into the parking lot and pulling into the space next to his battered truck. He didn't notice the car's cracked windshield that still had blood and black feathers sticking to it, nor the shadowy figure behind the wheel that stared at him.

Upon reaching the entrance of the Sunshine Harvest, Dennis did notice something out of the ordinary: the distant cawing of crows. In the back of his mind the little voice wondered *That's weird. Do crows fly at night?* But as was frequently the case these days, he chose to ignore it.

Dennis grabbed the door handle and looked at a paper jack 'o lantern grinning up at him from the door's window.

"Oh yeah," he muttered to himself, "happy fucking Halloween."

See? It's not that bad, the little voice said, and Dennis had to agree with it this time. Although the motel would never be called luxurious, with its faded green carpet, cheap brass fixtures, and well-worn furniture at least two decades out of date, it was, at least, clean and dry.

Everything inside was awash in a sea of orange and black for Halloween. Rolls of Halloween crepe paper ran across the borders of the walls and ceiling, joining with jack o' lanterns, both real and decorative, to set the color palette. Plastic skeletons, rubber bats on strings, and fake spiders on webs of stretched cotton added to the celebration Halloween.

Dennis, despite his mood, smiled. Halloween had always been his favorite time of the year. It's what sparked his interest in all things spooky and mysterious, which had initially fostered his love for magic. He knew he should hate the holiday, just for that, but he couldn't bring himself to do so.

His brief feeling of joy vanished in an instant when he saw that the motel was full of people Dennis recognized from MagiCon.

He sighed. *I should have known as much. Magicians are the cheapest bastards in the world, so of course they'd all flock here on their way home,* he thought. He then had his own train of scornful speculation derailed when the little voice in his head added, *Isn't that exactly why* you *stopped here?*

He shook his head and marched up to the registration counter. A candle inside a carved jack o' lantern flickered to his left, and next to it sat a plastic bowl filled with Dum Dum suckers. The guy behind the counter was in his mid-twenties and still had his boyish looks, though they were starting to mature. Despite that, the clerk looked all the more childish because he was drinking chocolate milk from a bright yellow carton with a rabbit's cartoon face on it. The cowboy costume he wore might have had something to do with the air of immaturity, too. The nametag on the man-child's chest read *Jim Stutton*.

Jim put the carton down and licked his lips clean. "Hey there, happy Halloween, can I help you?" he picked up the bowl of sweets and offered them.

Dennis debated for a moment, then thought, *what the hell*, and plucked a cherry sucker from the pile.

"Yes, I need a room for the night," Dennis said, putting his suitcase down and digging out his emaciated wallet.

"The Amazing Kraygen, huh?"

"What?" Dennis asked, then followed Jim's stare to his own chest where he was still wearing his MagiCon "hi my name is" sticker. *Oh that's just great,* he thought as he reached up to rip off the tag. "Yeah, I'm a professional magician and I uhm…" he stammered as his face turned red and his normally dexterous fingers fumbled to find an edge of the sticker to peel it off.

"I thought so," Jim said, paying no attention to Dennis' embarrassment. "Got a lot of you magicians in tonight after that convention you guys had down south. So, Mr. Kraygen, a room for one, then?"

"Yes, and it is Dennis. Amazing Kraygen is just a stage name I use." *Not to mention a stupid name I took from an old Dungeons and Dragons character I played once upon a time.* "How much will it be?"

"Seventy-five bucks, and you're in luck, only two rooms left," Jim said as he turned around and reached toward the key rack. Indeed, two old fashioned metal keys, not the plastic key cared you usually got in hotels these days, were all that were left on the rack. One was numbered three and the other nine. Without hesitation, Jim reached for room key number three.

"Well then it appears that we're both lucky," a cheerful voice called out from behind him. Dennis turned around to look at a man with long gray hair tied in a ponytail, a wisp of a soul patch beard, a gold Egyptian ankh dangling from one earlobe and eyes of undetermined color as they were behind honest-to-god, rose-colored glasses. Dennis pegged the newcomer as another magician, as only someone in showbiz could get away with dressing like that. The only thing that threw him off was the suit; it looked to be authentic Armani. No one in the trade who didn't have his own television specials or a gig in Vegas could afford that, and this guy was neither Penn nor Teller.

"Well I guess you are," Jim said and then added, "just a sec, let me get the vacancy sign." He then turned around to flip a switch on the wall. The stranger took the opportunity to smile at Dennis.

"Looks like fate, you and I arriving when we did."

"Yeah sure," was all that Dennis could think of as a reply. The stranger was starting to give him the creeps for some unknown reason. An air of oddness seemed to all but waft off of him, so Dennis turned back towards the reception desk.

"Where do I sign?"

ID was checked, a registration form signed, and crumpled bills changed hands before Dennis collected his room key and asked, "Does the motel have anywhere to eat?"

"Sure does. Just around the corner there," Jim pointed, "is the diner. It should still be serving."

"Thanks." Dennis turned to pick up the suitcase and saw Mr. Rose-Colored Glasses staring a hole into the back of his head. Caught in the act, the odd character smiled again, this time revealing a gold-capped incisor. Dennis nodded, collected his bag, and then headed to his room to drop off his suitcase before getting a bite to eat.

Dennis put the fork down and wiped his mouth. There were still three bites of pie left – pumpkin, in keeping with the Halloween theme – but after his big and surprisingly good dinner, there was no way he was going to finish it. For the tenth or so time since coming in, he looked around the diner at his fellow customers. At a guess, he would say that three-quarters of them were in the trade, and of them, fully half of the pretentious asses still wore either some part of their costumes or had their 'look' going in full effect.

Maybe they're just having fun for Halloween, his inner voice suggested. *You remember fun, don't you?*

Once more, Dennis' eyes searched out the good-looking woman with the spiky green hair. She was wearing a leather skirt, a studded belt, and a barely-buttoned tuxedo jacket with nothing on underneath it.

If you like her, you should go over and say hi. She's obviously in the business, so you can start out talking about that, the little voice began, but was cut off when someone at a booth near the diner's windows shouted; "Would you look at that shit?"

The man's three friends, one of whom wore a purple cape and another a black domino mask, were just as drunk as the astonished shouter, so all their slurred voices carried far.

"Yeah, look at that," said domino mask.

"It's like that one movie, with all the birds. What's that called?" Mr. Cape said.

"It's called *The Birds*, you dumbass," the first man said.

The fourth man said nothing. His head was down, his chin on his chest. He was either drunk or dead.

Mr. Cape grinned as only drunks, babies and the feebleminded do. "That's it - *The Birds*. It's like *The Birds* out there, all right. How many you think are out there, Sam?"

Dennis stood up, craned his neck toward the windows to see what all the commotion was about, and then jumped when he felt a hand fall on his shoulder from behind. Turning around, he wasn't surprised to find himself looking at two rose-colored lenses and a shining gold tooth.

"Hello there, I'm the Astounding Radu. You were at the con, right?" asked the motel's last guest of the night.

"What? Oh yes, I was. Hi, I'm Dennis." He offered his hand. He didn't want to, but it was the polite thing to do.

The other took it in a strong and cool grip. "Hello, Dennis. Nice to meet you. But what's your other name?" Radu asked, flashing gold-glinting grin.

"Oh, I'm the ah…Amazing Kraygen." Even after six years in the trade, he felt like an ass every time he said that out loud.

"Yes, that's the one. Would you mind if I joined you?"

"Sure, I guess," Dennis said, but was thinking the opposite. He'd had quite enough of magicians after MagiCon and now only wanted to rest.

Radu sat, produced a long-stemmed cigarette with the flick of his wrist, and asked Dennis' permission to smoke by arching an eyebrow over the rim of his red lenses.

"I don't think it's allowed —" Dennis began and then shut his mouth after the illusionist lit the smoke with a snap of his fingers. *Show-off*, he thought.

"I remember you from the convention. You did that water-bottle trick, right?" Radu asked, blowing out exotic-smelling smoke.

Wow, he remembered that! Dennis thought with more than a hint of pride. He felt a little kiss of the opiate that addicted all performers: recognition. It was tradition for all attendees of MagiCon to perform at least a few tricks, if for no other reason than to prove that they belonged to be there. The fact that someone remembered one of his amazed the Amazing Kraygen.

"Yes, I did that. I'm sorry, but I can't remember any of your work," Dennis began but then quickly tried to cover his faux pas with, "but I didn't get to the con until late, so I'm sure I missed it."

Radu smiled a gold-winking grin. "Don't worry about bruising my ego, my boy. The fact of the matter is that I didn't perform. I never do at those things."

"Oh, why not?" Dennis asked as he waved for the waitress to bring his bill.

"Most of the so-called 'professionals' aren't worthy to see my art," the older man said, and Dennis had to fight the urge to roll his eyes at the smug statement. He was about to write off the 'Astounding Radu' as just another pompous windbag, but was surprised when the man said, "But you might be worthy to see it. Want to witness something special?"

Dennis' insatiable curiosity got the better of him. "Sure. What do you got?"

"Watch what happens to our cute little waitress," Radu whispered, and reached into his pocket. From it, he produced an antiquated silver coin of some sort. It was wide, thin, and tarnished, with some long dead man's profile on one side, and a symbol carved into the other. The carving was a five pointed star; a pentangle which was the traditional symbol for magic. So common place was that knowledge, that many magicians had baubles and props inscribed with it. However, this pentangle was slightly different, it had something in its center that resembled both an eye and a flame. Radu then began to move the coin back and forth across the back of his fingers. It was an old test of manual dexterity, one that Dennis himself could do, and certainly nothing extraordinary.

The waitress came to their booth. "Can I get you fellas something else?" she asked with a sweet southern belle accent. The waitress was very cute, but also jailbait. At a guess, Dennis would have placed her age at sixteen, seventeen, tops. She had curly blond hair, dark hazel eyes, and a smattering of acne that she hid well with her makeup. Pinned above one small breast was a nametag that read *Sally*.

Radu cleared his throat to get Sally's attention as Dennis took a sip of his coffee. "Yes, dear girl. I'd like to bend you over the table right now and fuck you up the ass. Could I do that?"

Dennis' eyes went wide and he sputtered coffee out his mouth and nose. His head whipped up to catch the look of rage that was no doubt beginning to redden the young girl's face…and instead saw her wearing a mask of heavy-lidded serenity.

"Sure," was all Sally said.

"If my friend here wanted you to suck him off while I buggered you, could he do that? What if we wanted to take pictures and send them to your mother, would that be okay?" Radu whispered, then tossed a devil's grin Dennis' way.

"Sure," was the girl's reply.

Dennis was thunderstruck. He couldn't believe the filthy words coming out of the old guy's mouth, nor could he understand why Sally Schoolgirl was taking it so well. He looked once more at the girl's expressionless face then followed her gaze down to Radu's hand and the silver coin that danced over his knuckles.

Radu took a quick look around to see if anyone was hearing his whispered perversities, then continued, "And later, if we got a big Labrador Retriever and told you to get down on your hands and knees and…"

"Okay, that's enough," Dennis interrupted. "What the hell is this? You two putting me on or something?"

Radu looked at Dennis but kept the silver coin moving across the back of his hand. "No, Amazing Kraygen, it's not a con, a scam, or swindle. This girl and I don't know each other, nor did we arrange this beforehand." The magician's golden grin grew wide and predatory. "The fact is; this is magic. Not parlor tricks. Not sleight of hand. This is the real deal."

"Bullshit!"

"I'll tell you what – I could put the coin away, stop the spell, and then ask Sally those rather lewd questions again. But then, for your sake, I hope you're a fast runner."

The coin danced. The waitress waited.

"This is impossible. There's no such thing as magic," Dennis said. His little internal voice asked, *Are you telling that to him, or yourself?*

"Why is it that those in your line of work are always the biggest skeptics, yet also the ones who want most to believe?" Radu pondered aloud, then stopped the coin from flipping and made it disappear into his hand.

At last, Sally's face changed. She blinked a couple of times, took a look around with wide eyes, and then said, "Uh…sorry about that, fellas. I must have been zoning out or something. What did y'all want, again?"

"I said just bring my friend's check. We're ready to leave," Radu said.

"Sure," the waitress said again, then turned and left.

"I can't believe this," Dennis muttered to himself. He looked into Radu's red lenses. "So what, you hypnotized her with the coin or something?"

"Not hypnotized. I glamoured her, or, if you prefer, I charmed her. And my focus wasn't a mere coin, but a token from a civilization lost in time. Its like hasn't been seen by most since before the last ice age and this one came all the way from what is now Greenland."

"Okay, if what you say is true, and I'm not saying that it is, but *if* it is, then why did you show this to me?"

Radu grinned and performed the classic magician's gesture of trust: he turned his palms up to reveal that he had nothing in his hands. "Why, I thought that would be obvious: I'm looking for an apprentice, and I think you're perfect for the job."

Dennis was shocked by that, but before he could respond there was a *whump* and a loud *crack* from one of the diner's windows. The drunks at the booth next to the glass, the three who were still conscious at least, all let out a 'Whoa' in unison. Dennis turned and saw that one window now had a large spider web crack in its center and that on the outside of the glass something black and feathered was sliding down the window, leaving a trail of blood in its wake.

"It's *The Birds*!" cried the drunk in the domino mask.

"What the hell's going on out there?" Came a loud bellow from the kitchen area.

"Here's your check, fellas…hey, what's that?" Sally said as she turned to stare at the broken window.

Radu snatched up the check and rose. "Come on, it's getting too lively in here for my taste. If you wish to discuss my offer further, come to my room." Then, before Dennis could say anything, Radu was off towards the cash register, check in one hand, wallet in the other.

Dennis sat there for a moment, stunned and confused. *What are you waiting for? These aren't stage tricks the old guy's offering to teach you - it's real magic!* His little voice shouted inside his head. Dennis then sprung out of his chair to follow Radu.

The other magician - the only *real* magician in the entire motel - had already paid the bill and was walking down the main hall at a brisk pace to his room. Dennis had to jog to catch up, and as he did, his constant companion asked, *Why do you think Radu was so afraid of a kamikaze crow?*

To say that the rest of the night was magical would give someone the wrong idea, but it would be accurate. Radu has begun his instructions just after eight o'clock by producing an old book from his suitcase. No, it didn't have skulls on it and it wasn't bound in human skin. It was clothbound in green, obviously an antique, and had a title so faded that some of the letters had been worn away. Dennis could still make out what had once been there; *Cultus Maleficarum*.

"Well that sounds…ominous," Dennis said.

"If you knew the title of the book it was copied from, you'd really think so." Radu said with a smirk.

"What's that?"

"Never mind, suffice to say, it is a muddled and incomplete translation of the Latin, but it is in English and I assumed you don't read Latin."

"So this is what, a spell book?"

Radu let out a chuckle. "Not in the way you're thinking. It's not a proper Grimoire, but it does contain knowledge. Usually it can take weeks, even months to decipher the hidden meanings, but lucky for you, you've got me here to help you along."

It was now almost midnight and Dennis was both exhausted and exhilarated. He had seen, read about, and done things he had never thought possible. He levitated a chair with Radu sitting in it. With the aid of the room's mirror, he had scryed into another motel room and watched the girl with the spiky green hair enjoy some private time with a special 'magic wand' that she surely never used in her stage act. He had even summoned balls of flame that hovered over his outstretched palm and was only slightly surprised when Radu had told him that the fiery wisps were actually alive. Now Dennis stood in an elaborately-drawn magic circle of protection preparing to chant a spell that would bring forth a 'messenger of death', whatever *that* was. To say that he was scared would have been an understatement, but his ever-present need to know more kept him going, though the little voice in his head surprisingly wasn't happy about it.

You're playing with dangerous things and you don't even know this Radu, the voice warned. *Why is he teaching you all this? Would you show these secrets to someone you'd only just met by chance in a diner? Something is definitely wrong here.*

As much as Dennis hated to admit it, the little voice was right. This was all too much, too fast.

"Look, Radu, I don't think that I can do this."

"Sure you can," the wizard said as he carefully poured red sand onto the floor, making his own magic circle. "Now be quiet and be still. It's almost midnight on Halloween. That's a very special time. The ancient druids who first began the Feast of Samhain recognized the importance of the celestial alignment that occurred at that time of year. It's a time when barriers between the spheres are thin. It is a time perfect for contacting those from outside."

"Uh-huh," Dennis agreed without knowing what Radu was talking about.

"Of course these days it's all cheap masks and candy. Like so much of the old truths, it has been forgotten, almost purposely so. But that does not mean it is any less potent."

"Well thanks for the history lesson, but I really don't think I can summon up a demon." Dennis insisted. He wanted to leave now, but couldn't. He looked down at the intricate pattern of sand and knew that the slightest misstep would break the symbol and could doom him to eternal suffering. Or so Radu had told him earlier.

Who cares? The spell hasn't started yet, just leave, his little voice pleaded.

"My dear Kraygen," Radu started, as if he talked to a child, "It's not a 'demon', not as you know such things, anyway. Also before tonight you didn't think magic was real, and you were wrong about that. You didn't think you could cast spells or make charms, and you did that easily enough. This is really no different."

"This is crazy, and I'm…" Dennis began, preparing to leave the circle, when Radu whirled about, glaring.

"If you know what's good for you, Kraygen, you'll stay right where you are." Radu's words dripped with menace, and he aimed a finger at him as if to stress the point.

"Goddammit, my name is *Dennis!*"

"No, it's not. You've always been Kraygen. The other name was forced upon you by witless parents. This is exactly who you were meant to be." Radu sneered. "Do you think our meeting was chance on this night of all nights? Do you think someone with my power would waste my time going to a convention of buffoons and charlatans if I wasn't looking for someone special?"

"What do you mean?" The question came out tiny and terrified, as if Dennis' little, inner voice had at last spoken aloud.

"I need someone like you, someone with the spark. It is the only way this will work, the only way they will mistake..." Behind Radu's red lenses, his eyes widened: the look of someone who'd almost said too much.

Before Dennis could ask Radu what he was going to say, the room's window began to rattle. He turned his head toward the quivering glass. At first he saw only blackness, but soon he could recognize shapes: wings, feathers, gleaming obsidian eyes, and dark beaks far too many to count. A huge mass of large black birds swarmed at the window, crashing into it, trying to get in.

"What the hell is that?" Dennis cried out.

Radu laughed a joyless laugh. "That would be the murder. You know, a group of crows? Interesting that when crows gather they should be called a murder, don't you think?"

"What are they doing?" Dennis turned back to the old wizard. "What do they want?"

Radu snorted, went back to pouring sand to finish his circle and said nonchalantly, "They want me. Do you know what a psychopomp is?"

"No."

"They escort the souls of the living to the underworld at their time of death. They can take many forms; usually birds like sparrows, owls, and whippoorwills, but crows are the most...tenacious. Those damn birds are here because my bill is way past due. You see, I should have died many years ago but I decided not to, and that really pissed them off. But don't worry, that window is warded and it will keep them out for as long as I need it to."

Radu was now done with the sand, so he placed the bottle into his suitcase and withdrew an ancient papyrus scroll. He then stepped into his magic circle. Once there, he removed his red spectacles and threw them onto the bed. He did the same with the gold cap, sliding it off his tooth. "There," he said. "That's better." He unclipped his fake ponytail, tossed it away. "You see, after I cheated death, the psychopomps didn't go away. They knew I wasn't meant to be alive and they were determined to fix that. Now, one-on-one they're easy enough to deal with, but over time their numbers swell and swell until there's a huge murder constantly hounding me. That can be most problematic."

"So what has this to do with me?" Dennis asked as he raised his foot and tried to step outside his circle of sand.

Radu acted immediately with a wave of his hand and an utterance of alien sounds that could hardly be called words, "M'ng wal thuhey ia yog-sothoth cul xil'thatul!"

Dennis put his foot back down. He tried, but he was unable to lift it again.

"What did you do to me?" Dennis shrieked.

"Don't worry. I just wanted to make sure that when I cast this spell I'm not alone in this room. That would be very bad."

Radu unrolled the scroll in his hands and continued gloating to his chosen victim. "You see this? This is the original scroll of Everlasting Life I used all those years ago. It's absolutely ancient and priceless, penned by the Black Pharaoh, Nephren-ka himself more than a millennia ago. What am I doing with it now, you may ask? I'm going to use it to solve my crow problem. You see, that murder is here to take a soul away. If I give them one, they'll be satisfied and leave me alone – at least for a few years."

Cold realization of what was happening and worse, what was *going* to happen, uncoiled in Dennis' mind like a waking serpent. He willed his paralyzed legs to move, but to no effect.

"Unfortunately I can't sacrifice just anyone to the little black bastards to get them off my back," Radu continued. "I found that one out the hard way the first time I tried to bribe the psychopomps and it cost me dearly."

Radu motioned to his left eye, and now that it was no longer behind the red lenses, Dennis could see faint scars around the socket and that it didn't move. It was pale blue and made of glass.

"No, I have to find someone with a soul somewhat like mine in order to fool them. That means someone with a talent for sorcery. As you can imagine, wizards are none too common in this day and age, despite the popularity of Harry Potter. Luckily for me, I discovered that those with untapped potential often take to playacting the lives they were born to lead. That's where you and those other fools at the convention come in. Too bad that you happen to have the brightest spark in that pathetic bunch. You offer me the greatest chance of success with this."

"You're going to kill me?" Dennis croaked.

"Not directly. I'm going to call forth a Harbinger of Hermes, one of the Lords of the Wing, a Black Flyer of Yibb-Tstll. Oh they have had so many names over the countless centuries. Essentially they're just really big psychopomps, soul takers of the highest order. When these things are summoned they never arrive happy, and if you're not thoroughly warded, they'll tear your soul out of you and take it back to the stygian depths."

Radu gave Dennis a cold look, like a butcher appraising a cut of meat. "Ideally, *you* would cast the spell, as it would draw the Black Flyer's complete attention to you, but I guess that's out of the question now. But, as you should doubtless know, a good magician is always prepared, and that's why I purposely didn't complete your magic circle."

Radu grinned, the very image of Mephistopheles. "When the Black Flyer arrives and finds out that it can't get to me, it will be even more pissed-off than usual, and I'm afraid that it'll take that out on you, my unprotected, immobile friend. In doing so, it'll take your soul to wherever they take them, and those damned crows outside will disperse. That will give me a few more years of peace to find a better solution to my bird problem."

"Oh my God," Dennis whispered.

"No, my gods, the Old Ones, and they're listening," Radu said. "Now, let's get the show on the road." With that, he began to read the strange words from the ancient papyrus.

Dennis pulled and struck at his legs with his hands, even tried to force himself to fall over in order to crawl away, but all for naught. It was as if he was stuck in cement from the waist down. He looked around for something, anything he could grab hold of to either pull himself to the floor or use as a weapon. Unfortunately nothing was within reach.

Remember the water bottle trick?

Dennis stopped his frantic looking around and turned his head towards what his little voice was suggesting, an open bottle of water he'd bought from a vending machine in the hall and brought with him to Radu's room.

Remember the levitation spell Radu taught you?

Dennis nodded, focused on the water bottle and intoned the spell of levitation just under his breath in the hope that Radu wouldn't hear him. At first nothing happed, so he concentrated even harder. Dennis gritted his teeth and mumbled the alien sounds through his clenched jaws. He could feel pain starting to build in the front of his forehead, between his eyes, like a start of a bad sinus headache.

The water bottle twitched ever so slightly, but that was all.

What's going on? Levitating Radu and the chair was easier than this? Dennis wondered, and his little voice answered, *maybe he was helping you then?*

"No, I can do this," Dennis whispered and then started intoning the spell again. He balled his hands into fists, sweat gathered at his temples, and he started to tremble from the waist up. Then all of the sudden and without warning, the water bottle rose up and flew towards Radu.

It missed the wizard by mere inches, landing at his feet with a thud.

Radu stopped reading and arched an eyebrow at Dennis. "Trying to throw off my concentration, little apprentice? Sorry to inform you, but I've done this incantation so many times, I could now almost do it in my sleep."

He went back to reading from the scroll and the room became charged with ozone. The crows outside cawed and threw themselves against the magically-protected window. Dennis felt the air around him change, become heavy, press in on him from all sides. He saw the shadows in one corner of the room darken and solidify, elongate and take on the shape of something winged and monstrous. It appeared to be made as much out of darkness as it was out of anything solid. The creature's form twitched and blurred into the shadows around it. What little Dennis could make out was mostly piecemeal images: ebony feathers, a long and wickedly serrated beak, eyes fathomless and dark; each image was only an individual fragment of a terrible whole.

A sudden and total silence filled the room. Radu had stopped chanting and although Dennis could see the crows still crashing into the window, they made not a sound.

"Welcome, oh great Harbinger of Hermes!" Radu addressed the shadowy thing in the corner, then bowed low…and then abruptly stiffened in fear. Looking down, he saw the thrown water bottle lying at his feet. He also saw that it was open and had spilled its contents. The water had washed away some of the sand of his magic circle, breaking the protection it offered.

"Oh shit," was all Radu managed to get out before the thing in the corner lunged at him with a mighty, room-shaking caw.

You don't want to see this, Dennis' little voice warned, but Dennis, a slave as ever to his curiosity, couldn't look away.

The bird-thing landed within Radu's ruined circle trailing feathers and tendrils of smoky shadow. Radu straightened up and raised his arms in front of his face in a futile gesture of defense. He began another of his arcane chants, but was only able to utter the single syllable of "Yog" before ebony talons buried themselves in his throat.

Even from across the room Dennis could hear the sound of flesh tearing and the delicate *click* of claws scraping Radu's spine as the creature tightened its grasp. As jets of crimson sprayed the walls, the copper tang of blood filled Dennis' nose.

Then Dennis' head was filled with a sibilant whispering that cut ragged words into the soft folds of his brain. It was the voice of the Lord of the Wing.

Greetingssss, Grigory, it said soundlessly. *Long have you eluded ussss, but no more. To your final judgment I sssshall take you, but firsssst, assss payment for your insssolence, sssome pain. A ssssmall tasssste of what awaitssss you.*

Radu turned a wet, pleading eye towards Dennis. He extended a hand to the younger man, tried to beg, cry out, but the only sound that left his ruined throat was a red, bubbling gurgle.

The crow-thing ran a wicked talon slowly down the side of Radu's face, a lover's caress filled with malice. The claw peeled flesh off in a dripping flap, like it was skinning a blood-filled apple. Black eyes, devoid of mercy and filled with terrible wisdom, then followed Radu's outstretched arm and fixed on Dennis.

Your tale issss not yet at an end, the hissing screech scalded into Dennis' mind. *And thissss issss not for your eyessss. Look no further, lesssss you learn too much.*

The window shattered at last under the relentless assault and the murder of crows flew into the room, an undulating mass of darkness. Dennis could feel them all around him, their feathers rushing past, their claws and beaks scratching at his flesh. Now that the birds were in the room, it was filled with their deafening cries, but even still he could hear the Harbinger clearly in his head. It was mirthlessly laughing.

Almost simultaneously the feeling returned to Dennis' lower body and he toppled over, sending sand and black feathers scattering. His legs were cramped and unresponsive, so he dug his fingers into the matted carpet and slowly clawed his way towards the door.

Things wet and warm rained down on him and the carpet around Dennis became spotted with red as he pulled himself along. All around him were screams, the fluttering of wings, gurgling pleas in Russian, the snapping of bones, and the caws of the crows. Dennis kept his head down, eyes on the carpet, and focused on moving inches at a time out of this waking nightmare.

Did you think you could essscape the pull of the Black Gulf, little wizard? Your kind, ever sssince they crawled out of the muck have thought yoursssselvessss sssso sssspecial. All but the Great Old Onessss come before ussss in time, and you are far removed from them.

The crow-thing continued its psychic shriek as its claws made wet, ripping sounds in the quivering mass of bleeding meat with the one unmoving blue eye.

At the door at last, Dennis used one arm to lift himself up and the other to reach for the doorknob. Fingers wrapped around the cold metal and Dennis allowed himself a little smile of a job well done before twisting it. He then let out a curse and fell back down to the carpet.

The door was locked and he was sure that Radu had the key.

Ssssorry young one, but the ssssoundssss musssst ssstay within thissss room for I have only jusssst begun to play. If you were to open that door, you would let the ssssoundssss out.

"No, no more, please," Dennis cried, placing his hands against his ears in a vain attempt to block out the screeching in his head.

Do you wissssh an essscape from thissss?

"Yes, yes!" he shouted over the din of the murder.

Then witnessss what awaitssss your kind, until your mind can take no more and ssssseekssss the comfort of oblivion. Behold, my gift to you. Images then slammed into his brain so fast and strange that Dennis couldn't make sense of them, but even in half realized mental glimpses, they burned. Undulating masses twisting in the lightless reaches of space, an abandoned city both alien and coldly beautiful choked in yellow mist by a still lake with something monstrous just below the surface, another city beneath the waves wreathed in shadow, madness, and death, barrel-shaped monstrosities playing with the primordial ooze they found and not only accidently creating life, but the things that would one day consume it.

There was more, so much more, but as the Black Flyer had said, the rest Dennis lost to sweet oblivion as he slipped away into unconsciousness.

Dennis awoke with a start and a scream. His sudden movement stirred up the crow feathers that lay all around and on him, and seeing them flutter caused him to scream again.

He looked about the room, there were hundreds of black feathers, two scattered circles of red sand, gleaming shards of glass from the broken window, but not a single drop of blood, nor any other trace of Radu save for a pile of shredded clothing in a heap by the bed.

Dennis stood on stiff legs and limped over to the pile of torn garments. Bending, knees popping, he riffled through the torn and blood-free cloths until he found the key attached to the plastic tag with *Sunshine Harvest Motel* pressed into it.

Straightening up, he looked at the ancient papyrus scroll that lay where it had fallen, and then to the green covered *Cultus Maleficarum* on the bed next to Radu's – or was that Grigory's – suitcase.

Dennis looked at the old book with its terrible, wonderful secrets and thought long and hard about the possibilities it offered.

Then the image of the Harbinger of Hermes peeling away the old wizard's face from his skull like a rubber Halloween mask flooded Dennis' mind. He shook his head back and forth to clear it, and when the phantasm had left him, he was looking down by his left shoe where something round and blue stared up at him.

Radu's glass eye, like his torn clothes, was all that was left of the man.

"Fuck that," Dennis whispered and turned to unlock the door.

Once back in his own room he grabbed his suitcase, which he never even unpacked last night, and left for the lobby.

Out by the registration desk, Jim was still wearing the cowboy costume, minus the cheap felt hat, and was talking to an older, heavyset man, probably his dayshift replacement.

"Hey, Amazing Kraygen, happy day after Halloween. Getting an early start on things?" Jim smiled a weary 'I haven't been to bed yet' smile. "Yes, and it's just Dennis, not Kraygen. By the way, can you tell me whether anything…weird happened last night?"

Jim and the other man exchanged looks and then the younger one answered. "Nope. Nothing out of the ordinary. Why, you hear something last night?"

"No, nothing like that."

"Uhm, buddy, you got something…" The older man said and pointed to Dennis' head.

Dennis reached up and plucked a long black feather out of his hair.

"So, you off to do some more magic then, Dennis?" Jim asked, picking up the checkout paperwork.

Dennis thought for a second. "No. I think I'm going to go back home to Michigan and pick up accounting again. It's a lot safer."

He signed the papers, handed back his room key, and walked out into the sun-bathed, early morning parking lot toward his dependable old Ford. His little inner voice piped up, *You know, this is a good idea. Accounting is good, dependable, well-paying work. Why I bet if you went home and contacted the old firm they'd be happy to hire you back. Oh and you could look up Lisa, you know she always had a thing for you…* On and on the little voice went, and this time Dennis agreed with everything it had to say.

The Grey Rite of Azathoth

Robert M. Price

THE GREY RITE OF AZATHOTH
By Robert M. Price

I write in great haste. I must needs set down my recent experience while I am able, for I do already feel the memory fading and failing, as a dream flees with the dawn, as I was told. While no man is entitled to expunge from his memory any knowledge, even if it be possible, I confess I shall not mourn the flight of that recollection which I am presently to lose. And yet the knowledge may someday prove of value, even of great necessity, for the good of mankind. I shall not consult this account again, but shall lock it away for any who come after, whoever they may be, as Providence shall decree.

My name, John Checkley, will likely be familiar to you. Upon my arrival in the Colony of Rhode Island and Providence Plantations, subsequent to certain much-noised difficulties in the Massachusetts Bay Colony, I waxed curious concerning a notorious resident whose acquaintance I could not make in my new congregation of King's Church, as he frequented the Congregational Church instead. The man's name was Joseph Curwen. By all accounts, Mr. Curwen, a prosperous but secretive merchant prince, was the possessor of a keen intellect and of numerous esoteric scholarly interests. I ventured to call upon him and was welcomed quite cordially, contrary to all I had been told of his supposed reclusivity. I was relieved to find him wholly congenial as a host and convivial as a companion. I soon learned how much we had in common, as we had each traveled extensively through the capitols of Europe, sampling liberally the rich opportunities there afforded to the seeker after knowledge of the unseen realms. I, of course, sought an education in the field of theology, of which I made ample use in my later controversies with the Calvinists of Puritan Massachusetts. Curwen's quest inclined him to more arcane pursuits of a medieval character. I should not hesitate to brand the speculations implicit in his cryptical hints as heresy, but I have long championed sectarian tolerance, and if Joseph Curwen could be persecuted for unorthodox beliefs, so could the Quakers and the Baptists, a thing I decried in print. I now know, to my chagrin, that even enlightened tolerance must draw boundaries.

Joseph Curwen's manner of conversation produced in me strangely mixed sensations of expectancy and of apprehension. There was no guessing what he might say next. One was eager and yet frightened to receive the next revelations, mercifully cloaked in ambiguity as they might be. But things were about to become altogether too perspicuous.

"Dr. Checkley, I am of course familiar with your theological polemics and with the courage which moves you to advance them against those less amicable than yourself. I should like both to reward and to test that courage. Indeed, I have reserved to you a great privilege accorded to no divine in the history of Christendom."

I confess that the grandiose character of this utterance at once took me aback. In truth, Curwen's words were so extreme as to compel their hearer to question their speaker's sanity. And he had not even got to the hinted disclosure. I replied, "Mr. Curwen, whatever you intend, I am sure there are many who are more deserving than I. I would only puff myself up with vain pride should I accept the favor with which you tempt me."

"So you compare yourself to our Saviour and me to his diabolical tempter."

He had taken me by surprise, and I knew myself for a woodland creature caught in a trap. There was naught for it but to laugh and to let my host proceed.

"I dare say, Mr. Checkley, that, as a clergyman in the Church of England, you are a believer in the resurrection of Jesus Christ; am I correct in that opinion?"

"Of course you are, sir. And what of it?"

"Then I fear a grave duty has fallen to me. I must inform you of the error of your sincere belief."

As Curwen himself had already mentioned, I was no stranger to polemic and debate on religious subjects. I had met more than one Deist in public debate as well as in pamphlet wars. Their futile arguments aimed at refuting the resurrection of our Lord did not shake my faith in the least degree. I did not fear aught that Curwen, now seemingly revealed as an infidel, might propose. I braced myself to engage in the tiresome rhetorical motions entailed in these exchanges. But I quickly found that such was not after all what my host had in mind. He continued.

"Do you think me a religious skeptic? A denier of all things supernatural desirous of winning you to my opinions? Let me assure you: that is antipodal to the truth. In truth, I aim to confirm your faith, that and more! For in truth, Jesus the son of Joseph did not return from his death sixteen centuries agone. But rise he will. Today. And it shall be done by your own word."

I glanced over in the direction of the door by which I had entered. My one thought was now to take my leave with as little offense and mutual embarrassment as possible. It had become inescapably clear that Joseph Curwen was beside himself. What he might be planning next I could not guess, but I did not fear violence. Nothing in his manner, his words, or his movements suggested such. But I had no desire to be the audience of a sad spectacle of pathetic madness such as now seemed likely to commence.

Wordlessly beckoning me with a wave of the hand, Curwen strode into an adjacent room. It would now be a simple matter for me to head for the opposite door. Yet to do so would be unconscionably rude, as foolish as this may seem. Besides, my curiosity had gotten the better of me. I could not resist the lure of whatever charade he might have in mind. So, yes, I rose and followed him. The trail led through several small rooms and down a twisting flight of crudely hewn steps. My apprehension was growing as I realized that, the deeper we descended, the more difficult it would be to escape should there prove to be aught from which to escape. Perhaps we all have a dangerous dose of Faust inside us; I only hoped, in vain, as it would prove, that Joseph Curwen did not possess rather too much of it.

At length we arrived at what looked like a workroom, a makeshift laboratory of some sort. The nitrous walls were lined with rough shelves laden with ancient-looking jars and flasks. There were two or three tall posts upholding beams designed to brace the stone walls, somewhat reminiscent of the walls of a coal mine, and these featured a series of pegs and hooks from which depended various kettles, tools, and pitchers. Most of the jars bore labels emblazoned with numbers, Hebrew characters, or zodiacal symbols. All were crowned with metal stoppers. Curwen reached for one of these and emptied out its contents upon the stained and splintered table surface. The stuff was a very fine dust, none of it clumping together but instead resembling fine sand. Curwen commenced to explain.

"As is commonly rumoured, I have engaged and, in fact, still engage in a clandestine traffic in, shall we say, archaeological specimens… for my private collection, as you might say. I have learned that one stands to learn far more of the vanished past if one bypasses the stone monuments, which conceal as much as they reveal, and instead seek the wisdom of the ancients from the ancients themselves."

"You mean," I countered, "from their writings. Have you then made important manuscript discoveries?" He must have suspected, as I suppose I did, that I was offering him a sane and reasonable alternative, hoping to fend off some terrible truth he seemed on the point of revealing.

He paused and smiled in a way I cannot say I liked. "In truth, Dr. Checkley, I have. You might find several of them to be of deep interest. But that is not what I mean. I mean the ancients themselves. It is quite possible, you know. Does not scripture say that the Witch of En-Dor invoked the shade of the prophet Samuel to converse with King Saul?"

"Indeed it does, Mr. Curwen, but that episode is hardly meant as an example for us to follow! It is properly called Necromancy, and people have been put to death on account of it, as I am sure you know from your experiences in Salem."

"Of course I do, my friend. But you, yourself, abandoned the Puritan kingdom because of its rulers' intolerance of heterodoxy. Are you still so fair-minded?" He had me.

"I hope that I am. Proceed, then. What have you in store for me?"

"As I say, the rarest of treats! What God the Father would not or could not do, you shall do, here and now. Another voice from of old set me upon the trail of perhaps the greatest discovery of its kind: the very remains, such as they are, of the Nazarene Jesus. They are my newest acquisition, and I mean to give you the honor of initiating... the process. It is surprisingly simple. Now if you would just read the words written on this slip."

"Curwen, 'thy great learning hath driven thee mad.'"

"Ah, that is what I like so much about you, sir! Ever a jest at the ready! But I am quite serious. Let me prove it to you. Read on."

What harm could it do? When nothing transpired, I should at least gain some particular notion of the manner of my host's dementia. Presumably he should fancy to behold some spectre of his own fevered imagination. Then I must play along as best I could, humouring the madman as convincingly as I might till I could manage a diplomatic departure. So I took the paper from his hand and scanned the strange syllables. I will not boast if I remind the reader of my competence in the biblical languages as well as a passable knowledge of several modern European tongues. But I had never beheld the like of these. They did not appear to be phonetic interpretations of words in any familiar language, but were foreign altogether. Nevertheless, I began.

As soon as I had enunciated the first complete line, I found my concentration distracted by a sudden change in the room's temperature, which was now quite cold. I looked up at Curwen, who seemed in no whit surprised. He did betray a slight grin, nothing more. As I found my place and continued, he listened patiently, stopping me once or twice to correct my pronunciation. He said he might have recited the formula for me to imitate but that he wanted the results of the chant to be in answer to my intonation, not his.

Y'AI 'NG'NGAH,
YOG-SOTHOTH
H'EE-L'GEB
F'AI THRODOG
UAAAH

I got through it, finally, with passable accuracy. Or so I must have, for there were indeed results. As Curwen clapped his hands with childlike glee, a fumarole of mephitic smoke began to spread and swirl in the room between us, as the spilled powder sublimated directly into the air. Within the slow cyclone a definite outline began to distinguish itself. The unwholesome odor subsided in direct proportion to the increasing solidification of the human form before me. Naturally the whole business was most impressive, but I was not carried away by superstitious credulity. Instead my amazement consisted in admiration for the fantastic ingenuity of Curwen's showmanship. The ancients were quite familiar with all the tricks still performed by charlatans and entertainers of our own day, and I imagined that Curwen was demonstrating some striking spectacle salvaged from one of the ancient documents he had acquired. On this I hastened to congratulate him, but he was having none of it. He began to exclaim, I thought a trifle sarcastically, "He is risen! He is risen indeed!"

A scrawny figure of a man stood shivering before us. He was about five feet tall and without a stitch of clothing. His drawn face bore bloodstains, while his beard and hair were matted and shaggy. His extremities showed raw wounds. He stood unevenly, one leg being plainly shorter than the other, though not by much. I thought of the Russian Orthodox cross, with its slanted bottom rung, denoting their tradition, apocryphal I should judge, that the Saviour was a cripple. And at once I recognized that I was taking seriously Curwen's blasphemous claim to be retrieving our Lord Jesus Christ from the mists of the past. Consciously, of course, I knew the whole thing for imposture, and I pitied this poor stooge of Curwen and the physical suffering he had plainly been put through in preparation for the present farce.

"Dr. Checkley, do you not know your Lord?"

"I have never seen a portrait of him not the product of an artist's fancy."

"I charge you, Sir: do not squander this unparalleled opportunity! Have you no questions for the very Son of God? If so, you are a rare clergyman!"

I felt I was being made a fool of, but I thought to turn the tables. I did address the discomfited man, but I did so in the Aramaic tongue. I calculated that Curwen had expected me to forget myself and to speak my accustomed English, as if this "Jesus" should understand and reply in kind. Here is the translated sense of my question.

"What is your name, my poor friend? And how came you to suffer so?" I expected the man to stare blankly, uncertain how to proceed now that I had departed from the plan Curwen had designed.

But he answered me in the Aramaic. At first I thought he mispronounced the ancient words, but then I realized that my own

74

pronunciation was derived from the speech of modern Syrians, and that this strange man must be speaking in the ancient accents. I was dumbfounded. Now everything looked completely different to me. The challenges to my thinking and to my composure were dramatic indeed. But this is what he said, again in translation.

"I am called Jehoshua, son of Joseph the Nazarene. I have suffered many things and climbed up the cross of Tiberius. The sun above me became black as sackcloth, and with it my eyes darkened, and I gave up my spirit. All this was mere moments ago. How came I to be here? In this cold place?"

Curwen had stepped away to retrieve a shapeless garment from a heap in the corner. He draped it about the chilled form. The man nodded in gratitude. For his part, Curwen motioned me onward, urging me to continue.

"Why, O Jehoshua, did men crucify you?"

"I wrought wonders once I bound the powers of Baal-Zebul, prince of demons. I bent them to do my will, and so I healed many sick and possessed. I was one of many, and my rivals gave false witness against me to the prefect of Rome."

The man shook his head with understandable confusion, as if to clear his mind. I hated to pester him further, but I must admit I was seriously intrigued. "But if you were the Son of God, why stoop to sorcery?"

His eyes had cleared and now fixed upon me firmly. "Amen, I say to you, my Father vouchsafed me the power wherewith I bound Satan to despoil him of his goods."

"We have believed that you conquered death and rose from the grave, but it seems you did not, at least not until now."

His voice was acquiring a firmer tone. My own voice began to catch as I could no longer maintain a skeptical detachment. Good Lord, suppose Curwen had actually done what he claimed?

"My Father liveth, and all are alive to him."

"Bear with me, O Image of Jehoshua, and I will ask of you one question more. Did you come forth from the Godhead? Are you of a single nature with the heavenly Father? Mankind has shed blood over that question."

"You say that I am. Man, open your mind to understand the deep things of God, for he whom you call your God is a veritable Ocean of Light, and from him has wave after wave of angels gone forth to crash against the shore of crude matter. If you would seek my Father's kingdom, you must go up from earth and scale the Outer Spheres. The dark angels of Achamoth, who is also Azathoth, ever keep the gates. If you would surmount them, you must work the Grey Rite...'"

Just here Joseph Curwen interrupted our exchange, blasphemously silencing him who I was now on the verge of accepting as the very Word of God.

"Have I not given you a great gift, Dr. Checkley? Now you know what no Christian souls have known since the persecution of the ancient heretics! The churchmen of old were considerably less tolerant than you, kind sir. But you need not fear persecution for speaking the truth you now know, for you shall not know it for long. Are you feeling well, my friend?"

I took stock of my sensations and found that, in the excitement of the conversation just past, I had not noticed the entire ebbing of my physical strength. Indeed, I was virtually paralyzed! I tried to answer him but heard my own slurring speech. I realize now that Curwen must have poisoned me in some surreptitious manner, perhaps using some gas invisible to the eye. I was beginning to grow drowsy, and I understood that I should before long lose any memory of what had transpired here. The gift Curwen had given me he was not going to let me keep. I am very surprised to have retained even this much for this long. I know that I have lost some of the precious secrets vouchsafed me by the man Jehoshua, but I have managed to record what little has not yet flown.

One last thing I recall seeing and hearing in that subterranean den. Curwen took hold of the man and shook him violently. "Tell me the Grey Rite! For I would storm the heavens! I shall be as the Most High!"

This, too, was in passable Aramaic, as was the response. "I bestow my mysteries upon those who are worthy of my mysteries."

Whatever this Jehoshua might be that did not meet the eye of flesh, still, in the three dimensions that we occupy, he was a weak and wizened scarecrow; and it was with perfect ease that the doughtier Curwen seized and dragged him toward the wall, forcing him against the rough wood of the nearest bracing post. A blow to the poor man's forehead sent him into a semi-stupor. As the hammering began, the room commenced to spin around me. All I heard of whatever next transpired was one sentence apiece from each man.

"Prophesy! Who struck you!"

"Almighty, protect thy lamb!"

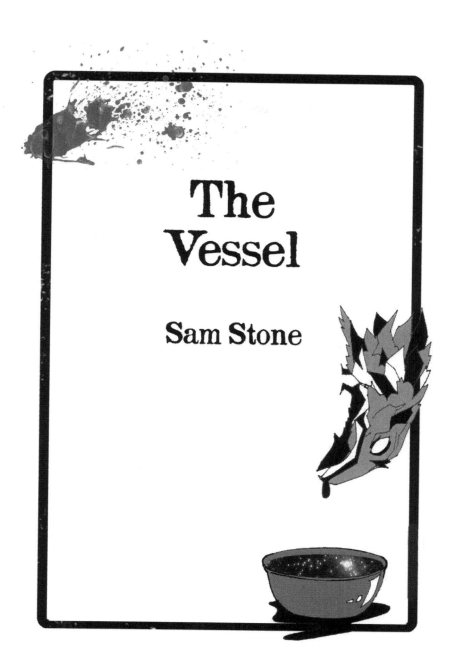

The Vessel

Sam Stone

THE VESSEL
By Sam Stone

Brent Jefferson pulled his hat down over his face and hurried through the dark and narrow streets of the French Quarter. Rain pummelled his head and shoulders. It was 10pm and a curfew had been imposed, which meant that all blacks were to stay in their homes after 6pm. But the Confederate military weren't interested in policing this area of New Orleans anymore. They had bigger fish to fry since the Federal Navy had opened fire on Fort Jackson. Jefferson knew it was only a matter of time before the Confederates fell and the Union Army broke through their defences to take over and occupy the city.

He knew he didn't have long before he'd have to flee the town and take with him the woman he loved. His biggest dilemma was that Carly didn't want to leave. She didn't even want Jefferson in her life.

Rain water dripped from the rim of his hat as he paused to look up at the tall building ahead. His eyes sought and found Carly's window. As usual she was sitting, semi-naked, flaunting her wares, even though on a night like this it was unlikely any trade would find its way into this dingy corner of the quarter. The soldiers were otherwise occupied, the local landowners were living in terror of losing their fine plantations, and the blacks were being whipped and locked up at night in desperate attempts to keep them from running away.

Times were changing and Jefferson knew that soon Carly's white owner wouldn't be able to force her to whore for him anymore. That was if the rumours of slaves being freed were entirely true. They only had the propaganda spun by the Confederates to back up any information on the war or the siege, but Jefferson suspected some of it was factual, if not all.

Despite the driving rain, Carly was cooling herself with a fancy Chinese fan. Jefferson recognised it as the one he had given her when she still let him visit. It gave him a strange kind of hope. Even from below he could make out the slender lines of her coffee-coloured thighs, as she sat, one leg crossed over the other.

"She's a whore, man. Why'd you even bother coming back here all the time," said a voice from an open door a few feet away.

Jefferson turned to see his old friend Matthew, a former slave who had managed to buy his own freedom some years before. He now ran an illegal bootleg store from the basement of his small house.

"It's not her fault," Jefferson said. "You know that."

Jefferson, Matthew and Carly had once belonged to the same plantation. The Beaugards had been cruel owners. Carly and Jefferson had wanted to be together, but fraternisation amongst the slaves wasn't allowed on Beaugard land – not unless they wanted you to breed more slaves. When their relationship was discovered, Michel Beaugard sold Carly on to the whore house. By then Matthew had bought his freedom and he thought it the cruellest punishment ever to both Jefferson and Carly. He had tried to raise the money to buy Carly's freedom from the pimp, but the white man wouldn't deal with Matthew. He saw the potential in Carly's half-caste looks and knew that the soldiers would like her. He would earn more from her by working her than by merely selling her on.

Even so, he kept Matthew dangling for a while: if the girl burned out quickly, he would probably let her friend buy her freedom. But Carly didn't burn out. In fact she took to prostitution so well that she was soon the best girl in the house. She was capable of dealing with twice as many johns in one night as any of the other girls. They all left satisfied, and came back for more.

When Matthew realised he couldn't help Carly, he helped Jefferson buy his freedom instead. Carly was some whorish princess now in an ivory tower that neither of them could climb.

"I don't understand what happened," Jefferson murmured as he stared up at her window.

"She weren't never what you thought she was," Matthew said.

Matthew invited Jefferson in out of the rain and handed him a glass of cheap brandy. Jefferson took off his wet coat and hat and sat down in a chair by the fire. The heat was welcome, but it couldn't touch the cold that sat inside him.

"The city's about to fall," said Matthew. "It won't be no bad thing for the likes of us. We have good times ahead. Carly will be freed then – if she wants to be."

Jefferson shook his head. He knew what was likely to happen – what should happen – but wasn't convinced the white soldiers from the North would treat the blacks any different than they did in the South.

"You knows I got a job at the Pollitt Plantation," Jefferson said.

Matthew nodded. The Pollitts were good white-folks who radically freed their slaves some years before. All of the blacks that worked the cotton plantation were paid. It meant that the Pollitts were infamous among the other landowners, but that they were also the only thriving farm in the area. There were no disputes or runaways, only happy families working, and living with the white landowners.

"The head house servant, Isaac, you know of him?"

"I knows him," said Matthew. "He the houngan."

"He says he can help me."

"If anyone can. He can."

Jefferson stared into the flames. Maybe Matthew was right. Maybe he should sit things out and see where it led. Carly would be free to make her own choices wouldn't she? But then, Jefferson wondered, would she choose to remain working in the whorehouse anyway? She certainly didn't look unhappy where she was.

Jefferson returned to the plantation and fell exhausted into his bed.

Despite the late hour, sleep was slow to come. Jefferson found himself tossing and turning, thinking about Carly and the hurtful way she had rejected him.

"I don't need no black boy in my life when I can play with all these white ones. They worship me, Brent. They buys me jewels and clothes and all they want is something I find so easy to give," she had said.

Jefferson knew that a life with him, the dream they once had of owning a ranch, would mean hard toil for both of them. But it surprised him that Carly found her new life to be so 'easy'. She had always been so shy, so reserved, and now it appeared that she was completely the opposite. He tried not to think of her spreading herself for other men: it hurt too much. But sometimes, when he lay in his bed at night, he couldn't believe she was the same woman he had loved so fiercely and risked so much for. Every scar on his back had been received because of his defiance, and his refusal to let her go and be used by the white overseers.

One time Beaugard's men had beat him so badly he nearly died. Even now he couldn't remember why they stopped.

He had a flash of Carly coming into the barn, the six overseers turned to look at her and Jefferson had blacked out cold. When he woke he'd found Carly pressing water to his lips, and felt the sting of salt on his back.

"You is such a fool sometimes," she had said. "Always comin' to defen' my honour. You gon' git yourself kil'."

But it wasn't cold, or distant. All her words were spoken with pride and love.

Carly was smart. She could read and write but she kept this mostly to herself, even though Jefferson knew about it.

"My daddy was a white man," she had told him. "He let me learn with his other chil'ren sometimes."

"What happen to him?" Jefferson said.

"Uprisin'. He had a taste for black flesh. Some of the men on the farm didn't like him messin' with their wives. The overseers beat the rebels down but by then they'd slit his throat. His widow sent me to the auction the very next day."

"She wanted you gone…" Jefferson said. He had taken her hand and kissed it to show how bad he felt for her.

"Yessir. She always hate how he paraded me around the house. How he bought me nice things, just like his other chil'ren, even though my skin was still too dark for him to ever admit I was his. She took all those fine presents back, too. Sent me out in rags."

Jefferson had always felt Carly was a lady but Beaugard's men had treated her like fresh meat from the start. It didn't matter how you were brought up. All that mattered was the colour of your skin.

"Jefferson …"

Jefferson jumped awake to find Isaac standing by his bedside. The Pollitts' manservant was a large man, and his dark silhouette was an unnerving sight.

"You want to help your woman still?" asked Isaac.

"Yes."

"You knows the sacrifice you has to pay?"

"Yes."

"Come with me. The congregation is waitin'."

Jefferson pulled himself from his sweat-soaked bed as he heard the drums pick up in the distance. He didn't ask what it meant. Even though he had been born on American soil, he knew something of the old ways by instinct. They all did.

He followed Isaac from his small shack and out towards the edge of the land. It was still night, but the dawn was tinting the sky and Jefferson could see the big old white house that belonged to the Pollitts up on the horizon. Nothing stirred over there. If the white family heard the drums they showed no sign of it.

"Isaac, how come the Pollitts free you all?" Jefferson asked as they plunged into the dense forest that formed a part of the plantation.

"That is 'tween me an' Massa Pollitt," Isaac said.

Jefferson swallowed any further questions and quelled his curiosity as Isaac led him into a wide clearing just as the Sun began to chase the night away.

They began a ritual, a dance of sorts, while Isaac, clad in a long white robe, shook a tall staff, covered in bone shards tied on with cord. The bones rattled together in rhythm with the drums. Jefferson saw no one playing them though, and even here the sound seemed distant, but part of the ceremony.

Bare-chested, Jefferson knelt by a blood-soaked altar while a young woman danced forward holding a live chicken. Within moments Isaac had taken the bird, cut its throat and splashed the still-warm blood all over Jefferson's face and chest. The rest of the blood was drained off into a round bowl.

As the last twitches of the bird ceased, Isaac stared down into the bowl and began to talk in the old tongue.

Jefferson listened to the lilting language, unable to recognise a word because his parents had never been allowed to speak it on Beaugard's land.

"I sees somethin' here …" Isaac said.

"What you see?" asked Jefferson.

"I sees Carly. She… *No!*"

Isaac's sudden gasp brought Jefferson to his feet. He looked into the bowl that Isaac held and for a moment he thought he saw Carly's face in the blood, only it didn't seem like her at all. She held the same, cruel, sneering expression she had worn when she sent him away the last time. There was a darkness crowded around her. Carly's lips moved, even though Jefferson heard no sound. A huge monstrous bulk appeared to be gathering momentum from the words she spoke.

Isaac abruptly tipped the blood out of the bowl and the vision was lost.

"What was it?" Jefferson said.

"You don't wan' to know what I seen. She ain't no good Jefferson. She into some bad voodoo. Somethin' like I never seen 'fore."

"You said you'd help me," Jefferson said.

"I can't. I never would have said so if I knowed what was goin' on …"

"Tell me what to do," Jefferson said.

"She gone to you," Isaac said. "You best for'git her."

No matter how much Jefferson pleaded, Isaac wouldn't change his mind. He sent the gathered congregation of semi-naked men and women away. And all evidence of their ceremony was removed, including the remains of the dead bird.

A few hours later the same people stood side by side with him in the cotton field, but no one spoke of the ritual.

The failed ceremony made Jefferson even more determined to save Carly. If something bad, some form of black magic, was responsible for the change in her, then maybe he could help. Maybe he should just steal her away, out of the city, as he had planned to do the night before.

When the work day ended, Jefferson gathered his possessions, his freedom papers and the small amount of money he had managed to save and set off from the plantation for the last time.

New Orleans town was in chaos.

"What's happenin'?" Jefferson asked as he saw a group of slaves running from the dock.

"The Union Navy done broke through the boom," one of them said.

"They is firing at anythin' that move. Git outta here fella or you is gon' git kill'."

Jefferson hurried away, but not in the direction that the slaves went. He carried on his journey to the French Quarter. Tonight, no matter what she said, Carly was going to listen to him. And, if he could, he would persuade her to leave with him.

As he did the previous night, Jefferson looked up at Carly's window. This time the balcony doors were closed, the room was in darkness. Jefferson felt a pang of anxiety as he hurried towards the building.

The building had once been a fine and expensive house, owned by a wealthy Creole family. Now this former regal home had been turned into a brothel. This dwelling housed girls and women on all levels of the spectrum and fees. Some catered to aristocracy, others – the basement whores – lay in cots underground and serviced the white-trash. White men, no matter how rich or poor, always seemed to need whores. Even so, girls like Carly were in the minority. She was favoured by the wealthy, and had entertained a fair amount of Confederate senior officers, too.

Jefferson pushed the thought of all those wealthy white men away. Her words still stung him but he couldn't give up on her. Not yet. Not until he was certain she was really where she wanted to be.

Heading around the back of the building Jefferson found the entrance to the basement rooms unlocked. Carly had told him about this entrance on one of the few occasions she managed to slip out to meet him. That was before the brothel changed her, but even then she had difficulty in being around him.

"Bein' with you makes me feel bad," she had said once. "You is everythin' I *thought* I wanted."

"I love you, Carly. I'm gon' git you outta here," Jefferson had promised.

"That's a nice dream, Brent. I'd like to believe it could happen. But you try takin' me from this place you is gon' git yourself strung up. I'm white man's property. You knows that would be stealin'."

Her words were intelligent like always, but Jefferson didn't want to hear them. It was on their second to last meeting when he had been the most insistent. Begging her to come with him then.

"You don't wan' somethin' that's been all used up," Carly said. "You deserve better'n me. Don't come back here. Forget about me. This just ain't gon' work out how it was s'posed to."

Jefferson couldn't forget, though, and all the times she'd been kind, juxtaposed with the one time she had rejected him, made it harder for him to let her go.

Now, he paused at the back door wondering what had gotten Isaac so spooked. What was it he had seen in the chicken's blood? Jefferson pushed away the weird and blurred image, convinced it was all his imagination, brought on by his desire to find the help he wanted. The thing was, Jefferson was a practical man. He didn't believe in heaven, hell or voodoo, he had just been so desperate he had hoped for a miracle.

A creeping doubt entered his mind when he recalled Isaac's reaction during the ritual. The houngan had been truly afraid of something.

Pushing down the nervous adrenaline that flooded his body, Jefferson tugged on the door, and as he expected, it opened effortlessly.

Once these downstairs quarters would have belonged to privileged serving slaves of the Creole household. Now, the interior of the basement smelt like hot sex and perspiration. All the time he was certain someone would see him there. One of the white pimps, or maybe one of the whores would raise the alarm. But no one came out of the rooms, and though Jefferson listened outside one of the doors, he heard no sounds from within.

There was litter and spillages of unknown origin underfoot. His shoes felt tacky as he traipsed quietly through the narrow corridor, past the whore's dormitory and up the staircase that led, he hoped, to the inside of the house. At the top of the staircase, Jefferson opened another door. He found himself in the main lobby.

Light poured in through a tall feature window illuminating a large circular hallway with an ornate marble floor and a grand staircase in the centre. Jefferson looked around at the many doors that came off from the hallway and up to the staircase and balcony that spread around the top. He could see several rooms in the gloom above and it didn't take him long to work out what direction Carly's room would be in.

The house was quiet though. Too quiet. Though he had timed his visit to coincide with the end of business, he had expected some customers, servants and whores to still be around. He went to the front door, found it locked up tight as though they expected the siege outside to surge inside. Maybe there had been no trade that evening. Maybe the whore house had remained closed while outside the world went to hell.

A surge of panic consumed him. What if the white man had taken all the best girls and fled? Forgetting caution now, Jefferson took the stairs two at a time. At the top he turned right and followed the doors around to the one he thought was Carly's. Then he paused. What if she was in there now with a customer? Could he bear to see it?

Jefferson floundered for a moment then he grabbed and turned the handle.

The door was locked.

Of course. It would be. They wouldn't let their best girl roam free would they? But then… how did she manage to meet with him in the past?

Jefferson pressed his ear against the door then tapped lightly. No sound came from inside at all. Then he heard a strange chanting coming from the floor below. He turned and walked back to the balcony, looking down the hallway. The sound was coming from one of the doors to the left. Though he had no idea what he was going to do, Jefferson hurried back down.

He could hear music now. This must be a ballroom. Perhaps some kind of debauched party was just beginning. He didn't know what to do. He couldn't just walk inside and take Carly. He wouldn't get within ten feet of her before some white man would shoot him down.

Jefferson heard a door creak somewhere behind him. He sank back into the shadows beside the staircase just before a group of people emerged from the room opposite. Three men wearing robes approached the door and Jefferson pressed himself deeper into the gloom for fear of being seen.

The doors to the ballroom opened releasing a flood of light into the stairway. Jefferson looked in, his eyes adjusting, and then opening wide. There in the centre of the room was Carly.

She was surrounded by several people all kneeling in a circle on the mosaic ballroom floor. She was wearing a long black dress and she stood before a tall table on which was opened a thick leather bound book. Her hands were raised, palms upwards as though in supplication, but her eyes remained fixed on the pages of the book.

As the other men joined her, two standing on either side, one joining the kneeling congregation, Jefferson was reminded of the ceremony that Isaac had performed. Only, Isaac had said something about daylight and dawn being crucial to keeping evil out of their magic. Carly was clearly involved in something more here than mere prostitution.

Jefferson realised he was trapped now in his hiding place unless someone closed the doors to the ballroom. But the open doors didn't seem to worry these people. Jefferson wondered if everyone in the main house was now gathered in this room and this was why there was no need to keep their activity secret. He cast his mind back to the whore den below. He hadn't seen anyone down there, his entry had been easy. Too easy.

"On dis night…" said Carly, "when the enemy is near, we call upon the Old Ones to help protec' dis house. Hide us, your servants, oh Great One."

Carly began to read directly from the book. It was like no language Jefferson had ever heard. The robed congregation shivered in unison as the idiom seemed to vibrate in the air. There was a substantial echo after each word, far more than the space should have created, mixed with the low timbre of Carly's voice.

Jefferson felt the hairs stand up on the back of his neck. He sensed power. Real magic which was nothing like the feeling he had experienced that morning in the clearing with Isaac. This voodoo was different. It was black magic, just as Isaac had said. It terrified him.

Jefferson felt an urge to run. An unnameable fear sent blood pounding through his veins. He felt like a buffalo cornered by hunters. It was a moment of clarity that made him realise he needed to get out of there before...

Jefferson swallowed. He forced his panic down and away. Before what? This was all just strange to him. What could the magic do to him or anyone else?

"On dis night ... when men die for their belief... we ask the Old Ones to protect' this house..." Carly repeated. "Destroy all those who enter dat do not belong here."

Carly slipped back into the strange tongue once more and the gathering raised their voices in a rehearsed response, not unlike the Christian chants that Jefferson had endured when he was a slave on the Beaugard Plantation.

Jefferson felt as though the words had pierced him. Whatever magic Carly was summoning – and he couldn't help but wonder how it was even possible after years of deliberate atheism – was presumably dangerous to any and all intruders, himself included.

Once more he began to wonder if he should leave before things went too far. He felt a real and genuine terror, though, that froze him in his hiding place while he watched the woman he loved.

The chanting suddenly stopped. A sense of anticipation rippled through the room. Jefferson could smell it, taste it, almost like the sexual energy he could sense in the basement.

"Bring in the sacrifice," Carly said.

A young white girl, face heavily painted, was brought in from a side room that led off from the ballroom. She was subdued, but afraid. Her thin arms trembled as she was brought before Carly.

Jefferson knew about forfeits from Isaac. Other than the death of a chicken – which Isaac had explained fulfilled the magic's need for life energy – the voodoo priest did not condone the taking of human life. *This*, he had said, *was black magic and it had no place in the rituals of good men.* Jefferson realised that this girl was, in fact, the equivalent of Isaac's chicken. Jefferson didn't know what to do. He had no responsibility to anyone but Carly. He couldn't risk being discovered for some white whore who meant nothing to him.

The girl was forced to lie down on the floor. The robe she was wearing was pulled open, and Jefferson could see that she was completely naked underneath. He wondered how she had come to be in the hands of these people. She seemed so young and he suddenly he wasn't convinced that she was the whore she was made-up to be, either. What if she were just some poor innocent who had been taken by these mad men? And how could Carly be involved with this?

Carly walked towards the girl. Now she was holding a dagger which glinted in the light from the chandeliers.

"You know what you have to do?" said Carly looking down at the girl.

Four men held her spread-eagled on the floor, each holding a wrist or an ankle.

The girl didn't struggle, but from his vantage point Jefferson could see tears roll down the sides of her face into her blonde hair.

"Dis is my sacrifice to you, oh Great One!" Carly announced. "My own blood sister, given in tribute. Give me the power to free dis city. Give me the power to seek revenge on those that have used me."

The girl squealed as Carly ran the sharp blade over her wrists, cutting viciously into the arteries.

Two more whores appeared with bowls. They placed them under the wrists of the girl and her captors twisted her arms viciously to ensure the blood seeped into the containers. Jefferson knew it wouldn't take long before the girl bled out. He had been shocked to see Carly inflicting the wounds but had forced himself to remain still and unobserved. Jefferson had heard of Carly's white sister. She had been close to her. Jefferson had even believed that Carly loved her. He couldn't believe that she had now, effectively murdered her for some obscure power.

The men and women were disrobing and all stood before Carly in their naked glory. As the bowls filled, the girl's captors let go of her arms and ankles and left her to bleed on the mosaic floor. Two of them brought the bowls over to the table and placed them before Carly. The knife was now lying beside the book, and Carly turned the page with a blood-stained hand. The blood stains disappeared as though the book was made of blotting paper and it had sucked in the blood.

Carly then dipped her fingers in the blood and began to perform a baptismal ceremony on the congregation. She daubed blood on the naked breasts of the women and smeared it on the erect penises of the men. When she had finished, she slipped the black dress she was wearing off her shoulders, dropping it down onto the floor.

Jefferson had never seen Carly naked before. He had wanted to marry her, have her as a wife and lover for life, not use her like a whore, even though he had thought she was no virgin: none of the slaves were, the overseers saw to that. Now he was fascinated with her beauty. The slender thighs, the full buttocks, the pert and round breasts that were so perfect he felt hypnotised by them. And so did, it seemed, everyone else in the room.

Jefferson began to think that this ritual was all some staged drama that would lead to sexual debauchery. It didn't though. And there was no doubt that the girl on the floor was a genuine sacrifice. Even so, Jefferson felt drawn from his hiding place, towards the ballroom and Carly. Her striking nakedness was like a magnet whose pull he couldn't resist.

Unable to stop himself, Jefferson stood and walked forward towards the open doors and into the room.

Carly was smearing blood on her own breasts and loins now. She paused to look up at Jefferson. Her eyes narrowed but she didn't stop the ritual and none of the white or black men present even acknowledged his presence.

"I'm here to take you…" Jefferson said. "The city is fallin' to the Union Army. Soon all black slaves will be free."

"I knows,' said Carly. 'I bin callin' this power to free us all."

"This dark magic?"

Carly nodded. Jefferson looked around. The rest of the horde appeared frozen, as though they were statues, posed in a garden of insanity.

"I knowed when we met that you were right for me," Carly said. "I seen it in your eyes."

"I love you, Carly."

"You went to Isaac to try and help me…"

"How did you…?"

Jefferson tasted blood as Carly pressed her fingers against his lips to silence him. It woke him from his confused trance. He looked around at the people again. They were like clockwork dolls that had run down.

"What is dis?" Jefferson asked. "Carly? It ain't right you kil' yor sissa."

"I had to kil' something I love in order to bring the power."

Carly backed away to the table. She stood before the book once more, arms held up, exactly as she had earlier.

"It's almost time," she said.

Outside Jefferson thought he heard musket shots. The army would be near. What would they do when they discovered the dead white girl? What would they think of Carly working her spell, covered in blood, like the men and women around them, standing paralysed like abandoned puppets?

"They ain't frozen," Carly said as though reading his mind. "They is in a dif'rent time from us right now."

"How?"

"I open'd a doorway… you might say… in another worl'. This is the worl' of the great ones. The ancient gods that hide in and around our worl' waitin' to be invited in."

"I don't understand."

"This book," Carly said. "My white daddy had it in his library. He had no idea what it was or of the power inside. I knowed. I seen it. I read it and unnerstood."

Jefferson looked at the book for the first time. He couldn't read, the words meant nothing to him, but he approached the table, looking down at the hand-scrawled patterns that filled the page.

Jefferson stared at the markings and he, too, began to understand. Carly's father hadn't been killed by an uprising but something she had done using this book. It all seemed suddenly clear.

He looked back at the body of the white girl. Carly's half-sister. Whiter now that she had bled to death than she had been in life.

"You wanted to free everyone?" Jefferson said. "Why don't I believe that is all you is doin' here?"

Carly smiled but her face wasn't the cruel sneer that had eaten into his soul nights earlier. It was warm and happy, the Carly he had fallen for.

"I done this for us to be truly together. I can't be with no ordinary man, Brent. I ain't no ordinary woman."

"What you sayin'? All these white men … All those overseers you went with … you think I don't knows what you did to stop me bein' beaten?"

"I couldn't let them ruin a perfect vessel," Carly said.

"*Vessel*? What you sayin'? Carly I come for you… you gunna leave with me now or not?"

Carly's eyes fell back down to the book and the text. She began to chant those alien words once more and then time seemed to restart. Around him the people were moving again. Two of the men caught hold of his arms, pulling him back from the table. Jefferson struggled and fought against them, but the words that Carly continued to speak made his limbs weak, his mind full of a deep thrumming sound and a heavy fog, and choked off the sound from his voice.

The men pushed him to his knees. Head bowed, all Jefferson could see was Carly's bare feet beneath the table. The air around him shimmered as though it were above the flames of a camp fire. The temperature became unbearable. Sweat ran down his forehead into his eyes. Jefferson felt an impulse to rip away his clothing. He felt as though the fabric was suffocating him.

Carly stepped out from behind the table. Jefferson raised his head and looked up at her perfect thighs, then her sex, and finally her face. She touched his shoulder and then his head as though bestowing some strange blessing. All the time her lips moved, and that peculiar guttural language poured out, hanging in the air and burning into his soul.

Jefferson didn't feel like himself anymore. He felt disembodied, and yet the pain he felt in his skin still reached out to him. He remembered the priest on Beaugard Plantation preaching every Sunday about fire and brimstone, the heat of hell, and he thought that somehow he had found his way there. Only Satan wasn't a man, it was a woman disguised as a human.

He saw through that façade now. Carly wasn't what she appeared to be and never had been. But how this had happened he didn't know. Maybe she was some demon born in the body of a child.

"My mamma knew the old ways," she said. "When my daddy forced his way into her, she cursed him and me. I wasn't born with a human soul. No human man can ever force me... I can only be given to a god."

Jefferson heard her words float to him through a miasma of choking sulphuric air. His body coughed, he felt a vague discomfort as the poison choked his lungs but his spirit was separate, gone from the physical form and only attached by a vague umbilical cord of light.

He looked down on the scene, saw Carly for the demon's whore she really was. In this state he knew so much of what had been going on. There were flashes of memory.

Carly stopping the overseers beating him, Carly going to the master and telling him to sell her to the whore house. The master was so confused by her soft voice, eyes glazed over by her hypnosis. Then Jefferson saw Carly in the bedroom upstairs. He knew this wasn't possible, but he was certain he was seeing her with her first client. The man came in, excited by her half-naked body. But Carly just touched his forehead and he stopped moving. For a whole hour the man remained sitting in a chair. Then he left, saying she was the best whore he had ever had.

Jefferson tried to call her name but his ethereal body had no capability to make the sounds his physical form could and now that was so far, far below, still kneeling at her feet.

He saw the darkness gathering around her. The words of magic still poured from her mouth like maggots swarming from a dead body. They ate at his soul and they pushed him farther away from the world of the living.

The black, roiling shadow thing that grew around Carly was now dwarfing Jefferson's body.

Carly looked up and smiled. Jefferson wondered if she could see him there, if she wanted him to see everything that was happening.

"It'll be you in body only..." Carly said. A rapt, fanatical grin spread across her face.

The darkness stretched over Jefferson's form. He felt a stabbing pain as the thing swarmed him. Then it was as though a thousand bees stung his skin simultaneously. His body jerked in protest. The thing squeezed him, forcing his mouth to open as it pushed the air from his lungs. But as

Jefferson's body heaved in new air, so it drew in the essence of this demon shadow.

Jefferson tried to yell once more, but he was growing more distant from the world of the living. The shadow disappeared inside him. Jefferson felt pain once more. This was the awful agony of his soul being expelled from his corporeal form.

He floated as high as the ceiling now. Carly picked up the blood-stained knife and pointed it upwards towards him.

Jefferson screamed inside as he felt the last tie sever and knew that his body was no longer a part of his existence.

The Jefferson-demon stood now. It looked around, as though seeing the men and women around him for the first time. It took the knife from Carly's fingers, and without warning, plunged it deep into one of the men nearby. As the man fell, the demon latched onto the wound, drinking and lapping at the blood.

When the blood stopped flowing, the demon attacked another worshipper, and another. Bleeding them all dry.

Carly stood, waiting until the demon was satisfied. Above, silently weeping, Jefferson watched his own body committing the atrocities. His mind screamed in denial as, having fed, the creature turned to Carly and forced her willingly over the table like a dog taking a bitch.

Carly screamed as the demon used Jefferson's body to pleasure her. She laughed and cried until her own orgasm shuddered through her, and at that point, the demon poured his seed inside her.

Jefferson wished his mind would go elsewhere, that he could stop seeing the woman he loved being violated by something using his own form. This wasn't what he had wanted for her, or himself.

When their violent mating was done, the demon took Carly's hand and led her naked towards the foyer. Jefferson tried to follow, but sensing him still there, Carly paused, looked up and raised her hand towards him.

"Stay," she said.

Jefferson tried to fight her will but he found himself unable to move.

Frozen in this one place, he could sense that Carly and the demon had left the house but there was nothing he could do but stay where she had left him.

Around him, the air seemed to boil and move as though, separated by a thin veil, monstrous gods held him in place with their unknowable powers.

Time slipped. Jefferson became aware of movement below. A group of union soldiers entered the room. They looked at the slaughtered bodies and shook their heads.

"Looks like some sort of madness went horribly wrong," said one of the soldiers.

"Bad voodoo," said another man as he entered the ballroom. Jefferson recognised Matthew. The black man seemed to be helping the soldiers.

"Sorry," said the first soldier. "We would have saved these poor slaves if we could have."

"I knows it. We is glad you're here anyways," said Matthew. "I only hopes my friend managed to get his girl outta here before this went down."

Jefferson watched them go.

There was nothing he could do. He was trapped and held there, incorporeal, powerless and hopeless. In his mind he screamed and screamed.

But the Great One, the elder god which had empowered Carly, and which had allowed his own body to be possessed by one of its nameless creatures, just tightened its grip.

Forever.

Like Comment Share

Don Webb

LIKE COMMENT SHARE
By Don Webb

So two years after my last friend had done so, I finally joined Facebook. Hey, I'm in IT, the last thing I want to see any more of is glowing screens. My wife had lots of useful advice: don't play the games, they're a time-suck; don't friend people you don't at least know; don't share every political or cute cat meme that comes along. I stuck by her rules for three days.

Ok, at first I played a few games – What Dr. Who Companion Are You? (Sarah Jane Smith). Which Literary Figure Are You? (Leopold Bloom). And I started getting "friend" requests from friends of friends of friends. And how could I not repost that picture of a black and white cat on a skateboard? I mean that's just too damn cute. So suddenly I had 332 friends. Then I got a request from Xulthan. I didn't know Xulthan, I figured he was some gaming geek I had known once. And Xulthan added me to a group "The Green God Game." I hate it when they add you to groups without asking you.

Xulthan posted a video link.

It was the strangest music I ever heard – vaguely Middle Eastern with songs in some language I couldn't place. I had been in Kuwait during Operation Desert Storm and could pick out Arabic. Maybe this was Yezidi or Martian. But it made the hairs on the back of my neck stick up when I listened. The video feed was pages and pages of parchment written in an alphabet unknown to me. I figured it was clues for the game, so I studied them closely, but nothing clicked. Except I did start dreaming about them. I would be walking in my neighborhood and all the shops would have signs in that weird script, for example.

Then the first game. Answer this riddle or agree to pay the consequences. "You are asleep in your home. It's 3:33 in the early morning. Someone is knocking at your front door, someone is knocking at your back door. Someone is knocking at your side window. What do you open first?" I put down window, I thought that seemed more like what a friend would do. WRONG – you open your eyes! For the consequence I was supposed to wear a green shirt on Wednesday. I'm a good sport, so I did. I saw three men and two women wearing green in the lunchroom. Three of them had already chosen a table. I walked over and said, "Green God Game?" They said yes and I joined them. The others drifted over. Then one man's phone rang. He had been texted:

READ THIS TO THE GGG. Welcome. The Green God smiles upon you! Soon your luck will increase if you continue meeting. Hour of the Green Ray. Day of Hermes-Yog. Year of the City 10,347,666. So it is done!

"Cool!" said one of the women – youngish, freckled, with red-brown hair. "It's an ARG!"

"What's an ARG?" asked Thomas Martinez.

I explained, "An Alternate Reality Game. The gamers are fed clues to solve a mystery. It usually ends in them participating in or witnessing a flash mob."

The older Chinese-looking woman said, "That's one of those spontaneous get-togethers? I've seen that on YouTube."

So we talked about ARGs, flash mobs, Facebook, and our history with computers. Mr. Martinez was the oldest among us – he had actually bought an Altair 8800 back in 1975. We talked about performance art. Bill Nadis' most far-out art experience was seeing the Trans-Siberian Orchestra's "The Lost Christmas Eve" with his wife a couple of years ago. Suzi Machworter, the redhead, had, on the other hand, been a nude canvass at a Dallas Museum of Art show. An artist had done an Aztec style painting on her naked body, and then invited members of the audience to cover her in black paint until his art was erased. We shared e-mail and FB stats and what part of the company we were from. Then we went back to our cubicles, except for Calvin Lee, the young black guy with the wimpy mustache who worked in Transpiration, fixing vans.

As fate would have it I ran into Calvin next Saturday. We were both eating at Taco-Taco. He saw me and motioned me to join him in line. At Taco-Taco, you get to shoot dice when you pay for your bill. If the dice come up Taco-Taco (tacos had replaced the one spot), you won a free lunch. A one in thirty-six shot. Calvin rolled. Taco-Taco. Then I rolled; Taco-Taco.

"Hey," said Calvin, "Maybe it's the Green God? The odds must be thousands to one against that happening."

"1,296 to 1." I said, "Pretty cool. Maybe we should play the Lotto today."

We had lunch, shared our life stories. I did buy Lotto tickets later, but no dice. That night, Xulthan posted his status.

Look to the northeast quadrant of the sky five minutes after midnight. A wonder shall appear. Say these words: "Zodicare Yog Sehresh!" and the Green God shall hear you.

I didn't intend to say anything, but it was a warm night, and Sally sat out our lawn chairs. We smoked a little weed and watched the sky.

Right on time, a beautiful green meteor flared across the sky.

"Say it! Say it!" Squealed my wife.

"Zodicare Yog Sehresh!" I was pretty dubious about pronunciation.

Next Monday we all wore our shirts. No one had told us to. We were all excited. Then Calvin brought up the free tacos. Then Suzi told us that she and Mrs. Wong had met at a convenience store and dared each other to buy scratch off tickets. Suzi won $75 and Mrs. Wong $100. Then they bought several more tickets and lost each time.

"So," I said, "How many of you said the magic words after the meteor flared forth?"

Everyone put their hands up. They had different expressions – Mr. Martinez looked ashamed, Mrs. Wong religious, Suzi ecstatic, Nadis embarrassed. Clarence grim – maybe even paranoid.

"Whoever is playing us is doing pretty good." I said.

There was some nervous laughter and then *my* phone rang. A text from #*xulthanrises.*

Priest Jough El Ayin has passed the boundary. Two Powers are seen. Eat no meat this night and you will see Ool Athag.

"What the fuck does that mean?" asked Nadis.

"It means eat fish like during Lent." Said Mr. Martinez.

"This is fucked." Said Nadis. "I don't like being made a fool of."

Suzi said, "No one's making a fool of you. It's just a game. You're just mad because you didn't win any money. Come on over to the Sac-n-Pac and I'll buy you a scratch-off. It will be fun."

Nadis was a balding single guy in his late thirties. He wasn't about to turn down being with a pretty girl. They rest of us went back to work, Pete Nunio made dirty jokes all the way back to our pod.

Oddly enough my wife had bought beer battered fish sticks for dinner that night, so I didn't have to make any decision about what to eat.

That night I dreamed a vast city, whose architecture was some fantastic blend of Angkor Wat and Giger prints – with a little Escher thrown in. The city was filled with strange looking men and women that wore glittering metal masks. At dusk, beneath two huge moons, we gathered at a great pit outside the city. A bright crimson ray came from the depths, and the people moaned in ecstasy. Then two green arms – hundreds of meters long – shot out of the pit. They fastened on an older man who carried a staff. They seized him, lifted him high in the air, and then pulled him down into the pit. His mask fell off as he descended. He looked like Thomas Martinez. Then people began dancing and embracing. It turned into an orgy. I rutted with a half woman, half goat and I saw Suzi nearby being taken by two hairy, apelike men at the same time. The air smelled of blood and cinnamon. Music – the music from the video – played.

I awoke aroused and tried to get my wife into it, but it was nearly time for the alarm to go off and she said, "Honey it's a workday. We'll do this on the weekend, when we can get into it." I let her go back to sleep and took care of myself. At the moment of orgasm, I almost always make a little noise. This time I said a word, "Sehresh!" I don't know why, and it scared me enough to keep me from drifting back to sleep.

That morning when I logged in at work, there was e-mail from Nadis inviting all of us to lunch at the Star of India across the street. We all showed up (except for Martinez). Nadis had won $1000 on a scratch-off game.

"It's all true!" he said.

We made a date to go buy tickets en masse that night.

Suzi was texted from #xulthanisrisen.

The time of Exchange is over. Priest Jough El Ayin has transitioned to your space and time. The Green God Game starts on the day of Hermes-Yog at the hour of the Cerise Ray. Odo kikale Nafatagn!

"That's helpful. Where's Martinez?" asked Calvin.

"What did you have for dinner last night, Calvin?" I asked.

"Big Mac and fries. Why?"

"No dreams?" I asked.

"Why? You mean that bullshit about don't eat meat? Why, did you have a dream?"

We looked at each other, our nan and curries getting cold.

"What's this got to do with Martinez?" asked Calvin. "You guys are serious bullshitters."

Calvin grabbed his cream colored I-phone and called Martinez. No results. Then he dialed Martinez's supervisor.

"He didn't come into work today. What do you bullshitters know?"

We stared at our food. Suzi and Nadis blushed.

"You guys are seriously fucked up. I ain't playin'."

Calvin got up to leave. Mrs. Wong said, "Sit down, Calvin. You are playing because it's how we will get rich. Sit down. Martinez was taken because he stood too close to something dangerous. That won't be our fate."

"What do you mean, 'taken'? Taken where? By who?"

Nadis said, "The God of the Pit, the motherfather of the Green God."

Pete Nunio asked, "What?"

Nadis said, "Look there's a text on Scribd. Google *The Seven Rays of Ool Othag*. Suzi and I found it this morning."

"Over breakfast?" I asked.

"Over none of your damn business. If you want to play a game, you better know the rules."

Lunch proceeded fairly quietly. We trotted back to our cubicles. I downloaded *The Seven Rays* but I didn't have time to read it. My boss piled it on that afternoon. None of us knew Martinez outside of the game. Well we were all Facebook friends, which meant we occasionally told each other when we made a road trip, saw a cute cat video, or passed on vaguely liberal political memes. Everyone but Calvin showed up after work and we walked to the Sac-n-Pac and bought tickets, and more tickets, and won nothing.

"The Time of Exchange is over." Suzi said.

"So when's the Hour of the Cerise Ray? That's like orange, right?" Suzi said, "At sunset comes the Cerise Ray down from the ruined planet searching for its opposite among the Hornless Ones. The unity being made in the Red Ceremony magic, all is balanced. Life for death, death for life, and the Daemons sleep in the Sixth Angle until the forces need be equalized again."

"What the fuck does that mean?" I asked.

"We need to get together at sunset on Wednesday. Day after tomorrow. We'll play a game."

"So is this an ARG? Is Martinez spoofing us? Or is this about life and death?" asked Pete.

Mrs. Wong answered. "It's a game. It's Facebook. And it maybe life and death. My aunt choked to death on a Mah-jongg tile. Death is never far away. Thousands die each hour, each minute."

"You guys are so much fun to hang out with," I said, "as a game, I'm not very amused."

I went home, said nothing to my wife, and when I saw the Xulthan had posted twice, I did not read them.

The next morning, I did not read them.

That night I clicked on the two links. Clicking wasn't playing.

The first was a very amateur shot of a boy being born. Parents looked normal. No occult significance. I always think the miracle of life looks a little gross on video. The second video looked very professional. A camera snakes through what appears to be a Stonehenge style ruin at night. Desert all around, three circles of stone. Great and spooky flute music playing in the background. The camera rests on the center stone the right size for a living room couch. I guess it might be an altar stone. The camera zooms in and we see a glyph carved in the gray-green stone. Simple, geometrical. Yet somehow it makes me fearful. I watch the video seven times in a row until my wife calls me to bed, calling herself a "Facebook widow." Nice one, Mary, real supportive. I start to tell her about the Green God Game, but realize how stupid and paranoid it sounds.

I spend thirty minutes getting dressed the next day. I am up and out before my wife. It usually takes fifteen minutes to dress, shave and grab a packet of Pop-Tarts. Should I wear a green shirt? Should I send a fuck-off? Is this a game that will end in a filmed scene, fifteen minutes of

YouTube fame and prizes? Is this an eldritch horror breaking into our world through a soft spot? What happens after a hundred years of monster movies, plush Cthulhu dolls, and prank spooky e-mails? When does the barrier that our ancestors' ancestors had so carefully set-up finally wear away? How many people had been like my great-grandmother who really said, "Speak not of the devil, lest he appear?"

Fuck it. It was the day of Hermes Yog, so I wore a "Kiss Me I'm Irish" t-shirt. Let the Green God deal with that.

We gathered at lunch. Even Calvin. We all wore green, although in Calvin's case, he had chosen a clip-on bow tie. Nadis and Suzi looked high on love, Mrs. Wong was prim and serious in a green dress that was the height of fashion twenty years ago. Pete Nunio looked younger than his 28 years. In his green and white dress shirt. I would've thought he was an intern reporting on his first day. We ate at Ruby's barbecue, because we needed to get away from work, and it was an eight minute drive.

"So?" I asked, "Are we going through with it?"

"With what?" asked Pete. "All we heard was that the game took place at the time of the tangerine or something. They didn't tell us to gather anywhere."

"The hour of the Cerise Ray." Said Suzi.

Nadis said, "All of you guys aren't thinking this through. There isn't a 'them' or a 'he' or an 'it' – somebody here is running a little game."

"I thought of that," I said, "could one of us rig the lottery?"

"Maybe that was chance." Said Pete.

"No. I think we were Chosen." Said Mrs. Wong. "It is like that Shirley Jackson story we all read in High School. 'The Lottery.'"

I asked, "What about Martinez?"

Clarence said, "I went by his house. He lives on the east side in a little house that used to belong to his parents. The lights were off. I knocked and rang the bell and shouted till the neighbors came out."

Suzi said, "Fred and I will be in the big truck bay by the north building at 6:35. That's sunset. Come if you want or not. It will be empty, it's Wednesday night, and all of those trucks are making deliveries until about midnight, right Calvin?"

Calvin said, "Yeah, that's right. It's unlocked because folks need to park their vans and trucks. It's got a break room."

"Great," I said, "we can meet the dread Green God with a Coke."

Calvin followed me back to my cubicle after lunch. He was scared – possibly more scared because he had not dreamt of Martinez. He wanted to know that I really had. He wanted to know if he was being fooled.

"Look, I don't know what to tell you. I feel we're all taking part in a ritual. Not as the players, not as the priest on stage, but just the folks in the audience. The people that stand up, sit down, and kneel."

"But those people feel good when it's over." Said Calvin.

"We might also."

He hung around for an hour. Twice my boss had walked by. I finally told him to beat it. His last words to me were that he was not going to be at the truck dock. I told him that I would probably bow out as well. So he waved pretty sheepishly when I met him at the door of the dock at 6:20. Suzi and Nadis were there, and Mrs. Wong. Pete held out until 6:33.

Suzi and Fred had chalked a diagram on the floor – looking a little like a hopscotch board in seven colors. At one end it was broad and orange colored. Cerise. Whatever. At the other end it was narrow and green. At the narrow end stood a rack with chains, winches, and hooks for lifting engines out of vans. It was terribly suggestive. Suzi had printed out *The Seven Rays of Ool Othag* and bound them into a green cardboard notebook. She read her lines.

"Welcome worthy players. As before, so now. The gods molt and break free of their larval shells. They teach us how to run and dance and scream. The real world breaks into the world of mirrors. Hear the mirrors breaking! Hear the drums of Ia Nath Thool!"

At that moment all of our phones buzzed, rang, or played music. We opened or activated them, fussed for a moment to remember how to work the loud speaker setting. Drumming filled the air, an odd time signature. Dave Brubeck would have been pleased. Clarence hopped up the diagram as though it were hopscotch.

"Not like that," said Mrs. Wong, "remember the video."

And that was when I realized that we hadn't all seen the same clips. We had been subtlety prepared for different roles. Clarence looked ashamed and said, "Show me, Simlisell."

Mrs. Wong bowed, and suddenly did not seem like a frail old woman that worked in Marketing. Suddenly she seemed wise and menacing. She stepped through the seven tiers striking a pose at each. Her poses were like Egyptian hieroglyphs. She was living letters – or rather words! At the last tier, with its deep hunter's green, she struck a pose that reminded me of the glyph on the altar stone. The air in the large dock suddenly seemed charged as though we had been running an ionizer or a Van de Graff generator for hours. Mrs. Wong bowed to us, and despite my burning desire to opt out of the game, I bowed back with the rest of them.

Then the air/space/our brains cracked. I could see a crack in the air, somehow floating in space over the suspension device. A long green crack. Pete Nunio danced the seven stations. A bigger crack started. Then Suzi. Then Fred. With Fred, fragments of the world passed away. I was looking on an alien world with a ruined planet in the sky and two small moons. The music now came through the cracks, not our phones. The tempo changed. Everyone but me had danced. I could see the Pit and what was left of Martinez was crawling out of it.

Fred Nadis said, "Shersess, it is your time."

I knew that word. I saw it flash into my mind from that first YouTube link. I could read the strange letters. It meant sacrifice. I started to run to the door, but Suzi and Calvin had anticipated my move. So I ran to the little room that held the snack bar. I wedged a rusty folding chair under the grimy doorknob. They began to chant, "Sheress, Sheress, zodicare entoia!" That meant *Sacrifice, Sacrifice, don't stay in your cave!* My being in this crummy little room was part of the ritual as well. They kept chanting.

I heard the outside door open. I screamed for help. Someone could help me. But their chant changed. "Xulthan! Xulthan! Qaa nadezzer, qaa Sheress!" *Xulthan! Xulthan, call the little one out, call for the Sacrifice!*

I wanted to look. I wanted to see Xulthan. He/She/It began singing. It wasn't a human voice. As the song grew unguided by the scales and chords and rhythms of Earth, I saw several of the images from Facebook. Not just things that I identified with the Green God Game. Posters of girls in futuristic green vinyl dresses. Volcanoes erupting. News items about asteroids hitting the Earth in record numbers. Biographies of weirdo painters and writers. Dirty jokes that I couldn't quite understand. Train wrecks. Burning school buses. Everything. Everything I had viewed on my quest from 0 to 332 friends. It was all part of a ritual. A ritual began long ago and farther away than I could imagine. It had been soaking into me, little by little. I felt it echo around my bones. It couldn't be written in a book, or maybe even in a thousand books.

I knew when Xulthan finished Its song, I would move the chair. I would leave my little cave as I had always done for centuries without end. I would walk into the crack between the worlds. I would bring balance. It would hurt. It would be squishy.

It would be Blissful.

(For the memory of Joel Lane)

With Death Comes Life

Scott T. Goudsward

WITH DEATH COMES LIFE
By Scott T. Goudsward

It is said the world would end in fire. That was wrong.
I'd like to say that it was fast and painless. It wasn't.

The morning started like every other. I rolled out of bed, turned off the alarm and padded to the bathroom for a shower and shave. Downstairs, I knew there would be breakfast waiting and a note from Jessica, my live in girlfriend. Later in the week, we'd be celebrating our sixth year together, little dancing, good meal, and dessert would be an engagement ring and a tearful "YES!" Or that's how I played it out in my mind.

Except when I walked into the kitchen, tightening my tie, she was slumped over the table, face down in the omelet she made me. A puddle of blood was spreading on the table, covering and soaking everything, dripping over the edge, saturating and staining the tablecloth. I ran over, slipping on Jessie's blood on the floor around the chair.

At one point I remember screaming her name, and then just screaming. I tried lifting her head, but there was so much blood. I moved her, just a hair and the scalpel that was still wedged between her limp fingers tumbled to the floor.

I saw the edges of the wound on her neck and pictured her all too clearly jamming the scalpel into her neck and slicing, pulling the perfectly sharp blade from one ear to the other, chewing her lips bloody to not scream out while tears rolled down her face. I reached for the phone on the counter, trying my hardest not to pass out before I dialed 911.

I woke up on the couch, though I don't remember walking to it. There was a damp towel on my forehead. I slipped it off and sat up. The apartment was crowded with cops, medics and photographers. A young man wearing a jacket with the EMT service logo on it, pointed a rubber gloved finger at me, then to a cop. In my pocket I felt the weight of the ring box; I'd been taking it back and forth from work so Jessie wouldn't find it.

"How are you feeling?"

"How do you think?" The medic grimaced, from my answer or his stupid question, I don't know. A cop came over and sat across from me on the ottoman. He looked at me like I was guilty, that I pressed the blade into her throat and killed her, watching as she cried, bleeding out and drowning in the blood filling her lungs.

"I need to ask you some questions." He said. No introduction, no condolences no business card. I sat back against the couch, deciding if I should cry, rage or just give up. It still didn't feel real to me. She had just kissed me earlier that morning before getting out of bed.

The barrage of standard questions began. "Did you notice anything strange? Was she acting peculiar? Was there a note? Why did you move the body? Where'd she get a scalpel?"

"No, no, no, I had to, she's a nurse, was a nurse." He stood and shook his head walking away as he slipped his notebook into his coat pocket. Jessie had been working day shift at the hospital for three years; I worked in the admin office. I never saw anyone at the hospital. She was in the ER, she saw and knew everyone. I watched, damp rag pressed to my face, as they zipped up the body bag and wheeled her towards the apartment door. I stood and walked over.

"Give me a minute, please." The EMTs looked at each other and then to the cops who nodded at them. I unzipped the bag, just to show her face, not the awful fissure in her throat. Her skin was pale, almost grey. Her lips would have been blue if she hadn't been chewing on them to repress screaming. I wanted to run my fingers through her hair and kiss her. The thought of kissing the cold bloodied flesh sent a shiver through me. Instead, I kissed her tepid, rubbery cheek and mouthed words "good bye."

When my lips touched her cold cheek, a flash of something ripped through my mind. A picture? The last thought trapped in her dead brain? I stumbled back and covered my face as the tears rolled down my freshly shaven cheeks. The cop came back over and ushered me to the couch.

"Is there anyone we can call for you?" There was a sympathetic tinge to his words this time. I heard the zipper on the bag closing and the squeak of wheels on the gurney as they wheeled Jessie out of the apartment.

"Call my boss, please." I tossed my cell phone at him and leaned back against the soft cushions. I tried to remember the image from the contact with Jessie's corpse. An old book, and a symbol on the page that glowed in the darkness or was it starlight? When the cleaning crew came in I went for the bedroom.

There was no way I was going to stay and witness them sloshing her blood across my kitchen floor with a mop, or whatever they used. In the ER, they used pads to absorb blood spills. In the kitchen, I had no idea. I sat on her side of the bed; I could smell her on the sheets, the scent of her shampoo on the pillow case. I reached for my cell, but the cop had it. I had the dubious task of calling friends and family and letting them know what happened.

A week after the burial, the apartment wasn't right. I'd gone through all of her belongings, looking for a note or a clue, anything to tell me why she would do that to herself. What possible reason could such a young beautiful girl have to do that? Despite everything, I still had that brief blurred image stamped in my mind of her last thought. She was trying to communicate something to me.

If it was a book, it wasn't on the shelves or the coffee table. I'd already gone through the closet and her dresser. Feeling deflated, I flopped on the couch. My time in the apartment was limited, I needed to move and escape her memory. Then I saw them sitting in the china cabinet, a brief reflection of the Sun streaming in through the window. Her car keys.

The green Toyota was still in the parking lot. Her nephew was coming to pick it up, it was going to be his first car. It's a shame he had to get it this way. I walked around the back of the car trying to not look inside at the faded green lei around the mirror or the curled photos taped to the dash.

I opened the trunk not knowing what to expect. It was empty except for a towel wrapped bundle in the middle. It seemed to glow in the dusky haze of the compartment. I reached for it, and pulled my hand back. What if it was something personal and treasured? Something for me? I still had the ring box in my pocket.

I picked up the bundle, the towels were hot from the Sun bearing down on the car. There was another flash, another blinding moment of searing pain, then orgasmic relief as the flash of an image faded into memory. I shook my head and went inside.

I stared at the bundle on the table as I slid my keys off the ring, the kid didn't need keys to the apartment or my car. I clutched each piece of metal in my hand to the point of being painful. I tossed the key ring on the table and put the other keys back in the cabinet, giving the bundle on the table a wide berth. I poured a scotch and then sat down across from it.

A low level vibration emanated from it, an almost inviting buzz. I smiled and sipped my drink. "You went off and got that box of sex toys, finally." I reached for the bundle. The towels were stone cold, the vibration stopped with the closeness of my hand. I unwrapped the top layer and let the towel fall to the floor.

A shudder ripped through my body, remembering the puddle of blood that had been there over a week ago. The second towel slipped off just as easily. This time it brought no reactions. An ancient book had been nestled within the towels. No name on the spine, no writing on the yellowed cover. The edges of the paper looked old and fragile. The vibration resumed, low and pleasing, when it was free.

I stared at it for a few minutes. Flashes of symbols, alight with energies, played across my mind. I leaned back in the chair when it ended. I knew why Jessie had got the book, if it made me feel this good. The thought of my dead girlfriend brought reality screaming back. I covered it with the towels and took my drink to the couch.

Her nephew came without much fanfare or conversation; we exchanged pleasantries and condolences, cold and practiced. After I handed him the keys, he was gone moments later. And I was alone again, with the book. There had to be a valid reason why she had this thing that gave off a slight miasmic haze when the light was direct on it.

I found Jessie's laptop under the couch where she always kept it, in case the place got broken into. "What were you doing with this?" I went through the desktop and the personal files. There were financial spreadsheets and a bucket list. At the end of the bucket list in underscored text *become immortal* with a smiley face after it. I sighed and closed the document.

"What the fuck did she want with you?" I asked the book. I was knocked back from the answer. It showed horrible and wonderful things, ceremonies and ritualistic sacrifice, cultists roaming the oceanfront during the high tide with torches bleeding themselves as they walked. The last bit of the answer was Jessie sitting at the table with the green-blue shimmer from the book, typing maniacally into the laptop.

"*Stupid question, Dan. She wanted to be immortal.*" I looked around the apartment for the voice. I was alone, windows and door closed, air conditioning humming in the background.

"*She found me in a very unsavory place, Dan. Jessie told you she was going on a business trip.*"

"There's no business trips for the hospital unless it's a nursing conference."

"*Good catch, but a little too late.*" I looked around again, convinced somehow it was all just an inner dialogue.

"Where did she go?"

"*You should also be asking yourself, what did she do? Remember, her walking with a limp when she came home. No sex for weeks, said she pulled something in her lady parts at the gym.*"

"But the membership had expired."

"*She laid down and opened her body, physically and psychologically for days, lying prone while body after body assaulted and invaded her. She bled, Dan. Bled and cried and screamed.*"

107

I looked at the book, my eyes rimmed with anger and hurt. Fear and rage surged through me. I wanted to pick it up and lob it out into the parking lot. Let some skater kid find it and be done with the horrible thing.

"Now you see."

"What do you want?"

"You, your soul, and to make you happy again. I want to help you get something back. And all you need to do, is gather some items and bleed a little. I can bring her back for you, Dan. Don't you want that? To have your girl back?"

"You did it." I said. "You put that image in my head. Not Jessie." Rage gave way to pain and grief.

"She was dead when you found her. If you had come down for coffee before your shower, you probably could have stopped me." I raised my eyes at the change. Me versus I. The voice was softer, more feminine. It was talking to me in Jessie's voice.

"Don't you want me back, sweetie? We can be together again. I'm in so much pain." I pictured her again, blonde hair matted with blood, facedown at the table with nothing: no warning, no signs, not even something scrawled on a paper towel begging for forgiveness.

"Jessie was strong and smart. She never would have listened to you. You tricked her. Promised her something."

"Life is made of blood. I wasted mine. Don't waste yours, Dan."

"You killed her and stop sounding like her!" I felt my throat constrict as my voice raised. Was this hysterics? Was it frenzy, or was talking to this damned book some way to heal the hurt, make the pain go away? The grieving process was horseshit and, in a couple of days, I would be expected back at my job, surrounded by everything and everyone that reminded me of Jessie, walking the corridors while they whispered behind my back.

I dry swallowed and got up from the couch. I poured two glasses of scotch, one for me and one for the book. I kept the bottle close to me. When this fit of insanity was over I was going to need the warming brown liquid to sooth me into unconsciousness.

I had to imagine what I looked like sitting there, drink in one hand, bottle next to me, staring at this book with the blue green haze. Like a child holding a flashlight with a blue bulb under his chin, making scary faces and casting long deep shadows over my eyes and cheeks. I finished the drink and continued to stare at the book.

The reds and golds of sunset spread like a quilt across my apartment through the sliders. For a moment it was tranquil, the eye of the storm. I was getting ready for whatever fresh illusion my mind was going to throw at me. Is this what going crazy felt like? Hearing voices? Conversations with inanimate objects? Having those voices change in mid sentence?

"What do you say, Dan? Want to fulfill my dreams? Make me immortal?"

"You're dead!"

"Not entirely." I ran my fingers over the book's cover, feeling the dry, rough leather. There was excitement to it. Just brushing against the hide made me hard. I reached for the bottle while imagining it was Jessie's skin I was caressing, the curves of her breasts and soft supple skin on her thighs.

"What do I do?"

"You can bring me back. Make me whole again." Images of symbols flashed through my mind, I fell into a chair, feeling each one as a sexual assault on my mind. *"If you're serious, only death and blood can bring life. I'll be back, immortal and yours forever."* There was something twisting around in my brain, the symbols were still flashing in the darkness of my mind, but in between were glimpses of horrific pain and endless dark miles in sleep and travel.

"We need my blood, Dan."

"I'll dig up your body. I'll do anything."

"Find it, we'll talk some more." I let my fingers roam across the book for a moment longer and then the assault stopped abruptly. My head cleared, it felt like someone had been rooting around my skull with a screwdriver, but I had to get focused for Jessie's sake. We were going to be together again. I took the ring box out of my pocket and set it on the table. When she came back to me, I'd propose before anything happened.

"Find her blood." Of all the things in the world. Where was I going to get my dead girlfriend's blood? I ripped through the apartment. The hamper was empty and most of her clothes gone and donated to Good Will. I checked the bathroom trash for an old band-aid, even an old tampon. There was nothing. I'd scoured this place clean and the cleanup crew did a good job, too. "The cleanup crew."

Somewhere in the city there was a medical waste bag with my dead girlfriend's dried blood on rags, mop heads, swabs and more. Where to start? I did another lap around the apartment. It had been too long since her death. Or had it?

"The book didn't say how I needed it, how much do I need?" I heard the madness in my voice and raced outside to the dumpster. There was still a chance to save her. My footfalls slapped echoes off the cooling pavement. The Sun was in its final stages of hiding. I ran around the side of the building to the access road behind. There was a shed of sorts, with chain link walls and a wooden roof. I opened the gates, threw open the black plastic lid on the dumpster and started fishing.

It wouldn't be near the top, it had been too long. I wondered if any of my neighbors noticed the crazed man digging through their trash. I went deeper, leaned in over the side until I was inside tossing bags over my shoulder not caring where they landed.

I looked out towards the road at the roar of a diesel engine. The trash truck was turning into the complex. I reached out for another bag, feeling the rumble of the approaching truck. In the lights from the building I saw my prize. Pressed against the side of a bag, making it near transparent, was a can of the soda I drank. I grabbed the bag, flopped over the side of the dumpster, and ran.

Bits of trash and papers trailed as I sped off, doing a complete circle of the building. I left the sliders to the apartment open, I hopped up on the small deck and ran inside, sliding the glass doors shut behind me. I tore the bag open and spilled the contents on the floor. The smell of rotten food hit me immediately. I gagged and forced back bile, sifting through the refuse on the floor.

At the bottom of the wrecked trash bag, was what I was looking for. There was a dish towel, under the breakfast she'd been preparing, soaked through and still slightly damp with her blood. I ran to the kitchen for a plastic zipper bag and stuffed the towel in it.

"Now what? Come on, book, tell me!"

"Now we need the next ingredient, Dan."

"Tell me you love me. That you need me." I barely recognized my own voice from the hysteria and desperation. "Tell me."

"I need you, Dan." A sense of calm and pleasure washed over me as I stood there in the trash scattered on the floor." *I need you to get me tears of the grieving."*

"What does that mean? My tears? Your parents?"

"You need to figure that out. Best hurry."

I grabbed the ring box and opened, looked at the sparkling gold band and faceted diamond. Nothing. I shook it free and held it. Nothing. I raced upstairs to the bedroom and got the photo album, the same one that had been on display at the funeral. I went back to the kitchen and sat down at the table. The glow from the book seemed weaker. The ghost flames were smaller. It was getting weaker, she was getting weaker.

I leafed through the album. Almost at first sight of the pictures I felt the tears welling. I ran from the table to the cupboard and got a shot glass, it was the only thing I had to store tears in. I'd spent three days choosing the photos while the funeral directors worked on the tear in her throat trying to see if they could conceal it enough for an open casket funeral. In the end, they couldn't. Even with a scarf part of the wound showed, no matter how tight the stitching. Instead we covered the casket with photographs and personal mementos.

I flipped through the pages feeling the emotions churn inside until the first tear slipped free. What was I doing? Listening to a "book?" Had I really slipped that far? I was imagining things. That had to be the only explanation.

"Have faith, Dan." I turned the pages until I felt the cool trickle of wetness. The tears slipped silently into the shot glass. The more photos I looked at, the faster the glass filled. I turned to the last page. It was a picture of us on the Jurassic Park ride at Universal, Florida, our first real trip together that lasted longer than a weekend. That trip I decided that I wanted to spend the rest of my life with her. Another symbol flashed through my mind, followed by another, feeling like gunshots ripping through my skull.

I fumbled the shot glass, catching it before it fell, and set it down. When I touched my wet cheeks, my fingers came back bloody. I had no idea what the symbols meant. They had to have some greater reason. They were the key to bringing back my girl.

"Take me, the towel and the tears someplace where there's room to walk. And bring something sharp."

The parking lot was too open, too many lights and witnesses. There was a school and shopping mall all in walking distance of the building, all too public. I walked around to the back of the building. The trash men had cleaned up the mess and left an angry note taped to the gates. I set the book down on a milk crate and stood there like a manic fool holding a bloody towel, a shot glass and a kitchen knife.

"Pour the tears into the bag, baby, we're so close." The soft purr of her voice sent chills through me. Goose flesh erupted up and down my arms. That purr commanded so much power. I opened the bag, the smell of coppery sweetness assailed me. Some of the remaining blood in the towel had seeped out. It looked like the bottom of a ground beef tray from the store.

"Here's looking at you, kid." *Casablanca* had been our movie, one of our regular date night DVDs of choice to watch. It was timeless, like Jessie, and like we were about to become. I lifted the glass so the tears could trickle in the bag. There was a chorus of voices in my mind, singing and chanting, I didn't understand a word of it. It continued to grow in volume until I thought I wouldn't stand it. I felt dampness on my cheeks again. Was I crying? I didn't dare wipe it away.

The tears turned luminous as they slipped from the glass into the bag. When I thought the glass was empty, the fluid kept flowing, seemingly endless into the bag. I blinked and dry swallowed. The chorus in my mind stopped. When the glass was empty and the last drop fell, I let it slip from my hand to shatter on the pavement.

The bag was heavy in my grip, the blood and tears swirled together in a luminescent kaleidoscope of colors and tiny lights. It looked like the posters of constellations I hung on my walls as a kid. The lights and colors churned. More images, more flashes of pain. I knew what this meant. I dipped my fingers into the bag, the "liquid" was ethereal and warm, and tendrils tickled my fingertips. I pulled my hand out and drew the symbols, etched like glowing tattoos in my brain, onto the ground. They were flawless.

"You're doing so good, Dan. Soon we'll be together forever."

"What do I do now?" In the movies and books you needed a body, a host for whatever came out at the end of the spell. Would my girl have to claw her way out of the ground at the cemetery and wander the streets covered in dirt and grass until she found me? Or would she just appear, like a ghost and coalesce into her old self?

Another symbol, another rifle shot through me. This time there was only one; one final rune blazing through me, searing my nerves and mocking my sanity.

"Draw it, make it big. One more task, baby." Her voice had a new artificial tone to it, metallic and fake. I reached into the bag, still full and took the towel out. I squeezed a little out as cars raced by on the road. I carried the bag with me, and drew the symbol made of blood and starlight onto the pavement. When I was done, the bag was empty and the towel dry. Blood trickled from my nose and ears. It was too much.

"Jessie, are you sure. Is this the way?"

"It's the only way, Dan. You have to do this for me, for us." I gave up, surrendered to the voice of what I prayed at the end of this ordeal was my girl. I looked at my handiwork on the ground. The rune was massive at least twelve feet long and seven across, with intoxicating twists and turns and impossible angles that seemed to fold in upon themselves.

"Walk the path, Dan. Don't veer off and don't stumble. If you fall from it, you'll be lost forever and I will never be able to return."

"I can't do that!" A faint hint of madness tainted my words.

"Remember, only death brings life. And Blood is the source of life." I looked over at the book, the ghost flames ablaze across the cover. Next to it on the milk crate was the knife. I nodded to no one in particular and grabbed the knife. I made a cut from wrist to elbow on each arm. I couldn't cut my legs, I'd never be able to finish.

The first step onto the glowing rune, the path I had to follow, was the worst pain I'd ever felt. It was like having the bottoms of my feet seared and the skin flayed off. There was resistance I had to fight against, like walking through powerful winds. The second step was easier. I heard the knife clatter to the pavement as I released it. Blood flowed down my arms.

I fought the resistance on the path, walking the turns and twists. Each step felt like a static charge waiting to shock me and make me fall off, or explode. I kept at it. Colors and starlight swirled around my feet and crawled up my legs as I walked. The steps became smaller, more precise. There, at the corner of one of the impossible angles I had drawn, I thought I saw an image of myself, arms out, blood raining from the gashes in my arms as my flesh was peeled away.

On the next turn I saw Jessie. Her beautiful smile coated in blood from the slash across her throat, her face caught in a perpetual scream. I watched her, staggered and caught myself before falling into nothing, forever. The image of her mouthed the word *no* and then faded away like a bad dream.

Two lines crossed and I didn't know which way to turn. I didn't remember drawing this. But so much of the day was a green blue haze burning at the very back of my consciousness, intruding upon my sanity. I was getting tired, weak. I'd lost too much blood. I wondered just for an instant what would happen if I failed. They'd find me face down, dead in the alley. I smiled, it seemed like an escape from this task that was consuming me.

I risked a look down at my legs, the color and lights had slithered up in tendrils past my waist to my chest. Among the swirls of color I saw my legs, bare, patches of skin gone, blood being stolen, a hint of muscle and a shiny spot of bone. I cried out.

There before me I saw it, the end of the symbol. The finality of this path I was seeking. I tried slowing, but I was being pulled along now. The book flipped open, the cover slapping against the plastic milk crate, the pages fluttered, as if caught in a breeze, and stopped.

The lights and colors left me then, stripping me of flesh, blood and marrow. They swirled and gathered at the end of the symbol. I started to fall. As I looked down, I saw myself dissolving into dust. At the end of the rune, a figure took shape, nude in the moonlight, hovering above the ground, surrounded by light and color.

"With death comes life." I saw Jessie then, her body caught in the stars spinning slowing, forming. Floating above the pavement she turned to me, faceless, hair caught in an endless static cascade.

With my last moments, her mouth formed, an endless gaping void full of stars. I saw it and understood. I saw the crystalline honeycombs burst, and the shards fly into eternity. There was a rush of wind as if from massive wings, a roar so mighty it crushed consciousness. And the first of many tentacles slithered through her mouth, through the dimensional portal into this world.

Then it all was gone. Darkness. Stars. Void. Pain.

The Dogs

Jeffrey Thomas

THE DOGS
By Jeffrey Thomas

There were two conditions March needed fulfilled when he entered into his search for a new apartment. One, was that pets be permitted. Some places, he had found, allowed dogs under a certain weight, or only of certain types, excluding such breeds as pit bulls, Akitas, and so on. This apartment building, a former factory in the heart of the city, followed the latter policy, but fortunately March's dog was a three-year-old retired greyhound, Snow, white mottled with faint brown. His wife had stayed on in their house. She had let him take the dog.

To determine the second condition, March took a sheet of paper out of his pocket, unfolded it, and held it against the brick walls of the apartment he was shown in the old factory, which like his dog had outlived its original purpose. He placed the sheet against one spot, spread flat under his palm, then another. Progressing from room to room, though the third-floor loft was mostly all one large room. The worn boards creaked under his feet as he shifted about.

"Is that a witchcraft symbol or something?" his prospective landlord asked as he watched March, chuckling nervously as he tried to make his apprehension sound like a joke.

"I'm an artist," March lied, though he had spent quite a lot of time getting the complex geometric figure on his sheet of paper just right. "This is one of my designs. I was just trying to get a feel for how my work would look hanging in here. I love the look of artwork hanging on brick walls." He turned to smile at the older man, to allay his fears. "It's great that you haven't over-gentrified this place. I love these old exposed pipes, the original wood ceiling and support beams." He gestured around him.

"They give the loft character, yes," the landlord said. "You wouldn't be the only artist who lives in this building."

March resumed pressing his sheet of paper to various places on the rough walls. The bricks had been painted over thickly, white, looking like scales in the flank of some immense reptile. Then, when he held the intricate design he had drawn against a windowless stretch of wall in the sprawling main room, he sucked in his breath sharply. He hoped the man standing behind him hadn't heard his little gasp, wouldn't ask if something were wrong. March could feel a current vibrating up his arm...spreading down into his chest and up his neck, as though some heavy piece of factory machinery – left behind, forgotten – still thrummed with power on the other side of this wall.

He snatched the paper away from the spot quickly, before the vibration could spread up into his head. He wasn't ready for that. Not yet. March looked around to smile at the landlord again. "I'll take it."

It had been three years since that day.

One wall of March's main room faced onto the gray street, admitting gray light through the large windows that ran its length. The other walls were covered in taped-up sheets of drawing paper, all of them crowded with arcane symbols and geometric patterns either copied from the esoteric books that filled his shelves and stood in precarious piles on the floor, or of his own design. Seen all together, the sheets of varying size partly overlapping each other, they looked like a strange web of ink surrounding him, enclosing this space in which he lived.

This space and the little it contained – himself, his six-year-old dog, his books -- was all that he had left, all that might define his forty-two years on this globe. Two months ago he had been laid off from his job of the last nine years. He was experiencing frustration in finding another that would pay adequately. Of course, he knew he wasn't the only one experiencing life's difficulties. Somewhere beyond the walls of his little cave, with their inked caveman's graffiti, right now someone was setting off a bomb strapped to their body in a crowded outdoor market. Some teenager was walking into his school's cafeteria at noontime with his father's shotgun in his hands. Someone was being burned as a witch and stoned with cinderblocks while other townspeople stood around taking videos of it on their cell phones. All the while, men in expensive suits sat around tables as large and glossy as ponds, laughing and laughing, like gods looking down at the entertaining cruelties of their playthings.

Thinking these things as he paced his creaking floor, with a mug of coffee in hand, March stopped to look down at Snow, curled on the floor near the foot of his bed. "If only we could aspire to be like your kind," he said to the animal. She lifted her head in her gently timid way, her protuberant brown eyes fixed on his. "But humans will never be as loving as you are. As devoted. As loyal. As noble." Snow perked her ears up. Was he babbling something about going for a walk, perhaps? He smiled at her fondly. "Isn't that right, my noble little girl?"

He still couldn't understand why his former wife, whom he had once thought was so in tune with his mind, his spirit -- now the wife of a man she had met online twelve years into her marriage with March -- hadn't understood his desire to know if there were other, better worlds or realities than this. Was it really "crazy" to hope for and seek such possibilities? Was it really "nuts" to be dissatisfied with the limitations of this floating ball of miseries? In the end she had flat-out called him "insane." As if it wasn't this world that was insane.

Just last night, in fact, according to a local news web site he had been perusing on his computer, a young woman had been found murdered in the city's largest graveyard, Hope Cemetery, savagely mutilated. Yes, right here in this very city. Hope indeed, he thought.

He hoped for something better. Or if he couldn't have that, he hoped for this all to end.

Still holding his coffee mug, he turned away from Snow, leaving her to lower her long snout onto her paw again, her hopes for a long walk, for the moment, crushed. March faced the wall where he had on that day three years ago held the page of a sketchbook, and known that a window could be opened on this blank space where no window existed.

It had taken him over a year to accomplish it. He had taped up innumerable drawings, which had since been moved to other walls or destroyed in frustration, entirely. Now, only one large sheet of paper was mounted there, by thin nails driven into the mortar between the bricks. He had learned that instead of erasing certain lines and drawing new ones -- in order to modify the view this window offered him -- he could alter the configuration with lengths of black thread instead. So he had driven other nails into the wall (fortunately his landlord had never needed to set foot in his apartment again), and he would unwind one end of a thread from a nail, shift the line of thread to another location, creating a new angle, and loop its end around a different nail.

The design as a whole was enclosed within one large circle extending to the edges of the paper, but other circles overlapped/intersected it, and complex angles created stars that subdivided into triangles. At various critical points and vertices in all these angles and curves he had handwritten words learned from his obscure personal library. Without these words to imbue the formula with power, it would all have only been black ballpoint on white Strathmore.

At the very center of the design there was a decagon formed from strands of black thread. This was, in effect, the window pane itself. It put him in mind of a porthole, which he now approached as if to stare out at a storm-tossed sea from the relative safety of his ship's cabin. But first, he picked up a pair of sunglasses from a little side table and put them on, resting his coffee aside.

March put his face close to the window, but he never touched it. He didn't even know what the sensation would be like. He didn't believe his hand would pass through – after all, he felt no breeze from the scene beyond, no whiff of air or scent from another land, and he never even heard sounds from the other side – but some intuition told him it was better to limit his curiosity to observation.

Ah, he thought, peering through, soon he probably wouldn't need the dark glasses anymore. Day by day the nuclear blaze of white light continued to diminish, where it showed between the vast black shapes that hung like continent-sized boulders in the sky. When he had first succeeded in opening this scrying lens, nearly two years ago now, nothing at all had been visible past the light streaming into his apartment like a concentrated ray beamed from the molten heart of a star, from which he had shielded his face with a cry. He had been blinded for over an hour, had feared he would never see again. The skin of his face had been burnt red and tender.

Gradually, over the weeks and months thereafter, as the brightness of the light grew less intense, he had been able to make out a city on the other side. And those looming black forms that hovered above it.

He couldn't tell how many there were; the one in the foreground blotted out most of his view of the sky, but other, similar shapes were suspended behind it. Slight adjustments he had made by shifting the angles of his threads had afforded him other views from the city's streets, but the position of the dark shapes crowding the sky hadn't noticeably changed, so tremendous in size were they.

It was not only a city out there…it was this city. His own gray city, grayer still, at some unknown future time. He had recognized the buildings, or the shells of them at least, since many had been burned charcoal black from within or without, while most had simply been abandoned to disrepair, their windows broken into silently howling fanged mouths.

When he had finally been able to make out the details of his city, he had realized that lying strewn throughout its streets were the bodies of its former inhabitants.

At first, disregarding the titanic hulks levitating in the sky because he couldn't yet process them, he had thought a nuclear war had transpired and these people had perished in the initial blast. But then he had grasped, scrutinizing the corpses from various different views of the city's streets as he tweaked his window's perspective, that all of them – whether man, woman, or child – bore the same strange injuries. Quite simply, their heads appeared to be smashed into unrecognizable pulp, bone and all, as if they had actually exploded… as if a grenade had been implanted into every skull.

Yet when the glare of light dimmed further over time and he was able to make out finer detail, he noticed that thin black cords, not so unlike the black threads he utilized in his formula, streamed out of each exploded head like sticky strands of web. These strands extended straight up into the sky. Though the silhouetted hovering mountains were too far up for him to see it, he felt intuitively that the far ends of the strands were connected to the amorphous titans themselves. It was, of course, not that these black strings had reached up into the sky from those myriad shattered skulls, but that the cords had been extruded from the shapeless shapes that almost occluded the sky above this dead city.

But the city, the Earth, wasn't entirely dead.

Whatever cataclysm had befallen humanity, it had apparently not annihilated other forms of animal life. Pigeons would waddle about this nightmare world as nonchalantly as if awaiting bread crumbs in the park. Gulls still wheeled in the sky, white motes against the unmoving black giants. March occasionally saw cats. But mostly it was the dogs that captured his attention. They skulked through the streets singly or in packs, their ribs showing ever more vividly through filthy coats. They looked lost, disoriented, and March imagined they were searching for their masters. He had always felt it was cruel that beautiful animals like his Snow were used for racing, so that humans might wager money on these sensitive unquestioning creatures, but seeing the stray dogs wander the stilled future city made him feel it was just as cruel that human beings had made dogs dependent upon them for food, for shelter, for the love they craved…too often, in vain.

Night never fell in this world beyond the brick wall; the steady radiance in the sky prevented that, or had the Earth been jolted to a stop so that it no longer even turned? The dogs stole about constantly, flitting from alley to alley. Sniffing through the streets, searching. Hunting, March thought, for cats and squirrels. He once saw a collie pounce upon a pigeon, successfully snatching it in its jaws then shaking its head wildly to kill it. Iridescent feathers floated to the ground.

Finally had come the day when the dogs had lost their inhibition, their sense of the previous order of things. March suspected, though, it had more to do with their desperation than any kind of breach in their loyalty. He saw a mongrel creep up on one of the corpses lying on a sidewalk – the body of a young woman in a short skirt turned to rags -- sniff at a withered and discolored leg warily, as if the woman might sit up suddenly and scold it as a bad boy, then lean in at last and bite into the half-mummified flesh.

After that day, he had seen the dogs eating human bodies on a regular basis. They fought over them, savagely. They dragged them off whole, like a leopard with a broken-necked antelope, or in dismembered pieces. The tethers that bound the near-headless humans to the overhead colossi snapped free and trailed across the ground.

Watching the starving dogs go mad with desperation, knowing how unnatural it was that they had been driven to feed off their very masters, made March's heart ache. As for all those dead humans themselves…well, their extinction was a fate they had earned, through their actions and their inaction and their unworthiness. And if his own future self lay in one of

120

those streets out there, his own head turned to mush, cables of black web running up from it to connect him to one of those Outsiders in the sky, that had manifested to reclaim this world – for he had later come to admit to himself that that was what those leviathans were: the beings that the rarest of the books in his collection had foretold – well, then that was okay, too. He didn't count himself all that much better than the rest of his breed. To his way of thinking, his own dog, Snow, was superior to him. And if Snow were out there hungry and afraid, then he'd want her to feed from his corpse rather than starve to death.

Today, March turned away from the scrying window and removed his sunglasses. Not much had changed out there over the past two years but for the slow dimming of the light that had heralded the appearance of the Outsiders. He felt a familiar itch, a deep grumbling hunger like that which had started him on this quest for knowledge back when he had still been married.

The need to know…to see…even more.

He had been too long content with his success in opening this window, doing nothing more radical than changing his street view from time to time. But now, finally, he had determined that he had to make more dramatic adjustments to his formula if he hoped to understand the destiny of his race more clearly…and exactly when it was that the Outsiders would tear their way into this reality. Once again, he had to truly experiment.

Then one day, more through that sense of intuition he possessed than through his exhausting reexamination of his book collection, he struck upon the answer. It was so simple he hadn't even considered it until now. What had really inspired him, ultimately, was a dream he had had the night before, in which he had been standing on the deck of a ghost ship at sea, the Mary Celeste perhaps, the only human aboard but with Snow faithfully by his side. He had taken up an incongruously modern pair of binoculars so as to scan the gray, stormy horizon for land. His view through the lenses had been blurry, so he had had to turn the diopter adjustment ring to sharpen his focus.

Yes! An adjustment ring!

First, with white correction fluid he painted over the ten words of power that accompanied each of the ten points on the formula's central decagon. The moment he painted over the first word, for the first time in two years the window was gone, leaving only an area of blank paper. He didn't panic, however, or bemoan his decision. As soon as the white fluid had dried he wrote the same ten words of power…but this time he advanced their position by one degree, clockwise, as if adjusting the focus of a lens.

The window opened again, and this time he had his dark glasses on from the start just in case he got kicked back to the beginning again, and that blasting column of light.

But no…his instincts had been correct. The lens gave him the same view of the city as last time, but from a point further, deeper, into the future.

He no longer needed the sunglasses, and removed them. The sky revealed in the spaces between the blob-like masses of the Outsiders was now a subdued, almost twilight violet. Faint rags of mist wisped between the buildings, and grass had grown up lush, if gray, through cracks in the pavement. Sizable trees had even sprouted, their roots displacing cement slabs, leaves dull and waxy. Walls were choked thick with grayish vines. Many buildings had crumbled in on themselves, turning into ivy-choked rubble. The city looked like a vast graveyard, overgrown, its long-dead occupants without surviving mourners.

He expected to see bones scattered in the streets. Surely no intact skeletons, but at least stray rib cages or femurs, for instance. No skulls, of course, though the occasional lower jaw was conceivable. Still, there was nothing. Had it all turned to dust?

He unwound one end of a string, shifted it to another nail an eighth of an inch over. It was like changing the channel on a television, with only a brief interruption of fluttering light/darkness between. As a result, he was given the view of a different street in the same demolished city.

Not only did he discover bones, this time, but he was introduced to the descendants of the city's orphaned canines, as well.

At first it was just the bones. They lay in the very middle of the street, heaped up in a neat cairn. He might have believed that dogs would leave them that way after having gnawed the last shreds from them and cracked them for their marrow -- just as a dog will bury a bone for future use -- maybe even as some new territorial behavior, but what then about the flowers?

The pile of bones was surrounded by a ring of plucked flowers of a type March couldn't name, with white petals. This was without question no accidental drift of uprooted flowers blown here by a windstorm. The circle was nearly as perfect as those he himself had inked on paper to design this magic lens.

So, there had been survivors of the apocalypse, after all! He was almost disappointed, but still anxious to see them…what they looked like, how they lived.

In the next moment, he did. And he gazed through his window with his jaw hanging slack.

A large dog, so thin it was emaciated – rather like an albino greyhound, but rougher in outline, more feral-looking, with striking pink eyes like a rabbit's – came loping out from between two tall mounds that had once been buildings. In its jaws it carried a human pelvis. Its intention was clear: it was going to add this prize to the cairn in the center of the street.

But as the dog neared the cairn, it rose up onto its hind legs. It walked upright the last few steps. With its front legs, which March now realized had something more like human fingers than the toes of a dog's paw, the animal removed the pelvis from its jaws and added it to the very top of the pile.

"Dear God," March said aloud.

Behind him, he heard the tinkle of Snow's dog tags as she lifted her head at the sound of his voice.

He placed a kitchen chair close in front of the window. Outside the actual windows of his apartment, night had fallen, galaxies of windows alight as if each building in the city had begun to burn up from the inside.

He saw other dogs come and go, as fleet and furtive as white ghosts in the unending violet twilight. Some galloped along on all fours. Some tiptoed past on two legs. No more bones were added to the monument to their dead, beloved masters while March watched, but one dog – and they were all of the same, strange new breed – did come forward to push the ring of flowers into a neater arrangement after the breeze had made its rim untidy. She bunted the blossoms with her nose and also patted them with her white-furred hands.

Was this, March wondered, a mutation caused by some emanation, conscious or accidental, generated by the Outsiders? Or could it even be that, having lived among human beings for so many generations, in their absence the dogs had begun to adopt human characteristics and behaviors as a matter of natural evolution? Even, in imitating humans, to replace them in some kind of tribute?

After a while March saw no more dogs in the street. He became conscious that his rump was sore from the hard wooden chair, and he realized he had neglected Snow for too long. He took her outside on her leash. She released a small pond of urine only a few steps from the old factory's front stoop. As he stood over her, March caught himself glancing up and down the dark street nervously...as if he expected that at any moment, some crouched figure as gaunt as a bundle of birch branches would come tiptoeing out from around a corner, its vivid pink eyes fixed on him hungrily.

When he was back inside he shuddered, bolted the door, unhitched Snow from her leash, and set about microwaving himself a poor excuse for a Thai dinner. While he waited for it to cook, he walked over to his computer idly and glanced at the local news.

He spotted the headline immediately: "Second Ghoulish Murder."

The body of a sixty-four-year-old homeless man had been found at the back of Hope Cemetery. He had been horribly savaged. A police spokesman was not confirming that these two murders were the work of a single perpetrator. They did not want to use the term serial killer at this time.

It wasn't the first time there had been murders in this city, March reflected. It was a big enough city, and the more people you lumped together, the more harm they did each other. It was just the law of Nature. Shadowy predators had always accompanied what passed for civilization, and always would. But somehow these two killings resonated with him on a deep level, unsettling him in a way he couldn't articulate to himself.

Naturally, the next thing to do was to white-out the words of power again, then draw them in anew, rotated one more degree to the right. He did this the following morning, after first making sure Snow had had her walk and her food and water bowls filled. He expected to be seated in front of the two-dimensional crystal ball he had created a long while.

He didn't know what increment of time had passed -- any more than he could judge the time that had transpired between now and the first view, and the first view and the second – but it was obvious that it was a great many more years (if one were still to portion time into a man-made notion such as years).

Buildings had lost more of their orderly shape, become more like natural formations of the Earth; he might not even have recognized them as having been buildings if he hadn't gazed on this scene from his apartment building's perspective previously. More trees had risen, almost forming a grove. Their leaves, and the grass and underbrush and rampant creeping ivy, still had that grayish poisoned look, but somehow the vegetation flourished. It wasn't so much that Nature was reclaiming the city, but that a new Nature had come about.

Yet all of this was secondary to his interest, because there was a new development that made him lean forward on his chair and murmur, "What the hell is this?"

In the center of the street where the evolving dogs had erected a monument to their masters – and he had decided it must only be one monument of many dispersed across the city, if not dispersed across the globe – the cairn of bones was gone, replaced by something which he couldn't identify. It appeared to be a two-dimensional black disk maybe six feet across, floating a foot or so off the split pavement, angled slightly away from March so he could see it wasn't a sphere. Its surface was flat black, featureless, but the edge of the circle appeared to be rimmed in a fringe of wavering cilia like that of a paramecium. In addition, maybe a dozen strands varying in thickness – from thread-thin to cables as thick as a wrist, perhaps – streamed upwards from various points in the disk's outer rim. Just like the strands that had once connected the decimated heads of human corpses to the Outsiders overhead, these various cords ran up into the sky to disappear in the distance, but March had no doubt they connected with the immense bodies still hovering above the Earth.

The sky showing in the gaps between the Outsiders was still that violet hue of early evening, and against its subtle glow he could see that after centuries or millennia of immobility the silhouetted outlines of the Outsiders appeared to be pulsing, throbbing amorphously. He noticed that long whip-like flagella had been extruded by the Outsiders here and there, lazily wavering as if the entities swam in place in the Earth's atmosphere.

He returned his focus to the hovering disk the Outsiders had apparently manifested. Just as in the case of the cairn of bones, March strongly suspected this wasn't the only such tethered disk that had appeared in this city, or upon the face of the Earth. Were those god-like entities at last, moving with the unhurried pace of the immortal, endeavoring to transform this reality into an environment that better suited their needs or desires?

A low rumbling behind March caused him to spin around on his chair's wooden seat to look back at his living space, jolted like a man abruptly awakened from a dream. For a disoriented half-second he didn't recognize his own surroundings, as if someone had bricked him alive in this box while his spirit had been elsewhere. Then he saw Snow. The white greyhound stood just behind him, her gaze fixed hypnotically on the lens as his had been. Her upper lip was quivering. At first he had had the odd notion that she was growling at him, but she had obviously sensed something in the scrying window. Up until this moment, over the past two years that it had remained open, she had never even appeared to acknowledge the window's existence.

March faced his lens again to try to ascertain what it was that had caused his pet to take note of it after all this time. The appearance of the levitating black disk? The undulating bodies of the Outsiders?

New movement, and March flinched as a figure entered the scene from the right, like an actor stepping out from behind a curtain onto a stage. It was one of the dogs, but that much further evolved from the last time he had watched them. It bore no vestige of a tail, and walked more erect than the tiptoeing creatures he had seen before; its upright posture no longer seeming tentative or unnatural. Though still lean, its musculature appeared more like that of a human than a dog. It was still covered in short bristly white hair, its snout still elongated and canine, its eyes still an almost luminous pink, but the creature's overall aspect conveyed a palpable intelligence.

The creature was carrying an armful of tinder, perhaps to start a fire. March had no doubt at all that these beings were now capable of creating fire. He realized, however, that it wasn't bare branches in its arms but a bundle of human leg and arm bones.

The strange being was moving straight toward the hovering disk. It didn't bend its path around it. Snow growled again, showing her teeth now, as the creature drew closer to the inky circle. March reached around behind him, without taking his eyes off the viewing screen he had called into existence, and stroked Snow's neck to calm her. Was the creature going to offer its burden of bones to the disk as a tribute, to appease its new masters?

Having created this scrying pane from a once empty sheet of paper, March was not surprised when he comprehended the black disk was a portal – though whether it was an intentional creation of the Outsiders, or merely a hole stretched open in the fabric of space and time as a byproduct of the Outsiders' new activity, how could he judge? However the portal had come to be, March's first impression when the dog-creature arrived at the disk was that it was going to throw the bones into it. Instead, the thing stepped over the rim of the disk and slipped its whole body into the blackness. In a fraction of a moment, the dog-being was gone, as if it had plunged into a vertical pool of ink.

No sooner had it disappeared than two more of the canine-things emerged from the same direction, their arms also full of human bones. Snow growled again, as the pair of creatures approached the disk as the first one had. They too, one after the other, hopped up into the black circle and were swallowed.

Like him, the dogs had figured out that the disk was the mouth of a tunnel.

"They're...migrating," March whispered to Snow, in awe. "And taking their masters' bones with them."

But, he wondered, migrating where?

Over the next several hours he saw one more dog-being disappear into the disk with a load of bones in its grasp. After that, March was too impatient to watch for more of them. Too impatient to wait until tomorrow to forward the words of power another notch. He decided to do that now.

First, though, he sat on the edge of his bed and stroked Snow and talked to her soothingly. He told her he was going to tear up some hotdogs for her and add them to her bowl of dry food as a treat, to keep her distracted while he inscribed the last of the ten words of power that would reactivate his decagonal lens. He said, "You're a good girl, Snow. You're the only living thing on this planet that I can count on. That I can trust. The only constant in my life. The only living thing in this world that truly loves me. The only thing that I truly love." His eyes were filling up in self pity, but also with the enormity of his affection. He understood he not only loved this animal, but admired her...and all her kind. To his mind, dogs were already the pinnacle of evolution.

He went on, "You don't live as long as we do. What will I do, someday, when I don't even have you anymore? I'll be alone. But I guess...I guess we're all of us alone. Most people just don't think they are." He smiled, and ran his hand along her neck again. "We'll just keep being alone together, I guess, huh? And see what the future brings."

She turned her head to lick his hand.

With Snow digging into her bowl of food at the other end of the long, single room that doubled as March's bedroom and living room, he penned in the last of the ten potent words.

March's initial impression was that he had been unsuccessful, that he had written one of the words incorrectly. The window only showed unbroken blackness. He was reminded, uncomfortably, of the disk he had seen floating above the street in the last view. He imagined a dog-creature's head suddenly thrusting out of the portal into his reality, pink eyes blazing, to snap at his face. But then he considered that perhaps night had finally descended over that future landscape.

Eventually, though, he realized he was seeing a churning sort of blackness within the blackness, a restless pulsing almost sensed more so than actually seen. Seen with his mind rather than his eyes. Thus, trusting more to his intuition than his paltry organs of sight, March came to understand that the Outsiders had descended from the sky at long last. Descended, and consumed. They had swallowed up all, until they were all.

He advanced the ten words another notch, to the fifth configuration he had attempted, so impatient that the correction fluid hadn't dried fully and the inscriptions were smeary. They still did the trick, but the resulting view was the same as before: only churning, sentient blackness. Nevertheless, he continued this way – sixth configuration, seventh, eighth, ninth, tenth, as though he were the master of time himself, forcing the arm of a clock -- until the only position that remained was the original one, setting number one, which had showed him the Earth still blazing with the white light of the Outsiders' eruption onto this plane of existence.

For now, he left the dial set at view number ten. For now, his mind couldn't assimilate any more than that seething black emptiness. It was almost soothing, that living oblivion. A kind of relief, like an afterlife of blissful nothingness.

That night, after he had walked Snow and then made himself a sandwich, he sat down in front of his computer to look in on the news. He almost expected to see that there had been a third killing in his city in or around Hope Cemetery, but there hadn't. He extended his search to other cities, then other countries, but of course gruesome murders committed in or around graveyards were so prevalent that they could have been the work of a never-ending supply of madmen. Still, wasn't it possible that some of these crimes he skimmed had been committed by another kind of predator? A predator that had lived in humankind's shadow for generations, maybe since the earliest days of human civilization? Going back as far, perhaps, as the time when primitive humans and wild canines had first begun living in conjunction?

The cosmic clock come full circle?

With the world all peacefully black outside the windows of his third-floor loft, March swiveled his computer chair to watch Snow as she slept, her snout propped on one paw as always.

"They don't eat us because they hate us," March whispered to the dog, while he wondered about the dreams that made her twitch one hind leg from time to time. Was she dreaming the primal dream of hunting prey? Was she dreaming of stalking on her hind legs alone?

He said, "They eat us to commune with us. Because they still love us."

Of Circles and Rings

Tom Lynch

OF CIRCLES AND RINGS
By Tom Lynch

It's a good bout, up to a point. We're pretty evenly matched, and this is the farthest I've gotten in the elimination rounds, so I'm stoked to be this close to placing first. Then, my opponent switches gears to Bagua Zhang. That's fine. No problem. He's probably getting tired, so he's looking to evade my attacks and let me tire myself out. Fine by me. I'll just wait till he makes a mistake, then I'll take home the trophy.

All of a sudden, he's doing an elaborate form, almost a dance, still moving in circles, spinning his hands and arms in some kind of demo thing, moving closer, closer. I don't know who he thinks he's going to impress, but it won't be m—

And I'm on the floor, sitting on my ass. My cheekbone is throbbing. It feels like he hit me, but what the hell just happened? I didn't see anything!

The ref comes into the ring, and raises my opponent's hand, pronouncing him the winner, and I'm still sitting there as everyone starts cheering for the other guy. Did I black out or something? I rub my cheek where he must have hit me, and my fingers come away bloody. He broke skin, too. Quite a hit. How did that *happen*? Why didn't I see it *coming*?

I roll up onto my feet and wander out of the ring, and meet with my sifu on the side. He nods at me, proud I've done as well as I have, but he can tell I'm disappointed. Years of training, practice, and meditation…to have come *this close*. I try to smile, but wind up shrugging, and head back to my car.

I get to the studio early to meet up with Sifu to review the video of my match. He meets me in the cramped office at the back of the studio, and moves some paperwork off a stool so I can sit next to him. He pulls up the file the tournament officials had sent him, and we get ready to watch.

"You did really well the other day. Perhaps the best you've done," Sifu said.

"But not good enough, hunh?"

"No matter how good you are, there's always somebody better."

"I guess. I just wanna see where I messed up. I was sure I was going to win that match."

Sifu nods and clicks play on the video. The whole thing is only a couple of minutes, so we don't have to wait long. I see a few spots where

I left openings, and grin a few times when I caught my opponent's lags. I watch the status bar, and there we are, coming close to the end. He starts his spinning dance thing, inching closer to me, and then I'm on the floor, and his fist is out.

I hear Sifu catch his breath. I turned to look at him, and he'd gone pale, his eyes wide.

"What—" I start.

"You must go," Sifu said. "Now!" And he practically chases me out of the studio. I stand outside in the slush, looking up at the sign for Kwan's Kung Fu, wondering what to do now. It's too early to go to work, and too long a drive to head back to my apartment to study. I pull out my cell phone and call the tournament organizers.

"Hi, this is Pete Jones," I say to the woman who answers.

"Hi, Pete. How can I help you?"

"Well, I was in the competition last weekend, and have a question."

"I remember you, Pete. You fought well. What's your question?"

"Thanks. Um…my opponent that final round. Can you give me his contact info?"

"Aw, Pete, you know I can't do that."

"At least his name. I'm really not looking to settle a score outside the ring here."

"Yeah, but how do we know that?"

"I want to know what happened! That's all! You saw the fight, right? Where the hell did that punch come from? I want to learn that technique, cuz I'm stuck between furious that I lost and awestruck that he won with one punch outta nowhere."

"I hear ya, Pete," she says, and pauses. "Look, I'll tell you his name, okay?"

I sigh. "I guess that's a start."

"And he's local, so you should be able to find him."

I perk up at that. She's clearly trying to help me out. I've been competing at their events for years, so they know be by now. Finally, I might catch a break, here. "Thanks! What's his name?"

"His name is Shun Jian."

"Thanks so much. I really appreciate it."

I sit in my car outside the address I dug up for Shun Jian. It's a simple apartment complex on the edge of town. As the late winter sleet comes down on my windshield, I try not to nod off while watching for this guy.

And then I see him. He has a backpack over one shoulder, and a baseball cap on, but it's him alright. I hop out of my car.

"Shun Jian?" I call.

He spins. "Who are you?" He speaks slowly, with a heavy accent.

Chinese, yes, but something else, too.

"Pete Jones. We fought at the tournament last weekend."

"The match was not personal."

"I know, I know…I just…"

"This is not a good time for me, Pete."

"I need to know how you did it."

Silence. He just looks at me. "Are you sure you wish to know?"

"Damn right I am." I feel the heat rising.

He just looks at me, then he steps forward. "I am not sure you are ready."

"Who the fff—"

"Do you want to learn this? This is not everyday training."

"Fine with me."

"You do not understand."

"How can I? You haven't said anything!"

He lets out an exasperated sigh. "I must go. Meet me at Edgewood School, Saturday morning at 8. Can you be there?"

"Yeah, I can be there."

He turns to walk away.

"Hey," I call. "Thanks."

"We shall see about that," he says over his shoulder.

A dusting of snow lies on the ground around the school buildings as I lean further back into the shelter of the entryway, trying to keep from shivering. I can see my breath as I watch the parking lot. I'm early because I don't want to miss this chance, and some people can be particular about timing.

"You are here. Good," comes a voice from my left.

I try to conceal the fact that I jumped by coughing into my hand. "Yeah, but the building is closed. Do you have a key?"

"We do not need a key for where we are going to be working." He leads the way across a courtyard and over to a covered walkway. The whole school was very modernist, and decorated with brightly covered squares and rectangles in the windows and on some of the walls. Every single building seems to be made of brick and right angles, and the walkway, covered by slabs of concrete held up by metal-pipe columns, connects each of these buildings.

Shun leads me over to a corner of the walkway near some stairs, and he vaults onto the metal-tube stair railing, and then up onto the top of the covered walkway. I follow. I'm as nimble as he is. Mostly. He's probably done this before though, so it's kind of cheating.

Anyway, I see him on top of the walkway, and we're now on a tar-covered strip that runs all the way around the courtyard, and changes in height a few times, where there are stairs in the walkway underneath.

"Are you warmed up?" he asks me.

"Not r—" I begin, and find myself pulling back from his first punch. I sweep at his lead leg. He pulls it out of the way and kicks at my knee. I hop upwards, and flick a front kick at his abdomen. He steps back, just out of range, and lunges in just as I'm coming back down. I stumble backwards, and he takes advantage of that, punches at my face and gut, kicks at my legs and hips, and even throws a blade-hand strike toward my eyes. I manage to get out of the way of all of them. One or two of them tag me, but it's nothing serious.

I fall backwards as something hits me in the calves. I hop up and back, and realize we've gotten to an area where our walkway has abruptly risen a bit. Shun continues attacking, and I keep backpedaling, fending him off.

Until I finally get a shot in. I sidestep a straight punch, duck down and dart forward with my elbow leading. I land a solid shot on his floating ribs. I hear the breath *whuff* out of his lungs, and I press on. I knee him in the thigh, and shoot out three quick punches: solar plexus, sternum, and throat. I feel him teetering backwards, and cock my leg for an epic, finishing sidekick.

Shun steps back and rights himself, quicker than I thought possible. "Good. It looks like you're warm now." He grinned at me. "So, you want to know how I beat you last weekend?"

"Yes. I *need* to know how you did that."

"You *need* to? This isn't a simple or easy technique. It involves pain and sacrifice."

"Doesn't all Kung Fu?"

"Not in this way. This is something else. This is more than just Kung Fu."

"Oookaaaay…" It finally hits me. I finally place what's been bugging me about his voice. Shun Jian talks like a much older guy. Sifu is in his early sixties, but Shun talks like some of those venerable old Chinese masters in bad Kung Fu movies. It's almost silly.

"I am serious, Pete. Yes, there are elements of it that hearken back to Bagua Zhang, but there is a completely different element to what is happening in this technique."

"I—"

"I can see that I am losing you. For now we shall focus on the physical aspect." With that, Shun demonstrated a series of moves that I mimic. He tweaks and corrects the motions, and we keep at it. For hours. It's far more complicated than I had thought, and according to Shun, the slightest deviation from the exact, means that the technique will fail and just be a series of pretty moves.

Despite the chill in the air, I'm dripping with sweat. After a while, my vision begins to blur. No, that's not it. I must be hungry or something because my hands are sliding in and out of focus, but everything else is crystal clear. I stop, knitting my eyebrows, and look over at Shun.

He's grinning ear to ear. As if reading my thoughts, he asks, "Are you ready for a break? Are you hungry?"

"Yes and yes," I reply.

"I thought we would be here for a while, so I took the liberty of preparing something for us. They are no longer hot, but should suffice." He gestures to some old-style stackable metal bowls, held together with a nylon strap. He squats next to them, and opens them up, offering me dumplings, noodles, vegetables, and broth. Simple, but delicious.

"So," Shun starts as we eat. "What did you see?"

"I musta been tired or something."

"Why?"

"Well, my vision got all weird. It happens sometimes."

"Are you tired?"

I stop for a moment. "No," I realize aloud. "I'm not."

Shun raises his eyebrows and flashes a brief smile. "So what is it you saw?"

"I saw my hands blur, as if they were moving too fast for a video camera to capture."

Shun smiles again, and nods. "Very well then, back to work. To stay familiar with the kind of movement you need, we will fight again, and you will only use the circular movements of Bagua Zhang, is that understood?"

"Yes."

"Then let us *begin!*" And he lunges straight for my throat. I step forward and to the side, slapping his hand out of the way, and dropping into a crouch to grab his lower leg. He pivots, cocks his leg, and brings his heel up into my chest. I hop back and around him. His foot swings out and locks my ankle as his forearm hits me in the throat. I drop backwards into a roll, and come up, grabbing at his lead hand, and spinning into a lock, pushing him away.

The dance continues. Fists fly. Feet snap out. Limbs are locked, and counter techniques applied. The Sun begins to set.

"Good work today, Pete."

"Thank you, Shun. I...hm."

"What is it?"

"Well, at first, I thought this was going to be a meeting of equals where I just learn one new technique, but this feels a lot more like I'm working with a visiting Master."

"You flatter me."

"No, I'm serious. You have a lot to teach me. Thanks for taking this much time..."

"I sense hesitation."

"Oh? Well..."

"What is it?"

I sigh. "I'm not trying to push the issue, but are we going to get to the technique you did last weekend?"

"Yes, but not today."

"I...understand."

"As you have sensed, Pete, there is more to this that you first thought. Happily for you, your skills are quite advanced already, and you are close. Practice. All week. Do not stop. Practice the form I taught you, and if you go to study with your sifu, practice the Bagua Zhang in class. We will meet here next Saturday morning at the same time."

Shun raises his hand, so I put mine up for a high five. I realize, though, that he's holding his hand out for a handshake. I grin, and shake his hand. It's funny, though, because I first thought Shun was my age, but he's not: he's older. As he smiles before we leave the school, I see wrinkles around his eyes, and his black hair is peppered with gray.

It's been a long week. I pull into the Edgewood School parking lot about ten minutes before eight. It's a sunnier day this time. Warmer, more humid with all the snow turning to slush. Last week was cold and gray.

Between my part-time job at the local big book store, the two classes I'm working on for my degree, and Kung Fu practice, the past week has been busy. I couldn't focus on any of it, though. I'd been too caught up in practicing the form that Shun taught me last week. Not only was it a problem that I was more interested in this than anything else, but it appeared to be messing with my perception of things. I'd get into my car after work, and then be home eating dinner, with no memory of anything in between. Then there was the time that I was sitting in the lecture hall, and everything *stopped*. I sat there, and wondered if I'd dozed off and everyone had left, but no. They were all still there, but sitting and standing like statues, mouths open in mid-sentence. And I blinked and it was back to normal. It was as if time had stopped and started again. The worst was when I'd stopped, but time kept going. One of the junior students punched me in the eye while we were sparring. Everyone said I'd suddenly stopped moving. I'd gone by Shun's place to try to find him to talk to him, but never found him.

We have lots to discuss today, cuz this is too weird, and I need to know what's going on. At first I thought I just needed more sleep or something, but as the week moved on, I realized that these *episodes* became more frequent the more I practiced the form Shun taught me. I'd broken out in sweats when I first realized that. Crazy. Too crazy. How could any of this be real? It feels like a dream as it all happens, but it's all *real*. Scary. Maybe I should have stopped. Maybe it should have made me crazy. Honestly, though, I kinda get excited. I suddenly make a connection...

"You arrived early again," Shun says from around the corner.

"That's how you did it," I say.

"I beg your pardon?"

"How you won the match two weeks ago."

Shun just watched me and raised an eyebrow.

"You...you somehow manipulated time. That's what this technique does! Oh my God! I kept slipping in and out, speeding up and slowing down while people around me wondered what the *hell* was going on. I can't...I mean...I finally get it."

"You are quick to understand, Pete. We only need to take the final step now, and you will be able to do it, too."

"And control it? Cuz I'm not loving the whole spontaneous thing in the middle of sparring."

"So I see from your black eye. Yes, there is an element of control."

"Yeah, good. I'm gonna need that."

"Indeed. Now, to get us into the proper frame of mind..." And he sucker punches me. Or tries to, anyway. The thing is, I have time to think about it as it happens. I'm used to fights seeming slower when you're in them, because I've been doing it for years. This time, though, I actually have time to observe the fist oozing forward. I watch it approach my face, and observe Shun's body as it starts to settle. I then look to see if I would be better positioned inside the punch, right up against Shun, or outside the punch possibly by his back. I even have time to think back over the week, and I realize this is the first time this is happening to me at the right moment. I step down and inside the punch, grabbing Shun's wrist and ankle, and I wait for full speed to resume. It does, and I twist and lift Shun. The result is nothing short of stupendous. I no sooner rise from my crouch than Shun is flying beyond me into the slushy mud.

I jog over, trying to hold back giggles. Suddenly I feel like a new superhero. I need to think of a good superhero name. And an outfit. Do I need to keep my identity a secret? Hee-hee! Or is there some way to cash in on this? Most importantly, and I almost trip as this one hits me, why am I thinking any of this is even close to normal? I stop where I am, and chills run through me. My gut drops. How the heck can this be *happening*? I look over at Shun. He's getting to his feet, wiping mud and slush off of his clothes, watching me.

"You look pale, Pete."

"I feel like shit, Shun."

"Why is that?"

"I—"

"You have suddenly realized that this is not accidental, yes? That this is real. And yet, this cannot be reality."

"Sure...I...I guess. Something like that."

"Walk with me." Shun turned and walked to the edge of the school grounds, and steps out into the woods beyond. He set an aggressive pace, and I am half-jogging to keep up with him. I watch how smoothly he's moving and realize he knows this path very well. He comes this way often.

Beyond the dancing over roots and ducking under unexpected broken branches, I notice that there is a fog building up. The temperature, too, is rising. The woods take on a hazy, dreamlike quality as I follow Shun deeper into the forest.

Finally, Shun stops and turns to me in the middle of a clearing. "Close your eyes and clear your mind, Pete."

I stop, and suck in deep breaths, closing my eyes. I let my mind quiet. Doubts and fears about what's happening continue to come up, but I let them slide by. I feel my heartbeat slow and my breathing come back down to normal. I open my eyes.

"There are just a few more steps, Pete. You are almost there, having progressed far faster than others I have trained through the years."

I grin. "Just how long have you been doing this, Shun? You're not that much older than me, y'know."

Shun looks sad for a moment, then he chuckles. "Let it suffice to say I am older than I appear to be. Now..." Shun leaps at me, but the way he moves chills me to the bone. He appears to *stretch* across the fifteen-foot space between us with a giant leap/step, and his fist is flying at my face. As I have been practicing, I spin and twist out of the way, dropping into a crouch, and I thrust my left leg out at his lead leg.

My eyes pop wide. I see my foot about to trip Shun, and then his leg melts and bubbles around mine, as if it's made of liquid mercury. I struggle, but let the moment by, staying in the fight, even though part of my mind is *screaming*. Shun spins and brings his leg up and then down into a hatchet kick at my neck. I leap to the side and roll, coming up onto my feet already punching at my opponent. I feel my left jab connect briefly, but slide off as Shun twirls under my punch. My right cross punch meets only air, and I feel him shove me. I stumble, looking to where he just was, but he is now a blur moving around me faster and faster, flickering punches and kicks at me as I do my best to dodge and counter.

I realize that I hear him whispering something, but it makes no sense. His murmur becomes a chant, getting louder and louder. For all the world, it sounds like he's saying "I stand at the Gate of the Silver Key and call to open the Gate. Yog-sothoth! Blur the Spheres of Time, and Open to Me."

Still makes no sense. But I have bigger problems. I still can't see Shun. I hear his voice, and feel his attacks coming, but even those appear more now to just be thrown out there, not really meant to hurt me, just a part of whatever form he's doing. All I really see is a gray blur of iridescent spheres in the mist.

Then I'm on my knees. I think Shun may have hit me like he did that first time, out of nowhere, but I realize there is no flash of pain. But I feel weak, like I've been sick for days, and not eating. I look up and I can see something at the edge of the clearing. It looks like two columns that weren't there before. I'm sure of that. They're too out of place for me not to have seen them as soon as we got here. I waiver, and drop so I'm sitting on my feet, supporting myself with my shaking arms. My head and shoulders feel heavy, and my muscles threaten to go limp. My upper lip is wet, I realize, and I look down to see that blood is dripping from my face forming a crimson puddle under my chin.

As I watch, something more comes into view between the columns. It looks like a wrought-iron gate…and it's swinging open. I squint, and my breath comes in pants. I force myself to keep watching. The mist in the gateway seems to whirl and coagulate into what looks like sea foam, twisting into a stretched mass of grayish…something.

"Yog-sothoth! Yog-sothoth! Yog-sothoth!" cries Shun as he continues his invisible spinning.

The something grows as lights throb and blaze from beyond. Empty sound begins to roar in my ears with deafening silence. Multicolored ball lightning bubbles out into the clearing, floating around the foggy grassy field moving opposite Shun's dervish dance. A form materializes between the columns and a black-shrouded, impossibly tall figure steps forward, and Shun stops his whirling so suddenly I fall again, now lying on my stomach, propped up on my elbows, not allowing myself to stop watching.

Something is different about Shun, though, now that I can see him again. His hair is snow-white, and he stands with a bit of a stoop. I see him drop to his knees and open his arms wide in front of the form. The giant reaches down with a gaunt hand, and touches Shun's forehead.

Shun stands and turns to me. He walks over and stands behind me. "I am sorry, Pete," he whispers, and yanks me up onto my knees by the back of my collar. "But I need you for something else. If I am to keep going, I need to offer one who has glimpsed the Spheres and begins to understand. You showed such promise, but the millennia weigh heavily upon me, and I must do this if I am to continue walking the Earth."

I'm too tired to do anything but tear up and let the tears fall. I have no strength left. Shun hoists me to my limp feet and guides me to the giant. He looks down at us, his face still hidden within the cowl he wears. The figure opens his arms, and Shun lets go of me. As I wobble and start to fall, I feel Shun's foot shove me at the lower back, forcing me into the creature's embrace. I drop forward into darkness.

The arms close around me and I am falling, falling.

Anger, fear, resentment drift away, and the darkness is no more.

The Gate opens.

Now I can see.

Forever.

The Bride of the Beast

Glynn Owen Barrass

THE BRIDE OF THE BEAST
By Glynn Owen Barrass

What a hell of a place, what a god-awful hell of a place. Robson took a nervous drag from his cigarette and squinted. The cemetery grounds were layered in mist, lying thick on the gravel path he walked down, coating the ancient, ivy smothered slabs he passed. The trees loomed like a canopy above him, allowing a ration of early morning light to filter through, and making the whole scene surreal, dreamlike, as if he hadn't been pulled out of bed at five in the morning to come see the murders at Highgate Cemetery. He was really just back in bed, tucked up with his wife's warm shape beside him, snoozing away for a few more hours before work.

Footsteps approached, muffled by the mist, followed by a thin shape. Balding, combover, long tan trenchcoat, mid-fifties. *Bill Hookham, good man*, Robson thought. The pathologist sucked on a cigarette, smiled around it as he stopped before Robson.

"Hey chief," the man said. "Came looking for you. Heard your footsteps." He removed the cigarette with one woolly-gloved hand and raised the other to shake Robson's own.

"Bill. Always a pleasure," Robson said, and they walked side-by-side the way Hookham had come from.

He turned to Hookham as they walked.

"So what's it like there? Jessup was vague in his call." Jessup, a Detective Sergeant and Robson's assistant for three months now, was still a little wet behind the ears, but...he was a good man.

"The lad's there already," Hookham said, "With four of my boys and a couple of beat bobbies. This is ugly, chief, the worst I've seen. Three kids naked and dead and..."

"And..." Robson looked at Hookham again.

The man sucked his cigarette to the filter and tossed it into the mist.

"Witchcraft," he said. This one word was all Robson needed to make his day a thousand times worse.

"Oh fuck," Robson replied.

Still with the mist, it wasn't lifting, but at least the trees had parted, bringing more light to the scene as the pair approached an aged crypt, grey, cracked and weatherworn. Four of Hookham's men, dressed in white coveralls, stood to the right of it, smoking. One uniform stood before a copper door green with verdigris. To the left stood Jessup in his grey suit, making notes on his pad while the other uniform spoke. The uniform nodded in Robson's direction and Jessup turned, waved, and hurried over. Robson shook his head and tossed his cigarette, pausing to stub it out before continuing forward.

"Detective Inspector!" Jessup said, a beaming smile on his face. Early thirties, clean shaven with blonde hair a little too long for Robson's liking, Robson gave Hookham a look that was reciprocated at the man's unwarranted enthusiasm at a murder scene. "You should see this place!" Jessup continued, "weeping angels and gravestones shaped like dogs and pianos, and—"

"And let's just get to the nitty gritty of it shall we?" Robson said. Hookham snickered. He approached the crypt, nodded to the surrounding men, and paused before the officer guarding the door.

"Detective Inspector," the man stood to attention like he was in a parade.

"You might want to brace yourself sir," said Jessup.

Robson snorted and stepped forward. The officer pushed the door open and stepped aside. "Was the lock on the tomb forced?" he asked the officer.

"No, sir," the man said, shaking his head.

The lintel above the door bore the name 'De Racine.' *Spanish? Italian? Yeah, Italian*, Robson thought and went to enter.

"Oh, hey." He felt Hookham's arm on his sleeve, turned to see the man had retrieved a large rubber-coated torch from an open toolkit on the ground. "You'll need this."

"Thanks." Robson nodded and stepped forward, pushing the door open further while finding the torch's 'on' switch. The tomb interior filled with illumination, and he grimaced.

The press are going to have a field day when they hear about this. Robson squinted his eyes shut. Footsteps behind him opened them again; Jessup squeezed passed him and cleared his throat.

Three corpses lay upon the flagstone floor, two women and a man, the male's feet facing the door while the women's heads did likewise. The women's arms were positioned so that their hands, right and left respectively, touched the man's genitalia.

The women, a long-haired blonde and a brunette, had scratches across their exposed stomachs, swirls and dots and triangles. The man, long brown hair, moustache and sideburns, had a pentagram painted across his stomach, a pentagram in a circle done in either red paint, or blood. It shone in the artificial illumination, so unless it was still fresh Robson guessed the former.

Jessup cleared his throat again and stepped further into the tomb.

"Looks like the, um, residents weren't interfered with," he said. "You remember that thing some years back? The vampire scare? You don't think this is connected, do you?"

Oh, great, this just gets better. "Hope to God, not," Robson said. He raised the torch and shone it upon the walls. Alcoves holding old dusty coffins, dead, mummified flowers tucked in around them, no vandalism upon the walls, no witchcraft graffiti. "The surviving De Racine's will be so happy," he muttered, and stepped forward, kneeling before the recently dead. A dark, ugly bruise lay around the blonde woman's neck. He turned the torch to the other woman. Same thing, and he found the same on the man's throat.

"Death by strangulation, the pathologist's first guess," Jessup said.

Robson nodded, looked to the marks on the women's chests and the pentagram. *I'll want photographs of those.* "You know what, Jessup?" he said and dusted his knees before standing.

"What sir?"

"I really wish I was still in bed."

"So, old chap. You see the reason for quiet and caution in this case?"

Robson nodded at Chief Superintendent Strange's words. He'd been getting it in the ear for two hours now; he prayed they were nearly done. Strange – balding, white hair, handlebar moustache with a hint of sandy brown within the grey, was an old private school boy with a clipped accent that constantly intimated the words: "I am better than you." Dandruff dusted the shoulders of his black suit jacket; not for the first time Robson quelled the urge to tell his superior to dust himself down.

"The press have been very reasonable, since the last trouble at Highgate."

Robson nodded again.

"So please, no leaks from your men, or it'll be someone's meat for the grinder."

Robson had turned his attention to Strange's desk; elaborate, old, like the man himself. These words had him lifting his gaze to send Strange a steely-eyed stare.

"My men are airtight, Hookham's too. If there is a leak to the press I'll have guts for garters myself sir. You don't need to worry about that."

Strange met his stare for a few moments with one equally as steely, then he smiled. "Jolly good Robson. And what do you think your next plans are?"

"I'd like to go through this, first." Robson indicated the brown paper folder Strange had handed him earlier. It was thick with information on the Highgate Vampire debacle from earlier in the decade. "And then I'd like to see what else our boys found at the scene."

"And the cause of death, of course," Strange said.

"Of course," Robson said, and retrieved the folder. "If that will be…"

"Just that the owner of the crypt is a very wealthy, respectable fellow. Try not to step on any toes out there." Strange rose from his seat. "Keep me appraised of the progress, and remember: mum's the word!"

Robson left Strange's office, turned left down the corridor and passed three doors before arriving back at his own. His office was far less regal than Strange's, with a threadbare carpet and a metal, laminate-topped desk. His filing cabinets were steel, not oak, and screeched and complained at their use on a good day. He retrieved his mug from the top of one of them and swigged a mouthful of cold coffee. He dropped the folder on his desk, poured the leftover coffee dregs in the wastebasket and poured a new cup-full from the percolator on the table behind his desk.

He took a heavy swig, washing away the taste of the last cold, sour mouthful and sat, feeling the mug's warmth fill his hands as he stared at the brown, dog-eared folder. He put the cup down, cleared a space on his desk by moving his ashtray and case notes, and pulled the file forward, opening it with distaste.

There were lots of newspaper articles, going back to the 1960s. These he skimmed through, seeing lurid headlines like: *'Caught on The Moonlight Trail of the Highgate Vampire!' 'Ritual Sex Act and Cat Sacrifice,'* (this article made him squirm uncomfortably), and *'Does a Vampyr Walk in Highgate?'* He didn't want to read them, but had to. So, he reached into his pocket for his cigarettes, lit a new one, and got down to reading tabloid trash.

Five cigarettes and two mugs of coffee later, he had the gist of what had happened in Highgate. A group of local young people interested in the occult had taken to prowling Highgate late at night, one of them claiming to have seen a strange figure, another claiming that this figure was in fact 'A King Of Vampires.' There had been vandalism, mass vampire hunts, desecration of corpses, all perpetrated by a group of idiots looking for publicity. One of them had gone to prison three years earlier, in 1974, for damaging memorials and interfering with dead remains, and after that, the crackpots had disappeared off of the radar.

"This is nothing to do with our case," he said aloud, wanting to give truth to his thoughts by saying them. He hadn't been around during the Highgate Vampire phenomenon, and from what he read, Strange was right in not wanting a resurgence of that sordid, long standing affair now that it was dead in the water. Still he took his notepad from his jacket pocket, noted down the two principal antagonists in the affair, and thought to send someone to snoop around and see what they were up to.

Just as he was putting the notebook back in his jacket, his door knocked, followed by Jessup bustling in.

"Hey sir!" Jessup said. Full of enthusiasm, he held a large brown envelope in one hand and his coat in the other. He closed the door behind him with his foot.

Robson indicated the vacant seat facing his desk and Jessup draped his coat on the back of it and sat down.

"We have the photos as requested," he said with a beaming smile on his face. He leant over and placed the envelope atop Robson's Highgate material.

If he was a dog I'd pat his head and say 'good boy,' Robson thought, then, "Good work Jessup. Anything from the scene?"

"Funny you should say that sir," Jessup said. He patted his jacket pockets and removed his notepad from the inside one. "Just hold on one second," he continued and leafed through it.

Robson took the opportunity to open the envelope and pour the contents out. There were six large glossy photographs, three of the Highgate corpses at different angles and three of the women's and man's mutilations up close. Teenagers. Barely more than children really. Just what did they—

"Ah, this is it," Jessup said.

Robson looked up from the photographs. The other man was reading from his notebook.

"Two twelve-volt car batteries were found in the bushes near the scene. Six cigarette butts, Pall Mall brand. The batteries are in the Met Lab right now – they're looking for fingerprints… And that's it."

"Car batteries, hmmm," Robson said. "There were no signs of torture apart from the flesh wounds and ligature marks, were there?"

"You thinking car batteries to the genitals, sir?"

"Hmmm, possibly. Just thinking aloud." Robson scanned the photos again. "Anything proving identification? Missing Persons Bureau contacted?"

"No on the first. Their office said it's too early to tell on the second," Jessup said. "Oh, and Hookham says he'll have his report on your desk later this afternoon."

Robson tapped his hand on one of the female close-ups, realized he was tapping the breasts and moved his hand. "Fancy a drive, Jessup?"

"Of course, sir. Where are you thinking?"

"See if you can find me a phone directory," Robson said, "And we'll take it from there."

There were four De Racine's in the Greater London Directory, and after discreet phone enquiries Robson found one that did indeed have ancestors interred in Highgate Cemetery. Robson played it cool on the phone, friendly and professional, and told the man there had been some vandalism and could he make a visit today?

Half an hour later he and Jessup were driving his weathered Ford Anglia through Kensington with Jessup using his A-Z to guide them to Chelsea Crescent.

They found it soon enough, a row of four-storied, white stucco-fronted terraced buildings with neatly trimmed rows of box trees lining the second-floor balconies. Expensive cars dotted the street, including a couple of Rolls Royce's. Robson realized his car would look a heap beside them.

"Looks nice," Jessup said.

"Expensive," Robson replied, and pulled up outside number fifteen.

"You know sir, we could have easily sent one of our uniforms to deal with this." Jessup said.

"I don't think so," Robson said. He pulled his keys from the ignition and left the car.

A few minutes later, after knocking briefly and being let in by the butler, an elderly, hollow cheeked man with wispy white hair, the pair stood waiting in an oak-panelled foyer. The room was opulent, with ancestral portraits lining the walls and thick tortoiseshell carpet underfoot. The butler knocked on the door to their right, announced the two, and then made his precarious way up the stairs facing the front door.

The door opened, and Robson was taken aback at the apparition that appeared there.

Tall, very thin in his brown tweed suit, the man's skin bore a yellowish cast to it. His eyes were sunken, dark with circles as if he hadn't slept in days. His thick black hair was combed back, his forehead lined with veins, his nose hawkish above a black goatee surrounding thick, red lips. The ghoulish face smiled, and Robson cleared his throat.

"Mr. De Racine?" he asked, and stepped forward, proffering his hand. De Racine accepted, shaking back with a warm, slightly moist grip.

De Racine said, "yes, and hello," in a slightly accented voice. He nodded at Jessup, and ushered both men through the door.

Another oak panelled room followed, this one lined with books. Recesses between the shelves bore glass book cabinets, topped with potted plants and Roman busts. Robson was impressed - De Racine had quite some taste. At the centre of the room stood an elaborately carved desk covered in newspapers and books. A freshly lit cigarette burned in a silver ashtray on the desk but it was too far away to see the brand. De Racine walked towards the desk then turned.

"Would you like a refreshment?" he asked, revealing that ghoulish smile again.

"Yes I—"

"No, thank you," Robson said, interrupting his junior. "We won't be here long, I just wanted to tell you in person about the vandalism at your family tomb and ask a question or two regarding it."

"Yes, yes of course. Terrible news that." De Racine grimaced and leaned his buttocks against his desk. "Were the bodies in there...interfered with at all?"

Jessup gasped. Robson gave him a look and replied, "No, your ancestors were untouched, if that's what you mean, just a bit of red paint on the inside. But can you tell me, do you know why the door to the crypt was unlocked?"

De Racine stared at him blankly, then shook his head.

"No, the door should have been locked, but then again, I haven't been to the family crypt since Uncle Arthur passed some thirty years ago. I assume the council or Highgate's people will be cleaning up this vandalism?"

Robson, who had turned from De Racine to examine the bookshelves, answered absently. "That's something you'll have to take up with them, I'm afraid. This was just a courtesy call really." He turned back to De Racine and added, "You will have to see about securing that door yourself though."

De Racine nodded. "Of course, gentlemen. Now, if there is nothing else...?"

"Well sir, he seemed like an okay chap," Jessup said as he fastened his seatbelt. "What did you think?"

Robson harrumphed and continued staring at De Racine's front door. "Those books in there, on the shelves... *The Gospel of the Witches, The Key of Solomon*... witches and demonology all over the place. So no, I didn't think he was an 'okay chap.' I think that the man is completely iffy."

"But do you think he's connected with the murders, Sir?"

"That," Robson removed a hand from the steering wheel and started the engine, "Is something I would love to know."

When Robson arrived back at his office he found Hookham's preliminary report waiting for him on his desk. It was short, but not very sweet. Hookham's notes said the three victims had recently had sexual intercourse, no surprise there, really, and the cause of death, until Hookham could get inside and check further, appeared to be manual asphyxiation. There were no signs this was performed by hand (no telltale bruising) or a rope (no marks indicating such). Hookham was also getting tests done to see if the victims had been under the influence of anything. Murder it surely was, with the killer, or killers, still out there.

And, Robson thought, *the killer just might possibly be a witchcraft fanatic.* This, and the strange man De Racine, remained heavy on his thoughts for the rest of the day, and after he had gotten home. He spent most of the following day dealing with a rape on the London Underground and interviewing five suspects. It was dark outside when he arrived back at his office and sat down with an exhausted sigh.

To his disgust, Jessup burst in before he even had chance to make coffee.

"Sorry I disappeared earlier sir, but I got a call from Missing Persons over the Highgate matter."

"Oh?" this perked up Robson's interest.

"Nothing on the man yet, but it shouldn't be long now. The blonde girl is called Deborah Wilson, the brunette, Tammy Brinkley." He rushed the words out in his excitement. "And another thing, sir. I asked Missing Persons whether they had any reports of girls around that same age reported missing the past few days. One name, Loretta Thomas came up. So I phoned her parents, and she knows Deborah Wilson."

Robson bit his bottom lip and thought for a few moments. "Jessup, Strange be damned about us pussyfooting around. Get some men watching that crypt at Highgate. Once that's done, meet me at my car."

Jessup nodded. "You have a hunch sir? Where are we going?"

Robson stood and retrieved his coat from behind his chair. "To pay De Racine another visit."

It was a chilly night in Kensington, with a layer of mist carpeting the streets Robson turned down towards De Racine's. He pitied the three men on duty at Highgate, and while Jessup hummed to himself beside him, he pitied himself for coming out without a cigarette. He turned onto De Racine's street and noted that all the houses were illuminated apart from De Racine's.

"Looks like he's out," Jessup said, "think we should wait?"

"No, I think we should go right to the door," Robson replied. He parked a few doors down from the silver Rolls Royce outside De Racine's house, hugged himself from the cold as he and Jessup approached the door.

Robson knocked, waited a while, then knocked again. Getting no reply, he rang the bell.

Not looking good, he thought, *and perhaps—*

He heard bolts removed and a key turn. The next thing, the wizened butler answered holding a large brass candlestick holder. The illumination was meagre. The man looked nervous.

"Power cut?" Robson asked.

The butler hissed through his teeth and said, "Master's orders."

"Ah, so he's in then? Good." Robson stepped forward and moved past the man into the dimly lit foyer. There were candlesticks here too, barely dispelling the gloom. He heard Jessup come in behind him. "Sir, don't you think—"

There was a loud, dull thump, and Robson turned to see Jessup crumble to the floor; the butler, with panic on his face, stood behind him with the candlestick holder raised.

"I, er…" the butler mumbled, and although still in shock, Robson stepped forward and slammed the old man square in the face. The butler went down, unconscious to the floor. Rubbing his smarting knuckles Robson kneeled. He felt a momentary regret for hitting someone so obviously feeble, then took handcuffs from his coat pocket and cuffed the man's hands behind his back.

While he was checking on Jessup, who he found was unconscious but breathing steadily, a voice issued from upstairs.

"Wendell, bring me more candles."

The voice was unmistakably De Racine's. Edgy over this turn of events, Robson steeled himself, checked Jessup once more, and crept up the stairs, slowly, taking two at a time. No candles illuminated the shadowy upstairs, but a door to the left of the top of the stairs stood ajar and more candlelight flickered from within. He approached with caution, for he could hear movement inside. When he reached the door he paused, for inside he spied a strange looking device stood upon a table.

What on earth?

The size of a typewriter, the thing was formed from tubes of copper and clusters of unlit bulbs. Metal cylinders were visible beneath the outer fittings, and it appeared inert. Still, it bore a slight violet glow about it. Robson had never seen anything like it. Stepping closer, he saw it was connected to two twelve-volt batteries.

He flinched as the door swung open, De Racine appearing in the gap. His face ablaze with anger, he was dressed in a scarlet smoking jacket. He held a revolver pointed directly at Robson's chest.

"I do believe you're trespassing." He said with a snarl. "Raise them, slowly."

Robson raised his hands and stared from the revolver to De Racine's face.

"Just a moment, sir," De Racine said, and keeping the gun aimed at Robson, he edged towards the strange machine. He placed his hand beneath the cluster of bulbs and Robson heard the click of a switch.

The machine started to sputter, a strange liquid sound that made Robson queasy. Then the noise levelled out, becoming a low drone that made the hairs stand up on his arms. The violet tint grew, throbbed brightly, and then became other colours he couldn't put a name to.

"Now come in, then remain still," De Racine said, "I will shoot the second you do anything."

Robson stepped into the room, saw candles on low tables and bare plaster walls flickering with shadows in the candlelight. The floor was bare board beneath his feet. Adding to the lack of illumination, his vision dimmed as whatever sound the machine emitted had a strange hallucinogenic effect on him. He blinked and shook his head as the room faded completely, replaced by something cathedral-sized, filled with twisted stone pillars and deformed statues. The black, titanic stone blocks throbbed with a violet aura, the statues; things resembling mutated women wrapped with violating spidery limbs and tentacles, mouthed silent obscene ecstasies. Swaying on his feet Robson looked up, saw deep space between the cathedral's broken roof filled with red suns and stars and planets oscillating in deranged dizzying motion that coalesced into De Racine's leering face.

"You like my temple? It was seeing this that gave me the idea of using Highgate for the rituals. And wherever I take the machine, the temple follows. Now again, don't move."

Robson couldn't if he tried. Ashamed of it as he was, he was utterly terrified of this unearthly turn of events – hallucination or not.

"Machine, what sort of machine?" He said with difficulty. "What's its purpose?"

"Bringing our worlds together through miscegenation," De Racine said and backed away. The temple faded, the usual contours of the room re-appearing in its place, although they were starker now, brighter than before, the colours subtly wrong.

"Loretta? Loretta, come in now," De Racine said and a moment later, a door to Robson's right, almost invisible in the earlier shadows, opened.

A young woman, late teens, stepped into Robson's field of vision. Long blonde hair, she was slim, beautiful, and wore a scarlet kimono decorated with flamingos. The colours on the kimono throbbed like the machine. She smiled at Robson, and embraced De Racine.

"These types are so easy to get hold of you know." De Racine said. "Hang around a book shop reading Aleister Crowley and they appear like bees around honey. Are you ready my dear? Ready to commune with the Devil?"

The girl nodded, and De Racine undid her kimono. It slipped to the floor to reveal a naked form that De Racine proceeded to kiss, from her neck down to her breasts before he backed off, turning to Robson with a lascivious grin.

"You want to join in?" he said. "Always better when more than one performs with the Beast." He raised the gun to Robson's head. Behind De Racine, the room faded, became the cathedral-like place again, and then returned to its usual form. Usual, except that eerie shapes had begun coalescing from the walls, rubbery lumps of multicoloured matter that seethed and shuddered as they filled the room.

Robson felt sweat building on his brow. The shapes, obviously alive in some form, moved through each other, or bounced off their companions. Some were congregating above the girl, growing feelers to stroke and explore her vulnerable form. She moaned, her head tossing around as her body convulsed in obscene ecstasy.

"These are mere minions, minor devils curious of the gateway between realms." As De Racine spoke, one of the shapes passed through his head. As it did so, his eyes glowed violet.

"You're a stranger to them, for now, so I cannot guarantee your safety should you move." De Racine lowered the gun and backed slowly towards the girl. With his free hand he reached into his smoking jacket and produced a small, curved knife. He smiled at Robson. "Blood is needed to summon the Beast, blood and sigils. But you have witnessed that already, yes?"

De Racine knelt, stroked the girl's stomach sensuously with the tip of the knife, then placed the gun on the floor beside him. He pressed down with the knife, the girl yelped, and De Racine began carving ugly, twisted shapes into her flesh. He said, "The Beast can be eager, destructive with its failures, but, there is always more beautiful fodder."

Entranced by this sordid scene, Robson didn't notice a closer, more insidious threat, until one of the entities was right beside his face. In a flash it entered him, and he screamed both inside and out as pain unimaginable tore his brain to shreds.

Robson found himself on his knees atop a blasted black mountain, dead grass like brittle white fingers surrounding him, thrust from grave earth blackness alive with squirming forms. The winds about him roared, howling in rage, screaming in his ears. His clothes buffeted about, he clutched his pounding head, screaming back at the wind and rolling onto his back. What he saw falling towards him from the sky froze the scream in his throat. His eyes watered, his jaw locking as his mouth issued a hoarse croak. The thing, the *Devil,* coming down on him resembled an obscene inkblot against the dark blue parchment of lightning-filled sky. And the blot had tentacles, flashing round like angry cats' tails, shivering spider limbs and shiny black horns and gaping mouth upon mouth upon mouth...

"Come, Master!" De Racine screamed, and suddenly Robson found himself back in the room, on the floor beside the prone girl with De Racine squatting atop her, his arms raised to the ceiling where something black and horrible seeped through.

"Defile this virgin," the maniac continued, as black tentacles roped into the girl. She shuddered and moaned at the violation. "Take this my—"

152

Robson cocked the hammer on De Racine's discarded pistol, aiming it squarely at the man's head. De Racine turned to him, wild eyed, his parchment-skinned face resembling a grinning skull. "Do it," he said, "take me closer to my god."

Robson turned the gun from De Racine's head and aimed it at the machine. He pulled the trigger.

*   *   *

De Racine was arrested, dragged from his house in cuffs by a dazed but not too injured Jessup. He was eventually charged with three counts of murder, although Robson knew the truth, that it wasn't a man that had killed the three youngsters at Highgate but something he had summoned from…where? Hell? Robson didn't know, didn't want to know.

He was just glad he survived that desperate encounter in De Racine's house. The girl, Loretta Thomas, left the house hopelessly catatonic, just another victim of De Racine's perverse lusts. Robson received a call from the mental hospital she was admitted to two months later. Loretta Thomas was pregnant. They suspected De Racine to be the father.

If only that were true.

But as the girl had left the house irreparably changed, so had Robson, for even now, six months later, he still saw those floating, amorphous shapes De Racine had summoned From Beyond. Mostly he saw them in the corner of his eyes, but sometimes, when he awoke shaking in the middle of the night, he would catch them hovering over his wife, and sometimes, leaving her body.

He tried explaining it away as delusion, the after-effects of the mental trauma he had suffered at the hands of De Racine. The things *couldn't* still be here, not when he had so totally destroyed the machine, shooting it repeatedly while an agonized De Racine wept and begged for him to stop.

For the most part, Robson could deal with seeing the entities, but the other thing, the horror he had witnessed coming for him and the girl before her mind had broken and he had fired his shots? Sometimes he could feel it, on the peripheral of his senses, and he would look to the bedroom ceiling and wonder whether the moans his wife made in her sleep were mere nightmares alone.

The Nest of Pain

C. J. Henderson

THE NEST OF PAIN
By C. J. Henderson

"Forty years on, growing older and older,
　Shorter in wind as in memory long,
　Feeble of foot and rheumatic of shoulder
What will it help you that once you were strong?"
　　　　E.E. Bowen

"You heard me--"

It was not that those present within earshot had not heard what the man had said.

"I want a refund."

It was simply that they could not believe their ears. A refund? For a house de-ghosting? While the confrontation escalated in the front room, back in his office Franklin Nardi closed his eyes--briefly. At least, that had been his intention, to cut himself off from the world for no more than, say, an extended blink. Really. He simply needed a second of darkness, had to remove himself from the world of light and reality for at least a moment.

Although, ultimately he had to admit, to do so was dangerous. The cool and comforting black was seductive in its feeling of relative safety. Some days, it seemed that every time he closed his eyes he felt a boiling apprehension he might never open them again. It was not a fear of dying, but rather of simply retreating from the world--of finding the appeal of separation from all mankind was too seductive, and that he had finally decided to give in because enough was enough.

"It seems to me, Mr. Douglas, sir," the voice of Mark Berkenwald, one of Nardi's partners in the Arkham Detective Agency, the sound of his words accompanied by the rustling of papers, "we have your signature here, signing off as an indication of your satisfaction with the job in question."

Nardi chuckled within his head at his partner's voice--Mark, always so calm, always able to put off an aggressor with little more than an excess of words. He also remembered the Douglas couple, remembered the job. He remembered losing his cool just a bit on the night he had spent in the old house. Arkham, like any town with an abundance of top drawer types, had money to burn. Recently among the well-to-do in that corner of New England, it had become fashionable for new home purchases to not be considered finished--or at least dignified--until said structure and its lands had been inspected for aberrations, both physical and other-worldly.

"On top of that, Mr. Douglas, Sir, the date of your signature here is over a year old. So, even if you hadn't approved the work, there are limits-_"

For some reason he could not explain at the time of that inspection, Nardi had opened himself to the house--or more correctly, to whatever might have been lurking within it--to a risky degree. Madame Renee, formerly Ms. Brenda Goff, his associate for that evening's examination, had assured him the next morning that if there had been any kind of dangerous presence on site it would have come after him.

It should have, he thought, told himself, hiding behind his closed eyes, behind his mostly closed door.

Should have?

What the hell did he mean by that... should have?

"I don't care about any of that," came Douglas' voice, quieter, less assured. "You just don't understand..."

"Should have?"

Nardi heard himself say the words aloud, a part of him shuddering at what he knew that meant. It had been almost seven years since he had retired from the NYPD, he and his fellows. Each having put in their twenty years on the force, moving to New England and opening a security firm had seemed like such a bright idea. Low risks, simple work, and what they had called back in the day, clean-air-lives. Each of them had been able to purchase a far more spacious private home than they had enjoyed in New York, one with land on both sides. Shoveling snow, raking leaves, planting a garden, joining the Knights of Columbus--

Their uncomplicated suburban dreams had materialized for the most part, but as in so many things, there had been unforeseen... complications.

"Mark," Nardi heard himself calling out, a part of his mind cursing him for doing so, "bring Mr. Douglas in here, if you would, please."

The head of the Arkham Detective Agency forced his eyes open. Forced himself to straighten his body in his chair. Forced himself to pretend the normal rules of the world still worked in the ways he used to believe. The ways he knew things worked before he had left the safety of Manhattan and its blessedly sterile concrete. Before he had discovered that there were things that lived in the darkness beyond any understanding. Before he had apologized to his mother for making sport of her for hanging garlic above the front door during his years living at home.

"Mr. Douglas," said Nardi in his most welcoming tone, pointing toward one of the chairs before his desk, "good to see you again. What seems to be the problem?"

Edward Douglas did not look good. Oh, physically he still appeared much the same as when Nardi had seen him last--a year, year and a half earlier--just before his wedding. Now he seemed gaunt. Worn. But mainly, what did not look so good to the security man were his former client's eyes. Nardi could see it without any trouble--the confusion. The fear, nesting there in the corners, attempting to overwhelm the entire iris in its effort to manifest, to envelope all of its host.

"Mr. N-Nardi, isn't it?"

"That's right. How can we help you?"

Douglas slipped into the offered chair, holding onto the armrests as he did so. His movements were weak, his motions jerky. If he were still a cop, Nardi thought, he would have pegged the man as one intimidated by neighborhood thugs. His instincts assured him there was something terribly wrong going on--at least in his visitor's mind, if nothing else. When he sat quietly, twitching slightly--nervously--seemingly unable to organize his thoughts, Nardi offered:

"You were askin' for a refund--"

"No, God--no." Douglas sat forward quickly as he spoke, clamping his lips shut after his brief explosion of words. Shaking his head slightly, more of a trembling than anything else, his eyes avoiding Nardi's, he continued, saying:

"I, I did say that. But, I didn't mean it. I mean... that's not what I want. I mean, I mean--"

"Mr. Douglas, please," offered Nardi, his tone as consoling as possible, "relax. Take your time. There's no rush."

"It's Julie," he said, too quickly. The fear in his voice forcing its way through the knot in Nardi's stomach. "Something... I don't know what, how to describe..."

Nardi's breath froze in his throat. It was partly his two decades as a police officer, dealing with people, listening to them, knowing when they were lying, knowing when they were trying to fool themselves--knowing. Then also, it was partly his years in Arkham. The things he had seen. The horrors witnessed, and those only felt. He knew something was wrong at the Douglas home, something beyond Douglas' poor ability to put any of it into words. Most likely beyond his ability to even comprehend it.

"She's... she's like, I don't know..."

The detective had no legal responsibility to do anything for the man on the other side of his desk. He could chose to send him to this or that organization, or offer to charge him for the company's services once more. He could also turn him out, ignore him completely. It was a thought that was certainly present within his mind--within the part of his

158

brain chiefly concerned with self-preservation.

"Get him out of here," that segment of his mind hissed. "What're you thinkin', you stupid wop? Forget this. Goddamnit, you remember what almost happened last time."

Last time?

While he offered Douglas various non-committal lumps of comfort, Nardi wondered at his thought. Last time... nothing had happened the last time. It had been open-and-shut. He and the witch went in, did all the tests, checked the place out, it was clean. It was.

You went the extra mile, ten of them, he reminded himself. You opened yourself up to that place, dared it to bite your ass. What more were you supposed to do?

Should have

Again, the same words, half-terror, half-accusation, echoed in his mind. Yes, he had tried, had done everything he could--he had. But still, his brain chose to remember the night not as a time when something could have happened, but should have.

Nardi stared across his desk at the man sitting there, softly crying. Edward Douglas was so distraught, so filled with frustrated self-loathing over his inability to articulate his situation, that his pathetic showing was almost comical. Except Nardi was not laughing. Inside, his bowels were churning, threatening to embarrass him. His fingers curling into involuntary fists, he tilted his head sideways, grinding his teeth, forcing himself under control.

He wanted to say the right words to Douglas, but had no idea what they might be. He wanted to comfort the man, but... how? What did he know about haunted houses, he asked himself, about creatures that could turn human beings inside out? That could break inter-dimensional barriers? All the things he had seen, all the horrors that had tried to kill him, how could he expose himself to any of it once more? And moreover... why would he do so?

"Perhaps," he said softly, his tone a thing of concern, his brain screaming at him to not release the words forming within his mind, "I should come over and check things out myself..."

"Oh, oh my God... could you, would you?"

Every part of him slipping into frenzy, Franklin Nardi used all of his control to assure his former client that nothing could be easier. Laughing with embarrassment, Douglas dried his eyes, agreeing that eight o'clock that evening would be perfect. Stumbling on his way out the door, the younger man said some five different "thank yous" before he was out of earshot. Nardi was only able to offer him one "you're welcome" before he began to shed his own tears.

Nardi sat outside the Douglas residence for some twenty minutes before finally leaving his car. He had not arrived early through any kind of accident or miscalculation. He had wanted some time to simply observe the house, to be within its presence. To see if anything felt different to him than it had a year earlier.

"And, detective," the cynical side of his brain asked him, "feel anything out of line? Got your cosmic mojo workin' yet?"

Using his anger to propel himself, when another vehicle pulled up on the opposite side of the suburban street, Nardi finally exited his own car and ascended the stairs to the Douglas' front door. He chose the knocker over the door bell, giving it three politely sharp raps, then waited for a reaction. Within a handful of seconds Douglas responded, welcoming the detective into his home. The two exchanged the usual greetings and then, before anything more could be said, she entered.

"Mr. Nardi... how good it is to see you again."

Julie Douglas' voice crept into the security man's ear, blurring his memories of the woman, transfixing him.

"Ummm, yeah, Ms. Douglas. Ah... you too. Been a long time." Taking his arm, the young woman--her hair dark, long, and radiant, her smile entrancing, her touch warm and lingering--guided Nardi forward into the Douglas home. Her husband trailed behind them, offering commentary which was ignored by the others. Seated in the living room, the woman asked;

"So, are you here because of Eddie's little obsession?"

"Ah... ma'am..."

"Oh, don't pretend. It's all right. The quicker we all get this out in the open, over and done with... why... the better for everyone--no?"

Nardi gulped. It was a small, barely noticeable action, but there was no doubt in his mind that the woman had seen it. Her grin was too perfectly timed to have been in reaction to anything else. Making certain his voice was calm, that it would not crack, he answered:

"I would say so. In fact, I must admit, I'm not certain why I'm really here. Mr. Douglas didn't actually explain what he thought the problem was."

"He thinks I'm different. That I've changed. That I'm not his blushing bride anymore." Leaning closer, leaning far too revealingly forward out of her chair, reaching toward Nardi, she asked:

"What do you think, Frank?"

The security man lowered his head slightly, closing his eyes to slits. Not looking directly at the woman, merely checking her position with his peripheral vision, he said:

"Well, we all change in time. Marriage makes us all a little different."

"Diplomatic, isn't he, Sweetheart?"

Her husband did not answer. Nardi did not waste any effort in even glancing to catch the man's reaction. He had to concentrate on the woman. There was no doubt in the detective's mind that Julie Douglas had changed. She had been a sweet girl. Not naive, but not jaded, either. Now, Nardi did not know what to make of her. She was aggressive, acting as if she could barely contain herself. But, he wondered, what was it she was trying to contain?

Nardi shook his head, working to clear the fog he could feel working its way into his brain. He could not identify the sensation within his mind. It was something like the beginning of a headache, the kind one felt in the morning, tiny stabs of pain just noticeable enough to force one awake. He tried to concentrate on the feeling, but no matter where, within his skull, he focused his efforts, the small slivers of agony would somehow dissipate, reassembling elsewhere.

"Got to make this stop," he told himself.

"Darling," the woman pretended to call to her husband, obviously using her words to taunt the security man, "our guest seems to be having some sort of difficulty. Whatever should we do?"

Whether Edward was about to respond to his wife's words or not, all attention within the room was suddenly redirected by the jarring sound of Nardi's cell phone going off. Fumbling it out of his pocket, the security man listened for a moment, then blurted back at the voice coming through it;

"I, I understand. On my way." Shoving the phone back into his pocket, Nardi forced himself erect, staggering for the doorway, shouting, "Sorry... emergency... have to go. I'll, I'll come back. I'll... I have to go--have to, have..."

The sound of Julie Douglas' laughter followed the security man to the door.

Nardi sat in the passenger seat of the car which had pulled up across the street earlier, trembling--unable to focus. His shoulders were hunched, his body drawing in upon itself, a fright he could not name or comprehend shriveling him. Reducing him. Forcing him to question his very sense of reality.

"I'm thinking I called you just in time."

"Y-Yes... yes... yes..."

"Jesus, Frank," replied Madame Renee, her eyes going slightly wide at her realization, "I know things were sounding weird in there, but just what the hell--Jesus, Frank."

Nardi had brooded over going to the Douglas house throughout the day. Finally he had called in the agency's resident witch, asking her to go along in the role of psychic back-up. The security man had gone in wearing a double wire which had allowed Renee to hear everything clearly, and to get a bit of a visual as well. Sitting in her car with a company's laptop, she had observed the scene and, when she had felt Nardi might actually be in some sort of trouble, had called his cell to give him an excuse to leave. Looking at him cowering next to her, she shook herself all over, then said;

"Frank, we have to get you out of here. Can you drive? What do you want to do about your car?"

Nardi heard the woman's words, knew she was correct. He could not go back inside the Douglas home. Not that night. Not in the condition he was in at that moment. He also did not want to leave his car behind. The things he had seen since moving to Arkham--had learned--no, he did not want a possession of his near the house, out of his sight.

But, he wondered, could he drive? Could he take control of himself, actually get the keys from his pocket, turn on the ignition, and drive? Drive? Pilot tons of metal and glass, weave around others doing the same? Did he dare?

"Shut up," he growled aloud, startling Renee, even though she somehow knew he was speaking to himself. "You shit, you miserable coward. Get it together."

His eyes closed, he shook his head violently, then spat away a breath as he opened his eyes once more. The fingers of his right hand sliding around the door release, with his left he pointed out the window as he said to Renee:

"We did background on that goddamned dump last year. I need you to dig it out. Call Sammy and Mark if you need help goin' through the files. I want them in on this, anyway." Snapping the latch, he stepped out of the witch's car, feeling some of his old self returning. Taking a deep breath, he forced it in and out quickly, took another, and then said:

"I need a meal. I'll see you all in an hour." When Renee asked him "where", he told her:

"Miflin's. Where else?"

The restaurant Nardi had chosen was one which could never have survived back in his native Manhattan, but it had been one of the major selling points for not only him, but his partners as well, when it had come time to choose a city in which to set up shop. Freddie Miflin was a retired Navy man who had decided to open an eatery that ran on his terms. There would be no menu. When you went to Miflin's, all you knew is that the food would be hearty, and there would be plenty of it.

The owner was not an utter curmudgeon. He took such things as food allergies and ailments such as diverticulitis into consideration. Potential diners were not presented with but a single choice on any given evening. And indeed, friends such as Frank Nardi could make requests if necessary. That night, however, there was no need. Even though it was only mid-April, Miflin had decided to cook up Thanksgiving dinner. When the rest of the members of the agency entered the restaurant, they found Nardi enjoying seconds of the mashed potatoes and gravy along with a thigh which looked as if it must have come from a turkey that had weighed in at an excess of thirty pounds.

"I'm not even going to comment," said Berkenwald, marveling at the amount of food still before Nardi.

"Good," answered the security man. Popping a massive chunk of dark meat into his mouth, he said as he chewed, "So, what'da we know about the Douglas dump?"

Berkenwald left the details on the house to Galtoni as he was interested in celebrating Thanksgiving early, himself. As he went off to get a plate, the Agency's last surviving partner pulled out the research file on the Douglas home, saying:

"I remember we took that one pretty serious because of the history we dug up ... lemme see... yeah, here it is..."

As Galtoni thumbed through the pages, the story of the property in question unfolded. It seemed that, originally, nearly three hundred years earlier when the modestly-sized mansion had been built, it had been a single property situated in the center of some fifty-eight acres. Over the decades, as neighboring Arkham had grown, various plots had been sold off by the owners. The sales had not begun until the mid-1800s, when the original family had fallen into disrepute. At first, sales had been slow because of the rumors and suspicions which swirled around the property. By the 1900s, however, memory began to fade.

"What kinda rumors?"

"What kind ya want," asked Galtoni, a dark chuckle accompanying his words. "Yeah, okay sure, a lot of it can probably be chalked up to the usual hysteria, even in this loony tune nut factory we chose to move to... I mean, were-creatures--"

"You mean like werewolves?"

"Yeah, but that wasn't all," answered the detective with a knowing grin. "There's them that believes in everything from were-sheep and cows to things they don't even have names for."

"They have names," offered Renee softly, to which Galtoni offered:

"Not in the dictionary, they don't. Anyway, there were also charges of devil worship, alchemy, witch covens, when they chased down old..." the detective thumbed back a few pages, then read, "Jedidiah Mortonson... there's a Bible-thumper's name for ya, huh? Anyway, they were willing to hang just about any dark badge available on him--hell, they hung him in the end as it was--"

"Surprised they didn't burn the place down," said Madame Renee almost under her breath. Galtoni told her:

"Apparently it was suggested, but it was decided to turn the house into an orphanage." When eyebrows went up, the detective nodded, telling those assembled:

"Yeah, I know, but there were circumstances. Seems Jedidiah had been, what would be the politically correct terminology in this case... ah, let's go with 'acquiring,' yeah, acquiring children for whatever reasons he might have had. When the noble townsfolk raided the place, seems those they found were in a pretty poorly state, locked in one of the sub-basements--"

"Jesus Christ, what kind of a nutjob was this guy?"

"According to the paperwork, just your average child-sacrificing warlock."

"And he got away with this for how long?" Galtoni held up a finger to beg for time as he thumbed first forward, then backward through his pages, finally finding the section for which he was looking. Giving everyone a you're-not-going-to-believe-this grin, he said:

"I guess that part is up to who you believe. You see, it seems there are those who felt that the Mortonson who got hung, Jedidiah, who was supposed to be the grandson of the original Mortonson who originally built the place and started all the hocus pocus crap, was actually the original Mortonson. You know, stretching his days by living through others--"

"Life extension through blood sacrifice," said Renee. When the others all turned to her, she added, "It's not unheard of."

"Neither is getting a good night's sleep, either," growled Galtoni. "What's crawling around inside that place, anyway?"

No one spoke for some long time. No one ate, either. Finally Nardi, having stared at the forkful of gravy-rich mashed potatoes on his fork throughout the silence, dropped the utensil to his plate, exclaiming:

"Goddamnit, but what goes on in this damn town? What is it? Every ten feet there's either a haunted house, or some old crazy stealin' souls, or gods slippin' in from other dimensions--"

"Let it go, Frank."

"Let what go, Mark," snapped the detective. "Tony's death? His atoms jumbled by some thing--some nightmare thing that no one can explain? We came here to get away from all the crap in New York, and what? What'd we find? What?!"

"Please, Frank," Renee threw in. "There isn't anyone here at this table that didn't think the occult was some dodge we could use to make some extra bucks. This town taught us different. I'm not saying that everything from crop circles to the Loch Ness monster gets a free pass, but we've all seen shit. And Tony Balnco... died, was killed... by something no one here will ever be able to explain. But all that doesn't matter."

"Yeah," Nardi shot back, "then what <u>does</u> matter?"

"What matters is what you decide to do next."

Renee was right, and the security man had to admit it. What exactly, he asked himself, was he going to do next? Edward Douglas had asked for his help. Indeed, if he had missed something during his inspection of the man's home, a something that had now taken possession of the man's wife--something of which he should have taken notice, then didn't he have an obligation to do something about it?

Should have...

Despite the insanity of it all, actually taking the idea of a spirit living within a house that could claim the soul of a person seriously, there were those words again. "Should have." They had sprung into his head that morning, the notion that he had thought back when first he had been in the Douglas home that there was something there. Something black and evil. Something dangerous. Something that had hungered for him, but that had apparently waited.

Waited for someone younger. Someone less resistant. Someone like Julie Douglas.

Shit, thought Nardi. Goddamned to Hell shit...

After another moment of silence, and then a long, defeated sigh, Frank Nardi told the others exactly what they were going to do next.

When Douglas came to the door the next morning, the look on his face was one of utter surprise. Blinking twice, he stammered for a moment, then finally managed to say:

"Mr. Nardi, you've come back."

"I said I would."

"Yes, yes, of course, but I ... oh, no matter. And I see, my... I can be so bad with names--"

"Madame Renee," the witch answered in her mock central European voice.

"Yes, I remember now. Please, please come in."

The fact Douglas was more than willing to usher them into his home at 7:30 in the morning revealed much about his situation. They had arrived without even an email's worth of announcement, but such an oversight in protocol seemed not to matter to the beleaguered husband. As he ushered them into the kitchen, he asked if he could get them anything.

"No, no thank you," said Nardi. "We filled up on the way."

"No, I insist," countered Douglas. When both guests continued to refuse politely, he tried suggestions of "just coffee" and even "water," but

Nardi merely revealed the top of the water bottle in his bag, and the portly Renee begged off from the standpoint of not being allowed to break her ritual fast.

"We just want to see your wife, Sir," said Renee, "so we can try to help."

Conceding that such was probably for the best, Douglas left the room, insisting he would be back with her as quickly as possible. As he did, Nardi checked the remote in his pocket, making certain it was ready to switch on when necessary. The team had spent the evening devising a plan for driving a spirit away from a host, if indeed such were the case. Although the available evidence strongly suggested such, still the members of the ADA came from a firm, rational world background. Even after everything they had witnessed over their years in Arkham, they still felt it best to be certain--especially considering the fact that despite what most knew, or at least suspect about their town, they still needed to live in a world governed by law.

A moment later, when the Douglases entered the kitchen, those seated at the kitchen table were as certain as they needed to be.

"Here she is, folks, the old ball and chain."

Both Nardi and Renee made the mistake of looking where they had been directed. Julie Douglas was indeed present, but not to the degree she had been the night before. As the visitors, they found her greatly diminished--hair bedraggled, lifeless. Skin sallow, sagging. Eyes, without luster—wandering, pain filled.

"Wha--"

The single syllable was all the security man could manage. The woman shuffled wordlessly into the room, mouth hanging open, the slightest dribble hanging from her lower lip.

"Oh, you were expecting ..."

Edward Douglas' words collapsed into laughter. The tone and strength of his voice came at the pair at the table far stronger than previously. Both wanted to turn, to try and understand from where had come the sudden change in the man's demeanor, but they found they could not. Their minds had been ensnared by the sight of the broken, desiccated figure advancing toward them.

"Sorry, so sorry. Where are my manners?"

As he spoke, what remained of Douglas circled the room, ending on the other side of the kitchen table from Nardi and Renee. His formerly retreating, cowering manner now began to reveal itself as the physical deficiency it truly was. All became clear for Nardi in that moment. In his own way, Galtoni had been correct. At the time of his execution, Jedidiah Mortonson had prepared an escape route for himself. The black magic the old warlock had practiced had given him the means. Instead of reincarnating as yet another son, however, he had chosen a more subtle hiding place--the walls of his own home.

More than likely, the security man figured, he'd already been sucking the life from the children he'd had as prisoners. When the house was transformed into their orphanage, he maintained that contact through the furniture, the very walls--then continued on down through the years, latching onto each new orphan delivered to his door step.

"Ahhhhhh," hissed the Douglas-thing, "I see it in your eyes, Franklin. You understand. Like yourself, yes... I retired. It was so, what would be a good word... comfortable. So easy to simply drift along, helping myself to a psychic meal here and there, living so many different lives... boys, girls, matrons, guards, making them do such wonderful things..."

Nardi ground his teeth together. He had not expected to be taken so completely by surprise. Suddenly his plan had fallen into jeopardy from a completely unforeseen angle. He had been waiting to confront the wife--had never considered the force living within the house would have had them both under control. He had been so certain of his strategy he had not even turned on his electronics--cleverly making certain there was nothing about his person that might give him away. As he strained to move his hand, the Douglas-thing chortled:

"I'm sorry to disappoint, Franklin. You were determined to be so heroic, to save the girl, to free her for her helpless husband. It's why I came to you first. Since the orphanage was closed, your filthy modern age and its political correctness, I withered, trapped in here, Franklin. Starved--starved! Do you hear me?"

Forget him, Nardi screamed within his own head. Concentrate. Fight, you useless sack of shit! Fight!

"It took decades for this place to sell. I was reduced--spent. Desiccated. Then, the ages of neglect meant repairs had to be made. I had to wait for someone to move in for so long. By then even the spell I had invoked to keep me tethered here was starting to fade away. Without nourishment, I could not sustain its power. I was so tempted to take you when you opened yourself to me, but no, I waited. And do you know why, Franklin?"

The assembly was distracted as Julie Douglas slid down the wall, collapsing to the floor. Mortonson had pulled too much from her, leaving her unable to move under her own power. The distraction allowed Nardi a full four seconds outside of the monstrosity's control. The first one and a half were wasted as he struggled simply to reconnect with his own nervous system. The next two were lost fumbling to shove his hand into his jacket pocket. As the creature across from him finished chuckling over the woman's fate, in the final half-second his fingers closed on his control device--

"I'll tell you why I waited, Franklin--"

And suddenly the security man found his control slipping, fading like the colors of the evening sky as the Sun drifted behind the horizon, surrendering all unto night.

"Because I wasn't about to settle for an old fool's body." Screw you, Nardi screamed within his mind. I might be a fool--

"Death would have been better."

But I'm not old--

Rage fueling him--anger aimed squarely at Mortonson, fury at himself--Nardi forced his fingers together, sliding the contact button on the bar control in his pocket, hissing into his lapel mic at the same instance--

"Now!"

Outside in their company van, Galtoni and Berkenwald reacted immediately, the first jumping out of the vehicle and heading for the house, the latter flipping the switch that started their speaker system broadcasting. It had been Renee that had suggested loud noise as a way of cutting through the control of whatever power was inside the house. The crew had decided on a double series--one of random heavy metal clips, none more than ten seconds each, the second a blending of high decibel electronic screeches. As every dog within a half-mile began to bark or whimper insanely, the Douglas-thing staggered, clawing at its ears.

As the horror cried out in agony, Nardi snapped into action.

Without hesitation the security man placed his hands under the edge of the kitchen table and flipped it upward, pushing it in Mortonson's direction. As it struck, Renee regained her senses, hurriedly digging into her bag. She managed to pull forth a small plastic container of powder she had prepared the night before. As she pried open its lid, the monstrosity managed to fling the table aside. Crawling back to its feet, it moved on the witch, just as Berkenwald reached the kitchen. As Renee screamed--

"Do it!"

The detective clicked on the over-sized strobe light assembly he had dragged in from the van. The horror threw its arms upward, shielding its eyes--screeching as the witch flung her container of powder over the forms of both Edward and Julie Douglas, chanting as she did so:

"Gel bin, de'sey... brougher kumbi... brougher kumbi... Gel bin, de'sey... brougher kumbi... brougher kumbi ..."

Mortonson screamed--the sound pouring from him a thing of unimaginable agony. Shielded from both the creature's terrible noise as well as the sounds from the van by the earplugs all of the team were wearing, Nardi moved forward to where Mrs. Douglas lay sprawled on the floor, scooping her up and heading for the door. Renee followed him slowly, backing toward the exit, continuing to curse Mortonson with her chant. As she watched the creature writhe, she spotted the moment when her powder along with her spell forced the spirit form from Douglas' body.

"Grab him," she cried out to Berkenwald who, already struggling with the heavy lights, shouted back;

"Are you kidding me?"

And then, before either could react further, the house began to groan. Mortonson's monstrous soul had retreated to the only sanctuary left to it, the home it knew so well. Desperate for sustenance, it immediately began to draw strength from its foundation of massive stones, its timbers--new and old--the plaster, the glass and pipes, tiles, latches, hinges--everything. And thus was its undoing.

As the witch and Berkenwald managed to struggle both the lights and Douglas outside, the ancient structure began to groan horribly. They were barely a yard away from the door when the sharp cracking of multiple rupturing beams began to be heard. The end came with an unbelievable abruptness. Having stolen so much of the vulgar dwellings solidity over the preceding few decades, that which remained, even adding in the repairs made by the Douglases, proved to be nowhere near adequate to revive the retreating warlock.

As the team watched in near shock, the ground itself gave way, building and foundation and the very earth falling downward into a pit which swallowed not only the cursed structure but nearly all of its acreage, plants and trees, walkways--everything. The fire that erupted, engulfing everything combustible, was eventually blamed on the ruptured gas line. Neither the Douglases nor anyone from the Agency saw any reason to argue the decision.

Over the following few weeks, both Edward and Julie made, if not full recoveries, steps far enough back to normalcy that they were content not to bring suit against the Arkham Detective Agency. In the end, they decided that even in a town as dark as the one in which they lived, the law was neither backward reaching or far-sighted enough to award damages in such a case. The settlement from their insurance, the gas company, and the original surveyors who had certified the land as stable was adequate for them to relocate.

"Besides," the somewhat restored Edward decided, "it was a nest of pain. Better it rot in whatever Hell it landed."

The Douglases did not rebuild on their lot. That was donated to the municipality of Arkham, to do with as it pleased. The town elders were given sufficient warning as to what might still lurk below the surface.

It is believed that adequate precautions were taken before any excavations were attempted.

Black
Tallow

Edward M. Erdelac

BLACK TALLOW
By Edward M. Erdelac

I hadn't physically seen my old university roommate, Paul Woodson, in more than a decade, not since a few years after graduation when our lives really started to radically diverge. His began a rocketing climb that culminated in his establishment as the grand high financial wizard of a Fortune 500 multinational. Mine nosedived in a steady, occasionally desperate and perennial flounder that has left me what I always was, a translator of antique books, respected in circles much smaller than his, but nowhere near as successful, financially.

We kept in touch, of course, over the years, mainly via e-mails and the occasional phone call, perhaps mostly because of my extensive contacts in the rare book field, a subject which has never ceased its fascination for Paul.

That's because he believes everything he has achieved has been thanks to the practice of magic. That was how we met, as furtive, over-serious young initiates, dabbling in Tarot cards and the intricacies of the Goetia, pretentiously spelling magic with a 'k.' We pored over the writings of John Dee, Simon Magus, and Eibon, and the three A's of our higher education were Abramelin, Al-Hazred, and Alistair Crowley.

Yet when I, in my senior year, finally pronounced the whole business utter bullshit, and argued with Paul that no man can hope to harness and steer the chaotic winds of the universe by engaging in embarrassing tantric orgies and messy black chicken assassinations, Paul merely refrained from countering me, and continued on his path.

Time may judge which of us was correct.

That's not to say I believe in magic now, but I believe in the human mind, and that personal magnetism may be trained like a muscle when the will is there, and made to domineer over lesser personalities. Paul had that will, and now he commands that magnetism and worldly power.

He is a multimillionaire, perhaps even a billionaire, is married to an achingly gorgeous former Parisian cat walker, with which he has fathered a bright young daughter. He has a bona fide fleet of vehicles (notice I didn't say merely cars), and a senior officer's position in a financial empire which literally spans the globe.

For him, dedication to magic, training his personality and intelligence via methods both arcane and scientific, has inarguably borne fruit. Maybe his study of bold ideas and meditation on complex alchemical formulas somehow helped him divine the erratic movements of the chaotic economic markets. Whatever his pursuits, he resides in that position all men crave. He needs nothing.

That was why, when he called me one day at the rare book dealer where I am on precarious retainer in Chicago, I was surprised to hear the old hunger still unabated in his tone.

I guess hungry men strive harder than the rest of us, but it was never worldly success Paul had craved in those years of scrying and scratching pentacles on the floor of our dormitory to call down the powers and thrones. For him, the pursuit of magic had always been that old alchemical dream of self-actualization. His own soul was the lead he wished to turn to gold, and that divine transmutation, he always said, only came with the attainment of ultimate knowledge.

But how could knowledge ever be ultimate? I'd always argued. It was folly on the level of Faust. No man could know all there was.

"The universe, its true nature," he had told me once, a hungry, fiery look in his captivating eyes. "That's the final answer worth attaining. To know that, its origin, its purpose, answers all other lesser questions by default. Life, death, love, transcendence, they're all marginal concerns compared to that."

He had been like an addict then, transitioning swiftly from gateway magical systems to harder, more involved disciplines, casting aside traditions with exasperation when he rapidly mastered and consumed their most secret teachings and, in the end, found them lacking.

That anxious quiver was still in his voice. I could hear it even over the phone.

"Raymond," he said without preamble, when I picked up the line. "I want you to drive up to see me this weekend. I have a book I'd like you to take a look at."

Paul's name was not unknown at the shop. He was one of our most loyal patrons. But although the owner chatted with him from time to time when he called to request some obscure tome, he never came in himself, and an invitation was unheard of.

"Paul. This weekend? I don't even know where you live."

"I'm in Hinsdale. I'll give you the address. Do you have a pen? Or should I send a car?"

"No, no I can drive myself. What book is this?"

"I'd rather not say over the telephone. I'm sorry, Paul. I didn't even ask. Have you any plans?"

I can't really afford plans. When my rent and bills are paid, I have very little left over to entertain myself with, and usually spend my weekends at the shop cataloging and reading. The shop was only open by appointment on Saturdays, and there was nothing scheduled for this, the weekend after the New Year.

"I don't have any plans. But listen, wouldn't you rather have Mr. Zell or Travis look this book over? I'm not really the guy around here when it comes to assessing really rare books. I'm just a translator."

"No, Paul. It has to be you. When can I expect you?"

"Well, we close up in two hours. I'd like to stop to eat. I can be there at…."

"Don't. I'll have dinner waiting. Can you spend the night?"

"Spend the night? What are we, kids?" I laughed.

"You'll want time to look this over. I guarantee it."

"Paul, won't Cherie and your little girl…."

"They're out of town, Raymond. Visiting her mother in Bayonne. Will you?"

This was strange, but I thought about my shabby, drafty apartment on Lake with its ticking old radiator and shrugged. I didn't mind spending the weekend in an old friend's opulent digs, even if it would have me chewing my own heart out in envy on Monday.

"Alright, Paul. It's a date, I guess."

He rattled off the address so fast I had to ask him to repeat it.

The house was what I'd expected a one percent-er to reside in. Singular, secluded, multi-leveled, post-modern architecture, aesthetically spare but pleasing, lots of glass and hardwood flooring, set at the end of a tree-lined, private drive and festooned with all the ridiculous amenities extreme wealth afforded: a garage bigger than my childhood home, a pool that might have been for reflecting or swimming, a lush, sprawling garden no one living there could possibly have the time or inclination to tend, a tennis court, etc.

I was already chewing my bottom lip and keenly feeling all the wasted potential of my life when my hilariously out of place Civic was admitted through the electric gate. If prancing about under the moon wearing nothing but goats' blood had earned Paul Woodson all this and more, what an idiot I was to have disparaged it.

I'd barely cut my engine when the front door opened and Paul stood there, as if he had been anxiously waiting in the foyer the entire time, watching the approach to the house through his security cameras. Somewhere inside, a stereo was blaring a scratchy, noisy blues recording, the words strange, the background alive with the raucous, howling voices of a live audience. Something I'd never heard before, which interested me, as I'm something of a blues aficionado.

"Come in, Raymond!" he urged, as I went to my trunk to get my overnight bag. He disappeared for a moment while I rummaged, and the music cut out abruptly. The sudden silence was startling, as if the rowdy crowd had been cavorting in the house and instantly disappeared. He returned.

"It's good to see you, Paul," I stammered on his porch.

"Yes, good to see you too, Raymond. How've you been?" He asked, though it was all an annoying formality.

He desperately wanted me to get in the house, to see his wonder. His personal appearance didn't really live up to the place. His prematurely grey hair was a bit disheveled, and he didn't look like his press photos. His penetrating eyes had that wild, voracious look. Far from the expensive suits I always saw him in in the business section, he looked as if he'd slept in his sweater and slacks. Maybe he'd let himself go a little with Cherie away. A woman like that, I don't know if I could ever relax around her, entirely, either.

"Not doing as well as you, of course," I said, admiring the house's uncountable treasures. I felt like an intruder, no matter the invitation. I was not meant to see these things. Monday night in my sagging bed would be a hell. "What's that you were listening to?"

"Sorry. It helps me think. I forget how loud it is."

"It's alright, while the cat's away, eh?"

"Cat?" he said, looking confused.

"Cherie. I guess since she and your little girl are gone for the weekend…"

He blinked.

"Yes, of course. No, they hate my music."

"Was that Robert Johnson?" I asked dubiously, knowing well it wasn't.

"No. King Yeller. Just a flash in the pan from around 1964."

"I never heard of him."

"You woudn't have. That's the only recording," he said distractedly. "Your dinner, I ordered out. I hope you like veal scallopini."

I chuckled.

"I never had takeout veal before."

I wandered into the dining room adjoining the immense kitchen. It smelled wonderful.

"Oh they only do it for me, as far as I know," he said, opening the oven and pulling out the dish that had been warming inside.

It was delicious, but I felt hurried. Paul leaned on the marble island and simply watched me as I ate.

"Aren't you eating too?" I asked.

"I'm fasting," he said.

"Fasting? Some diet thing?"

"It hasn't been that long, has it Raymond?"

Of course. We had fasted together during my dabbling years. It was a part of magical preparation. I still didn't want to believe he was still doing that at his age.

"I'm sorry," he said quickly. "Please don't let me disturb you. Here, I'll get you some wine."

He uncorked a twenty five year old bottle of something called Romani-Contée and poured. I suspected I would choke on it if I knew what he'd paid for it.

We made no small talk. He busied himself with something in the kitchen while I hungrily devoured the best meal I would probably ever have.

I saw the object of my visit, though. It was on the edge of the marble counter, a modest sized book covered in a cloth of black velvet. I could see the gilt-edge poking out from under one corner.

When I had cleared my plate of tender veal and porcini, and drained my glass, he clapped his hands together.

"All finished?"

"All finished. Now what's so important?"

He moved to the book and removed the covering.

I leaned in close.

It was an ugly little thing, less than a hundred pages. It was bound in mottled, flaking, pale leather, and rather inexpertly, I thought. Some of the pages did not quite fit, as if they were mismatched, or taken from disparate sources. I squinted hard at the cover, which bore no markings. It was old, whatever it was.

"Anthropodermic bibliopegy," he mumbled, very close to my ear. He was standing near, hovering almost.

"Binding in human skin?" I wrinkled my nose. Claims of book jackets made from human skin usually turned out to be unfounded. Pig skin was often mistaken for human. I had once seen a copy of deSade's *Justine et Juliette* with a human nipple on the front board below the title, and another time, Carnegie's biography of Lincoln bound in a black man's hide. "Not very well done, is it?"

"It was stitched together by hand. By the same hand that did the fleshing and tanning."

"Whose hand is that?" I asked, reaching out to thumb the pages.

"No, don't open it!" he snapped. Then, more gently, "Let me."

There was no title, only page after page of densely inscribed text, all in various hands, languages, even hieroglyphs on what looked like brittle papyrus. There were strange diagrams inside. I knew it was some kind of grimoire, but it was impossible for me to guess where it originated from.

"What is this, Paul? Some kind of scrapbook?"

"Sort of. Have you ever heard of the *Infernalius*?"

"It sounds…familiar."

"Think back to the books we heard talked about in our college days,

Raymond. The books your own grandfather had from his great uncle."

That was great, great uncle Warren, the man family history had always told me I'd inherited my love of languages and old books from. He'd been a Classical Languages professor in Arkham, Massachusetts in the old days, and a chum of the somewhat notorious occult scholar Henry Armitage. Upon Warren's death in 1931, most of his books and papers had been donated to his university, though a few had been passed on to his brother.

It was the revelation that I was Warren Rice's great, great grandnephew that had started off Paul's fascination with me in school. He seemed to buy into the old story about how Warren and Armitage had had some strange mystical dealings in Dunwich in 1928 or so. The books my grandfather had let us peruse in his study one summer that had belonged to Warren were mainly scholarly treatises, such as Copeland's *Zanthu Tablets: A Conjectural Translation*, Casterwell's *Kranorian Annals*, and von Junzt's *Nameless Cults*.

Then I remembered.

"The Book of Books?"

Paul smiled.

"The Book of Books. Not some idle boast, but a literal description. A book hidden among the pages of seven other books." He held up his hands and ticked them off, finger by finger. "*The Book of Eibon, the Book of Karnak, the Testament of Carnamagos, the Ponape Scripture, de Vermiss Mysteriis,* and *the Scroll of Thoth-Amon*. Each one a rare treasure in their own right."

"Come on, Paul. It's a fantasy," I laughed. "The timeline's all wrong. How could something be hidden in an ancient Egyptian scroll *and* a book written in 1542?"

"You know of the Akashic Record. The ethereal library of all knowledge written and unwritten which men may tap into. And the history says that The Dark Man entity dictated *The Infernalius* to the Hyborean wizard Gargalesh Svidren, who dispersed the knowledge through time. Abdul Al-Hazred hid the assembly instructions in the original, unexpurgated Arabic *Kitab al-Azif*. They're only visible to those who already know it's there. A book which rewards the practitioner with ultimate knowledge of the universe."

"I thought it was supposed to end the world," I said, pursing my lips. "How much did you get fleeced for buying this, Paul?"

"It's the genuine article," said Paul. "Dr. Francis Morgan recovered it from Old Noah Whateley's personal library in Dunwich after the affair with your uncle and Professor Armitage. It's been in a private collection since 1966, along with Whateley's diary."

"Noah Whateley kept a diary?" I said, incredulous.

Whateley's reputation as a sorcerer was renowned, but like my own as a translator, only among certain circles. As students, we'd spent our junior year spring break in Arkham and Dunwich trying to learn all we could about him and run into a wall. I'd chalked it all up to being folklore. Paul had insisted the locals had protected us from the true knowledge.

"He did, and related his assembly of the book in 1882."

"Finding the right copies of those books, unaltered by translation...it would've been impossible for one man," I said.

"He was hired by a cult, the Order of The Black Dragon. You remember them."

I nodded. Von Junzt had mentioned them, some sort of apocalyptic cult with origins in ancient Israel and adherents all over the globe.

"Their members gathered the required books and brought them to Whateley. He assembled them, and once the Order had performed the ritual and taken what they wanted from the book, he was sent back to Dunwich with it. Apparently it was their intention to call something forth, something that should have ended the world."

"Well, so the book's a fraud," I said. "Obviously the world didn't end."

"The book's purpose isn't to end the world, but to grant the ritualist his heart's desire. The Order wanted the end of the world. The book gave them the means. The book *changes* to fit the magician's desire."

"A book that changes? That's crazy."

"Well, I don't believe the ritual changes, but the end result does. The desired effect is in the heart of the evoker. Noah Whateley was depressed after the failure of the Order of The Black Dragon," Paul went on. "He pored over the book for years, trying to figure out what went wrong. In the end, he learned that an outside party had interrupted the Order's enactment of the ritual. The fault wasn't his. His purpose was renewed. He decided to carry on where the Order had failed. He wanted to facilitate the return of the Outer God, Yog-Sothoth. He found the means in the book, using his own offspring. But he died before the long ritual could be completed. I don't think his grandson, Wilbur, could properly read the *Infernalius*. The ritual was imperfect again."

I thought of what was known of Wilbur Whateley's fate, how he had been killed trying to steal a rare copy of the notorious *Necronomicon* from the Miskatonic University library. A desperate act. Had he been trying to complete his grandfather's work?

"The man I acquired the book from was a kind of mercenary librarian," Paul said. "He made his fortune lending the book to aspiring magicians and recovering it after."

"After what?" I asked.

"After they failed. Most died. Malnutrition, heart attacks, one wound up in an asylum in upstate New York. That's where I learned about the librarian."

"So what do you intend to do with it?" I asked, looking down at the strange little book with new interest.

"What do you think? I'm going to answer the question whose answer has eluded me my entire life."

"But...even if this is true," I said. "Why? You have everything, Paul..."

"I have *nothing!*" he exploded, slapping his hand on the counter top. "*Nothing*, Raymond. Do you think I set out all those years ago to attain mere money and luxury? What kind of a fool would I be, to expose my very soul to the darkest undercurrents of the universe, open myself to the influence of malignant powers, simply to afford a ridiculous house to live in during my brief time on this earth? Do you think I'd do the things I've done, made the sacrifices I have, for *this?*" he finished the last waving his hands dismissively at his plush surroundings, as if they were my own cramped living room. "No, years of research and practice and abasement has granted me nothing but worldly pleasures. It's as if the true power behind the veil of the universe has amused itself by tossing me bones and scraps from its table in response to my meaningless barking. But now, with this book, I believe I finally have discovered an inroad to the truth. To true power. What I do now, I do in pursuit of the only thing that has constantly been out of reach my entire life."

"Alright," I said, though I wanted to shake him, remind of all the blessings he was neglecting with this insanity. "Alright, Paul. But again, if this is true, then nobody has successfully used this thing. What chance do you have?"

"I have a resource my unfortunate predecessors didn't. You."

"Me?"

"Who knows more about the alphabet of Mu and Tsath-Yo than you? You studied your uncle's work. I don't believe there was a more accomplished linguist alive than Dr. Warren Rice. You're his scion."

"Paul," I snickered nervously. "It's been years since I studied that stuff. I haven't read a word of Hyperborean in..."

"Let me tell you what I believe," Paul interrupted, touching my shoulder and fixing me with those drilling eyes. "The key to the Old Ones, to the forgotten powers, was left to us in these languages. These aren't just dead tongues. These are, in their own right, mystic formulas. God evoked Creation through the use of words of power. I think very few men can truly understand them, and those that do, once they do, cannot hope to forget them."

He turned to the book between us on the island, opened it to a certain page, and spun it to show me the archaic letters of one of the headings.

"Read."

I looked down at the page, doubtful. I would humbly say my mastery of the classical, Oriental, Germanic, and Semitic languages is considerable. But what I remembered of these supposedly antediluvian scripts, they had an internal consistency, but nothing in common with any other spoken word.

I'd studied them only a little. That one summer when Paul had told me fantastic stories about the beings that supposedly existed somewhere in the outer dark beyond empirical creation, the things whose power, he said, made the angels and demons of western magic look like Saturday morning cartoons. It was the summer I'd first read my uncle's books, and Paul had remarked admiringly that if there was an inheritable gene for language, I had it.

As I squinted at the ancient page, a haze descended over my eyes, and it was as if the twisted letters moved and the knotted meanings untied, revealing their truth.

"The Making of The Black Tallow," I read, surprised at how quickly the letters came back to me.

He snapped the book shut.

"You see?" he said. "I knew you could do it."

I admit I felt a wave of excitement come over me, and a little fear, too.

"Now what?"

"I'm no slouch when it comes to ancient alphabets," Paul said. "But translation and reading aloud are two different things. There's a key passage at the end of the ritual. An invocation. The pronunciation must be precise. There, I need your help."

"You want me to read it?" I asked, unsure.

"No of course not. As the evoker, I have to be the one to read it aloud. I want you to transcribe a phonetic pronunciation for me."

"A crib sheet?" I said, smiling.

"Essentially," he said, smiling back. "Raymond, I can't stress the importance of this step. I really believe the correct invocation may have been where my predecessors have all failed. I need you to do this for me, but I also need you to tell me truthfully if you're unable to."

"This is crazy…"

"Raymond, I'm rich enough to be crazy. I'm also prepared to pay you for your service. Handsomely."

I shook my head, "We're old friends, Paul."

"Please don't take it as an insult," Paul said holding up a hand. "It would be my pleasure. I'd pay Abraham's bounty for this. A seven figure remuneration for an old friend is almost a relief."

I coughed.

"*Seven* figures?"

"Seven for the seven books of the *Infernalius*. Magicians like synchronicity. Will seven million dollars secure your expertise?"

"*Seven million?*" I shook my head. "You're joking."

"Look at this place, Raymond," he insisted. "It cost me more to build this house, and I have four more around the world. I'm not boasting, just trying to put it into perspective for you."

"It's above and beyond my usual fees," I said.

"This is my life's work, Raymond. I only wish I could grant you some greater portion of the joy I'll feel once it's done."

Seven million dollars buys a lot of joy, I thought.

I had come in sight of this place with a stab in my heart thinking of what I would have to return to. Now, Paul was saying, to simply render some ancient text into a phonetic key, I wouldn't have to. It would be real work, and he was right, I was probably the most qualified expert he knew. I shouldn't feel guilty about the money.

I didn't. I wouldn't.

"Alright, Paul," I said.

"Let me show you to my Oratory," he said.

Paul led me through the house to a basement stair, and down into a surprisingly large sub-level, somewhat labyrinthine in design. There were passages that led off into rooms where I saw workspaces with assorted tools, some for carpentry, others for electrical work, and a pottery room with a wheel and kiln. We passed a strangely sweet smelling room where I saw a large vat of bubbling liquid.

"What's that?" I asked, craning my neck as we walked past.

"One of my wife's hobbies. She runs a candle making business out of our home," he said.

I looked at him askance.

"Idle housewife. She's picked up a lot of hobbies since she quit modelling," Paul said. "Anyway, that's for making tallow," he said, reaching in the doorway and slapping off the light switch. "She's always leaving it going."

He led me to a locked door and produced a ring of keys from his pocket and opened it. Beyond was a narrow concrete stairway, incongruously leading up.

We climbed the stair to the top of the house, and so came up through the floor of Paul's ritual lodge, a custom built single room Oratory on the roof of the house with shuttered windows covered in thick red drapery in every direction, and a terrace surrounding, like the top of a lighthouse. The structure was cleverly hidden from street level.

Paul lit a series of seven brass oil lanterns suspended from the ceiling by chains, illuminating the room, which was paneled with white pine wood. In the center of the chamber was a large uncut stone altar with a ritual silver censer atop it, and in a hollow space beneath, various linens and silks, phials of oil, a scarlet miter and wand of Almond-tree wood. A marble lectern, engraved to resemble a baroque pillar rising from the back of a reclining dragon, stood before the altar. The room smelled of myrrh and olive oil.

The floor around the altar was already inscribed with white chalk. A large circular device had been drawn there, a summoning or protection circle. I didn't know which, because it had been so long since I'd concerned myself with such things. It certainly wasn't any Solomonic ward I'd ever seen. There was a kind of many-pointed star design in the center, constructed of what appeared to be seven heptagrams overlaid. The fantastic geometric pattern managed to suggest both dizzying chaos and meticulous precision. On the outer edge of the circle, corresponding to each of the star-points, there sat a black candle, forty nine in all.

The candles were also of peculiar design. They were shining black in color, and molded in such a way that they tapered upwards. Each was flanged into six wicked outreaching points, like a spearhead, or the topper on some gothic iron fence.

I approached the circle and crouched down to peer at one of the candles. The wicks were of some braided, silken substance. Not cotton.

"Did Cherie make these for you?"

"I used her resources," Paul smiled thinly. "But I built the molds. The book called for specific design and placement."

"Are they wax or....?"

"Tallow. Calf suet," he said.

"From the veal takeout place?" I asked, grinning.

Paul smiled.

"I intend to start the ritual tonight, Raymond. Do you think you can provide me the pronunciation in time?"

"That soon? I don't even have any of my reference books."

"I'm paying for expediency. My own library has copies of every book your uncle had."

"Show me to the library," I shrugged.

The downstairs library was as well outfitted and aesthetically pleasing as the Oratory. The reading table was already piled with the books I needed.

He set *The Infernalius* down and opened it. He unfolded a sort of brass plate and laid it across the open book. The plate had an adjustable window which Paul centered on a certain paragraph. Effectively, the rest of the two pages were hidden.

"Confine your work to this passage," Paul said. "I'll be in the Oratory, preparing. When it's finished, ring this," he said, placing a small bell on the table. "I'll hear you."

I slid into the chair at the desk and glanced at the stack of reference books.

"Raymond," said Paul, laying a hand on my shoulder. "Thank you." Then he left me to it.

I call it work, but really, I was surprised how easily and quickly the transcription went. It was a short, though expressive passage, which required only a few glances at Casterwell and Copeland to suss out. I was surprised Paul couldn't do it himself. But of course, he was burdened with his own neurosis. He believed this would actually attain for him the driving need of his life. I merely thought it would make me rich.

Oh, I checked and double-checked it, to be sure. Both for Paul's sake, and for my own. Really this work would forever alter my life, if Paul actually paid me what he'd promised. But then, I thought, what if, once the whole affair is over and nothing happens, and he pushes over his marble lectern and breaks his wand over his knee, he decides not to pay me? Maybe, I thought, I should ask for the money in advance.

Was I being unscrupulous taking advantage of an old friend's eccentricity? Maybe. But I was tired of the book shop, tired of reading of places I would never visit. A million dollars would buy a year of exotic travel, a year or two of absolute freedom. But with seven, I knew I could live the rest of my life free of care.

I glanced down at my own reflection in the brass plate. It had only taken me an hour to transcribe the passage into a phonetic key. It was just a lot of pseudo-mystic babble, heaping praise and swearing loyalty to something called Yog-Sothoh and Azathoth, and offering sustenance to a thing called Krefth Daal Zuur, That Which Strains Against Its Chains.

Bullshit.

I grinned at the plate, picked veal from my teeth with my fingernail. I hesitated to ring the bell and tell Paul I was finished. Seven million dollars for an hour's work didn't seem kosher. Maybe I should wait a bit, make Paul think I was really breaking a sweat over the thing? Maybe he wouldn't trust the key if it was completed too quickly?

I flipped through the reference books a bit, but soon grew bored. I'd read these, after all. I touched the edge of *The Infernalius*, and noticed something poking out from beneath the brass. It looked like a bit of illumination.

I shifted the brass plate to the side and saw, with a flush of excitement, that there was a painting visible on the edges of the partially fanned book pages.

I turned the book on the desk and moved the pages to arrange the painting, which was not visible when the book was closed. I'd seen disappearing fore-edge fan paintings before in the shop, on sacred works. They often depicted pastorals, or religious figures.

I considered the mad genius of the book. According to him, it was comprised of pages from seven separate books (each from different locations and time periods), pages which only made sense when compiled with their scattered brethren. What kind of mind came up with such a thing? And what kind of mind could conceive of a piece of fore-edge art on those disparate pages which again, only appeared when the book was compiled and fanned out in such a way?

No, it was impossible.

The painting was strange in the extreme. It was actually a panorama that extended across three edges. It depicted a multitude of naked human figures surrounding a jutting black stone and cowering beneath a starry night sky that would put Van Gogh to shame in terms of its roiling expressionism. The entire painting, or rather the sky, was bordered with rows of jagged teeth, as if the sky itself were a gaping mouth. Further, the stars within the mouth were actually more like iridescent globes of sickly light. At the base of the altar, a man in the red and black robes of a magician stood within a circle of lit candles. Looking closer, I saw that strewn and broken over the altar, were the bodies of two female figures, a mother and child.

An inexplicable dread came over me, and I glanced up at that instant to see a family photograph hanging on the wall. Paul, looking grim as usual with only the hint of a smile, his hands on the shoulders of his lovely wife Cherie, statuesque, blonde, shining blue eyes. His twelve year old daughter, already reflecting the beauty of her mother.

I stood up, the chair groaning back. I don't know why, but things started to fire in my brain. Connections. That weird fore-edge painting. Paul's offhand joke about his willingness to pay 'Abraham's bounty.' The heading, The Making of The Black Tallow. I couldn't bring myself to find that heading again.

I stared at the bell for a moment, then left the library.

I crept through the immense house, fearful I would turn a corner and bump into Paul at any moment. I managed to find what I was sure, by its pink trappings and popular band posters, must have been Paul's daughter's room upstairs. The bed was unmade. It could be the slovenly habits of an adolescent, of course. I went to her walk-in closet. Rows of clothing. Nothing to be gleaned here. Except above one shelf there were two pink designer suitcases. The girl was wealthy. She might conceivably have more than two suitcases. She might have a different color suitcase for every day of the week.

I vacated the room and headed down to the basement, my pulse accelerated. What would I say to Paul if he caught me snooping around? Didn't seven million dollars buy a modicum of discretion? Apparently not.

I walked through the basement corridors, past the various rooms, till my nose detected that sweet smell again and I fumbled for the light switch in the dark candle making room.

The big vat of buttery yellowish tallow was cooling now, like old soup. On the workbench table I found strands of long blonde hair. Scissors. I opened the cabinet over the table. Nothing but spools of cotton, premade wicks, pillar molds, oils, and ceramic holders. I sat down heavily on the stool, and noticed the metal wastebasket next to the bench.

It was full of women's clothes. I arranged them on the table. A woman's and a girl's.

Heart sinking, all the saliva in my mouth evaporating, I went to the vat, found the wooden stirrer sitting outside on the concrete floor, splashed with old tallow and colored wax.

I broke the hardening skin and dipped it inside, stirred the thick mixture, ground against something on the bottom.

After a few tries, I dragged it to the surface.

A gory human skull broke through the yellow patina, the blue eyes still staring out of the mournful sockets.

I let the stirrer tumble to the floor and backed out of the room, deaf from the blood coursing in my ears.

I ran back upstairs. I had a thought that made me gag. When I'd asked Paul if he'd gotten the beef suet for the candles from the same place he'd gotten the veal…he had smiled without answering. It was just a thought, but I vomited on the floor.

I returned to the library. *The Infernalius* was gone, along with my pronunciation key. God, I should call the police. Paul had gone over the deep end at last, in his crazy pursuit of….of what? How could he do this? Throw all this away? That lovely woman, their child.

I don't know why, but I returned to the basement stair, suddenly more angry than afraid. I wasn't afraid of Paul, surely. I don't know what I intended to do.

I made my way down to the locked door, found it ajar.

My legs felt like they were strapped with sandbags as I slowly mounted the stair to the Oratory, where I could hear Paul chanting. A red glow permeated the stairway the higher I got.

I crept up to the top and peered over the edge.

Paul stood in the circle, decked in his silk robes and tall miter. *The Infernalius* lay open on the lectern. The curtains and shutters were open, the dark sky all around. There were no stars, no moon, only black clouds that blotted out the stars, like in the fore-edge painting.

He was turning slowly in the circle, chanting the old dead words I'd transcribed, over and over again, touching the braided human hair wicks of the black tallow candles made from the fat of his own wife and child with the lit end of a ceremonial candlelighter.

"Paul…," I managed.

He paid no mind to me. Didn't hear me, maybe. My voice was no better than a croak. The last candle was lit.

He lay the snuffer on the altar and raised up his arms, as I'd seen them in the painting. He roared the invocation I'd transcribed one last time. I couldn't have pronounced it better myself.

I stood and leaned in the doorway, sick at the mad spectacle.

Paul Woodson turned and faced me in the last, but he was looking downward. The horrid, flanged candles flared, and he was lit from below in the resulting blaze. I saw his expression fall slack in utter surprise.

Then he fell through the floor.

Or rather, into it, up to his waist.

From where I stood, I saw the floor on which he stood within the strange chalk diagram shimmer and fade to darkness.

It was as if a hole opened beneath his feet. A pit.

But it was no pit.

It was more like a throat. The walls pulsed with unnatural life, and were lined with whirling, counter rotating rows of teeth, like some kind of combine. The teeth were flanged, exactly like the black candles surrounding its outer maw. A black, inky breath seemed to exude from it, and the oils and incense of the room was overpowered by a stench of rot that made me gag.

He screamed as he fell, and the circle folded and closed on him exactly like a mouth, the burning candles snapping together, biting him in half through the middle with a sickly sound and a splash of copious blood.

The surrounding windows exploded inward, showering him with a hail of broken glass. A hurricane wind roared through the Oratory, extinguishing the candles, but not before the silk robes caught flame.

I saw his detached upper half ablaze, tumble flopping from the circle. Dying, he managed to lift himself from the floor by his hands, and I saw his expression, framed in fire. It was one of absolute, sublime ecstasy. He began to giggle, or perhaps scream. Both. I couldn't be sure. Then his flesh curled and he collapsed. The billowing drapes caught fire.

I turned and ran from the room.

I half fell down the stairs, careened from the basement, in total animal flight, staggered upstairs, and burst out the front door.

I saw the smoke rising from the center of the roof as the Civic turned over and I wrenched the wheel about and tore down the driveway, smashing through the gate and out into the Hinsdale streets.

Paul Woodson was dead. Devoured by…what? I didn't want to think about it. My brief stab at fortune was gone. The book was real.

The book.

Did that mean what Paul had said about it was true, too, that it would give a man his heart's desire? At the very least, it was physically worth a bundle to the right people. Mr. Zell at the bookshop could've set me up with a buyer, no doubt. Hell, I could've done it myself. Paul had said the previous owner had made a mint just lending it out.

Well it was gone now, consumed in the fire.

And yet....I found myself wondering.

The painting on the fore-edge. Paul hadn't seen it. Maybe it had been a warning, not to evoke the powers he'd called attention to. Or maybe, it had been a final, obscured step in the procedure. In the painting the sacrifices had been lain on the altar, not left to melt in a tallow vat.

Maybe Maybe Paul, for all his care and precision, had overlooked an important detail of the ritual.

Well, there was no way to test my theory at any rate.

The blare of a car horn broke me out of my racing thoughts, and I squealed to a stop near the entrance ramp. I lay my head against the steering wheel, I don't know how long, until a second bleat of a horn from an impatient driver behind me, roused me again.

I accelerated up the ramp, fancying I could hear the clanging of fire engines in the distance. I angled the car for Chicago and my miserable, empty apartment, thinking of the picture on the library wall, of Cherie Woodson and that grand house.

The streetlights pulsed down the length of my car like intermittent lightning, or the strobe of a grocery store scanner ascertaining my value.

Something caught my eye in the middle of the backseat.

Something pale, squarish, and mottled.

Paul, for all his care and precision, had overlooked an important detail of the ritual.

Well, there was no way to test my theory at any rate.

The blare of a car horn broke me out of my racing thoughts, and I squealed to a stop near the entrance ramp. I lay my head against the steering wheel, I don't know how long, until a second bleat of a horn from an impatient driver behind me, roused me again.

I accelerated up the ramp, fancying I could hear the clanging of fire engines in the distance. I angled the car for Chicago and my miserable, empty apartment, thinking of the picture on the library wall, of Cherie Woodson and that grand house.

The streetlights pulsed down the length of my car like intermittent lightning, or the strobe of a grocery store scanner ascertaining my value.

Something caught my eye in the middle of the backseat.

Something pale, squarish, and mottled.

The Mindhouse

Christine Morgan

THE MINDHOUSE
By Christine Morgan

What do they tell you about me, I wonder?

The truth, now that you're old enough to hear it? The truth, because families are about honesty, about trust?

Or do they tell you the same lies they told the rest of the world? The lies they wish they themselves could believe, the lies they wish were true?

Maybe it was with what they considered the best of intentions. To protect you. To spare your feelings. Why should *you* have to grow up with so much hanging over your head? Besides, it was easier for them. Preferable. Less painful. Safer.

At least I can be sure they've had to tell you *something*. You may not have been old enough to remember when I went away, but they can't deny I ever existed. No, you must know you have a sister.

Or ... had one, at least.

They could claim I'd died, I suppose. Who would have doubted it? And if so, how far did they go with the ruse? Was there a funeral? A faked death certificate? Would I see my own name on a headstone, or engraved on some urn, if I ever went home?

Not that I can leave Evergate.

Well, I *could*. Maybe. I've made great progress.

I *am* all right.

Now. I'm all right *now*.

That's the catch.

Well, that and the rest of it. What we do in the mindhouse helps *us*, but what about the long run, the big picture, the grand scale? The fate of humanity? The fate of the world?

It'll happen anyway, though. Why fight it? It'll be far in the future, long after we'll still be around. We can't change things. We can't stop it. We have to look out for ourselves and our own best interests. Is that so wrong?

My friend Nathan agrees with me. Of course, he also knows what would be waiting for him outside of Evergate. It's one thing to admit the guilt and feel the remorse. Having to be held accountable, to take responsibility ... it's daunting. It's daunting for people who've done lesser wrongs than his.

We can't help wanting to take the easier way, the less painful or less shameful way. It's just instinct, preservation, simple human nature.

Like our parents did all those years.

I was never sick.

Not that way. Not in the way they wanted everyone to think.

There was no cancer. Chemotherapy and radiation treatments didn't make me the way I was. That's just how they explained it away. It looked better, you see. It made *them* look better. How *brave* they had to be. How brave and noble and strong. To be pitied, and admired, for bearing up so heroically.

And did they make the most of it! Basking in the sympathy, milking the attention for all it was worth, if not quite to a Munchausen's-by-proxy level. They didn't try to *exacerbate* my condition. They didn't want to *keep* me like that. When it finally really got to be too much, they relented and sent me to Doctor Hasturn.

What I did to them was beyond unforgivable.

Worse than if I *had* gottten cancer.

Worse than drug habits, sex scandals, pregnancy or a criminal record. Any of those could be written off as a phase, the wild waywardness of youth.

Or joining a cult ... which would have been ironic enough, the way things turned out ...

These days, some things once deemed shameful carry a certain cachet; our parents would have earned bonus points among their social circle if I'd been a lesbian, and they could be just *so* very tolerant, so open-minded and progressive and trendy about it.

But, no. No such luck. Nothing that dramatic, exciting or politically correct. I couldn't even be something controversial like a vegan, a liberal, an atheist.

All right, at least I wasn't *fat*, but still!

Insanity is never going to be a cool stigma.

I don't mean eccentricity, oh, no. That's for the quirky, temperamental artistes. I don't mean ordinary mood swings or picky people calling themselves OCD. I certainly don't mean edgy but endearing sociopaths as depicted on television.

I mean mental illness. I mean schizophrenia. In the *real* sense of the word, not the usual stupid Sybil-joke misconception. Paranoia. Delusions. Hearing voices. Hallucinations, by no means limited to the visual.

Did they tell you your sister went crazy?

Somehow, I doubt it.

Oh, denial, that river in Egypt. Our father was the pharaoh, and our mother had her own personal Cleopatra barge.

They didn't want to admit it, acknowledge it. Of course not. It'd reflect badly on them. Cancer was one thing, but madness? Imagine the talk, the whispers, the gossip. Imagine the disastrous effect on the family's reputation! Business! Political ambitions! The country club!

And so on.

Yes, I was insane.

Either way, sick or insane, I suppose you're surprised to hear from me. At all, let alone after all these years of silence. I'm surprised, too. I expected it'd be discouraged from both sides. Our parents wouldn't have been in favor of it, and Doctor Hasturn says that contact with anyone from our former lives tends to be less than therapeutic.

An exception was made for us, though.

I'm better now. It won't seem that way once I explain, but you never saw me the way I was before. How bad things got, there toward the end. In the hospital. The psych ward. The locked unit. The restraints.

It was terrible. The suffering, the torment. I don't mean the way I was treated, or the drugs they pumped into me … the way they never let me have a moment's privacy, a moment's freedom. I don't even mean the food.

The worst of the torment was in my own head.

You have no idea.

Or … do you? Sometimes there are hereditary components. Sometimes these things run in families. And you are now about the age I was when I had my first major psychotic break.

But, no, if you did, you wouldn't be so accomplished already, so successful. There'd be signs. Early indicators I'm sure they would have been watching for. Watching closely.

Then again…

Well, someday you might have children of your own. You should know the risks, what kind of legacy you might be handing down to them. You've seen what it can do to a family. Whether you understood or not, you grew up surrounded by it.

I'm sure you'd handle it better than our parents did. I'm sure you wouldn't let any child of yours go through that. You'd do whatever you could to help, wouldn't you? To spare them the torment I suffered?

If not for Doctor Hasturn, if not for Evergate, I'd still be there, in the hospital. Doped to the gills, on meds for the symptoms, and on meds for the side effects caused by the meds for the symptoms.

Or I'd be out on the streets somewhere, me and the other homeless crazies, camping under overpasses, panhandling, scrounging through the trash, doing what's called 'self-medicating' on cigarettes and cheap booze.

Or I'd be dead.

Instead, I'm much better now. I'm cured. Thanks to Doctor Hasturn. Thanks to the mindhouse.

My hair's grown back, by the way. You've probably seen the old pictures; they must keep them around to shore up the sympathetic image.

192

Awful ones where I look like a skeleton in pajamas, all pallid and bony, dry skin, scabby lips, burning-mad eyes sunk in bruise-purple sockets. Ready for the debutante ball, right?

We kept her at home as long as we could, they'd say... but she needed the kind of care not even a live-in nurse could provide... see how thin she is, she could hardly keep anything down, they had her on those nutrition shakes... and her hair, her poor hair, it got so wispy, falling out in patches, so they shaved it...

That wasn't how it happened.

Look closer at those pictures next time. If they're the ones I'm thinking of, my hands will be wrapped up. Bandaged, or in these padded glove-mitten things.

Trichotillomania. How's that for a word? I pulled it, you see. My hair. Pulled it, twisted it, and plucked it out by the roots, one by one, strand by strand. Eyebrows, too. And eyelashes. Even with my head shaved and the mittens.

Some people eat it, too, chew on their hair, swallow it, risking it clumping up in their intestines and causing a blockage. Not me. That isn't why I lost so much weight. I wouldn't have eaten it. I wanted to get *rid* of it. To yank it out of my scalp, out of my face, and get rid of it. Burn it, if I could. Flush it down the toilet, if I couldn't burn it.

It's grown back now anyway, as I was saying. My hair. It's past my shoulders. I know I used to pull it, I remember doing it, and I remember it made sense to me at the time. It seemed like the only thing I could do. The smart thing.

I thought – don't laugh; I know how crazy it sounds – that it wasn't *my* hair. That it wasn't *hair* at all. That it was something else. Cilia, maybe. That it was alive, that these alien spores had burrowed into my head and were extruding themselves in these fine wiry filaments, threads that looked like hair, that fooled everyone but me. The longer they got, or the more of them there were, the stronger they'd become. Until they took me over. Replaced me, or kept me trapped inside while they used my body to do things. So I had to pull them out.

Crazy, I know. But that's why I didn't chew my hair, the way so many other trichotillomaniacs do. Mine wasn't a compulsion. I didn't do it without thinking about it, as an unconscious habit. I did it deliberately, because I had to, in order to save myself from the cilia spore aliens. And the last thing I'd want to do was ingest those filaments, take them back inside myself, like tapeworms. Bad enough they sprouted from my scalp and face and eyelids, where I could see them, where I could reach them to pluck out. I couldn't stand the idea of having hairy tangled knots collecting in my guts.

Would you? Would anyone?

But try explaining that. Try explaining that the reason you won't eat is because that only feeds the cilia spores and maybe if you can't pluck them out you can starve them instead. Try explaining that you can't sleep because the moon sings and the sun groans and the stars scream terrible words into your mind, words that would kill people or drive them insane if you said them aloud... day or night, it doesn't matter, because the stars are always there.

It was terrible. Imagine not being able to trust your own senses, your own thoughts. Imagine watching someone waste away, tortured like that. Someone you care about. Wouldn't you want to help? Wouldn't you want to do anything in your power to make it better?

Luckily, like I said, I'm fine, now.

Since coming here. Since Doctor Hasturn.

Since the mindhouse.

I want you to understand that. I want *someone* to understand that.

Someone who isn't also here at Evergate. Obviously, *we* understand. It just doesn't necessarily mean much, given our situation. What's that they say? Consider the source? Take it with a grain of salt? Maybe the lunatics aren't running the asylum outright, but, the rest of the world isn't very inclined to believe us when we try to tell them we're not crazy anymore.

We're not.

We're fine now. We're better. We're cured.

As long as we continue our treatments. That's why we can't leave. If we do, we'll revert. We'll go back to the way we were before. Nothing else will work for us. Nothing else has. Medication, ECT, behavioral modification plans, everything short of old-school lobotomies... been there, done that, no use.

Others have tried. They've decided that, hey, since they're cured, there's no need to stay. No need to continue treatment. Certainly no need to stay locked in the loony bin. You see that all the time, even with people who aren't suffering psychiatric disorders. They don't follow the full course of antibiotics, they stop taking pills as soon as the symptoms go away, and they treat the dosage instructions as optional. They sign themselves out of the hospital against medical advice. We all think we know best.

We're wrong.

Some choice, huh? Between madness and seclusion. Between a sane life in Evergate and a real life in the real world.

Here, we can be normal. We have clarity of thought. Focus. Freedom from the voices and hallucinations, the delusions. We can function. We can have valid interpersonal relationships.

We also contribute to the slow but inexorable downfall of humanity.

What kind of argument is that, in making a case for not being crazy?

Oh, we're not crazy anymore, because our doctor is a warlock cult-leader who's guiding us in rituals to siphon off our madness and funnel it through a psychic vortex…

Why, yes, that seems perfectly sane and reasonable, doesn't it?

But it's true.

So much for credibility, right? So much for proving I'm *not* delusional.

Doctor Hasturn doesn't *claim* to be a warlock. Or a cult-leader, for that matter. We don't wear robes. We don't shave our heads – ha, wouldn't that be fittingly absurd?

When we go to the mindhouse for our sessions, it is cognitive meditation and structured group glossolalic therapy.

Otherwise known as: we sit in a circle and chant.

Not in any actual language. They're just nonsense syllables, made-up words. Like mantras. They don't mean anything.

Except they do.

They have power.

Did I tell you earlier about hearing the stars scream terrible words that would kill people or drive them insane if uttered aloud?

It's kind of like that.

Power. Those sounds have power.

Yagth amur fthagn yagthos rullos orann'ti.

See?

Thig'alla haroun, haroun ob ik'shmai.

Do you feel it?

The shiver?

The power?

But the words… they aren't words. That's what glossolalia is. Sometimes known as 'speaking in tongues.' Though it isn't the kind of holy-roller frenzy you might be imagining. We aren't transported into states of euphoria or manic religious ecstasy. No angels, no sobbing, no wild hallelujah choirs, no stigmata.

We just… chant.

Doctor Hasturn doesn't preach, doesn't sermonize. The mindhouse isn't a church, strictly speaking. We don't have the usual trappings associated with ceremonies – candles, chalices, idols, relics. We don't drink wine. We don't perform blood-sacrifices or burn incense or have orgies.

There are books, sure. Books, but not Bibles. Not hymnals or tracts. An entire shelf of books, with worn leather bindings and gilt-edged pages gone yellowed and brittle from age. The covers are embossed, stamped with symbols and sigils. A few have titles in what appears to be some sort of crude, bastardized Latin. *Librios Turpis Atroxi*, for instance. And *Valde Vetus Res*. Others … others I can only guess at the pronunciation, let alone the meaning. *Zsossonoggos U'trys Deighrn,* and *Cthlotha Fthagnd.*

I suppose it *has* been a church, at times, in its fashion, the mindhouse. It was originally constructed as a private family chapel. You know how it is with these places. Starts off as a mansion built by a land baron or railroad tycoon, gets converted to a hotel, maybe repurposed as a military academy, turned into a hospital, used as a relocation center during World War II, remodeled into a boarding school, rented out for writers' and artists' retreats, and so on.

Yes, Evergate's gone through a lot of incarnations over the years. Additions, outbuildings, updates to the plumbing and wiring, periodic redecoration. But, always, at the heart of it, at the core of it, the mindhouse. Unchanged.

Nathan has read up on it. The house, the history. The Evergates themselves and the mysteries surrounding what happened to them, back in the 1900s or whenever it was. He's been here quite a bit longer than I have. You'd recognize his full name if I told you. They still hold memorials on the anniversary, you know.

He's not proud of it, his notoriety, what he did, the people he hurt that day, the lives he ruined. He hates to think about it. Like with me and the hair-pulling, what he believed seemed real to him at the time. He was certain that he was doing the right thing. Now, he knows how insane he was.

If anyone from outside saw Nathan now, they'd evaluate him and determine him fit to stand trial. He'd be sent to prison... where the effects of the mindhouse would gradually wear off. They'd be punishing a madman for deeds beyond his control.

It's one of the hardest parts about the therapy sessions... cringing at the now-clear recollections of your worst moments, your most painful choices and shameful actions. Having to confront and live with your own inescapable past.

Our illnesses, Doctor Hasturn says, can only *explain* our behaviors. Not *excuse* them. We can't look to others for forgiveness or absolution. We can't look to a benevolent God. There is no moral order to the world, and society's efforts to establish laws and justice are only feeble, crumbling bulwarks against the capricious entropy of chaos.

We are agents of it, that chaos. The very prevalence of insanity is a sign that we are on its path, a steepening speeding downward spiral into the abyss. As a species, we are mad. We always have been. In some of us, the madness is to an extent and of an excess that it can be tapped. It can be drawn off and channeled.

That's why we hold our sessions in the mindhouse. Something about the design of it serves as a prism, an amplifier. I've no idea why, or how; I don't understand the architecture of it, but it's curiously fascinating.

It's an odd-shaped space, situated where several of the mansion's other walls come together at angles that somehow don't add up. The roof tilts in uneven wedges toward an off-center peak; if you gaze up at it too long, the lines of the ceiling panels start to look like the strands of a web spun by a psychotic spider. I often wonder how they did that, whoever designed the room, whoever built it.

Of course, that might just my own ignorance speaking. Someone who's studied such things might look at it and find it simplicity itself. Then again, I could be wrong; maybe it would perplex even an expert. Maybe it'd pose a real challenge, a real puzzle. I guess that's far much more your department than mine. You are the educated one, after all. You'd probably take one look and be able to explain the mindhouse's peculiar geometric effects in the same way you could those of the House-of-Mystery varieties of tourist trap.

But I honestly believe there's more to it than that, than mere tricks of vertigo-inducing perspective and proportion. More than optical illusions and subliminal suggestions in the décor.

The floor's done in tiny mosaic tiles, worn and faded along the paths where people walk, but at the edges it's still as vibrant as the day it was installed. As with the ceiling, the longer you look at the random design, the more it seems to form patterns... indiscernible patterns with meanings that can't quite be grasped.

There are windows, but they don't admit daylight. None of the frames are the same size, and none of the panes have straight edges. Some of the glass is clear and some clouded, or frosted nearly opaque. The stained glass portions are jewel-toned, marbled, and swirled. They glow, as if from within, as if by their own eerie, eldritch illumination.

The mindhouse's acoustics are as peculiar as the rest of it. Sometimes a whisper will resonate like a gunshot; sometimes the loudest shout vanishes into thin air. It might be silent as a tomb at midnight in that room, or the very space itself might hum with a sourceless vibration, a deep bass-note from everywhere and nowhere. Footsteps echo as if the space beneath is a hollow chasm... or they thud as if on solid ground... or they are swallowed up as if absorbed.

Occasionally, we hear chimes. Silvery, horrible, musical yet atonal chimes. A few times, it's seemed like distant voices answer back, murmuring in multitudes. Once – thankfully, just that once – we heard a wet, heavy grunt and a slithery shifting I could have done without.

You might think that it's a weird, creepy place for asylum inmates to be brought for groups, and you'd be absolutely right. As crazy as I was my first time there, I wasn't so crazy as to realize that it very much was *not* the typical setting of durable stain-resistant carpet, fluorescent lighting, and folding chairs. No. I'd seen plenty of rooms of *that* kind before. The mindhouse was different, very different, right from the first.

Similarly, Doctor Hasturn is *not* the kind of psychiatrist I'd typically encountered before arriving at Evergate. Tall and slender, pinch-faced... jaundiced of aspect and bloodshot of eye, as the poets might put it... nothing of the caring, kindly counselor or the wise, nodding sage here. We never talk about our mothers, or our unresolved issues with potty-training and fears of abandonment. We don't discuss our anxieties or neuroses; lines like "mm-hmm and how does that make you *feel?*" are never said.

Dreams, though, we do discuss. Dreams, according to Doctor Hasturn, are the secret speech of the universe. They aren't to be analyzed with trite symbolism, nothing so new age or Jungian as that. They are deeper messages, far deeper than the sub- or unconscious. They are from beyond, from outside, from the primal currents of the under-psyche.

In the dreams, sometimes, the nonsense syllables of our glossolalic therapy chants aren't such nonsense after all. They begin to seem like words, like a language just beyond our comprehension. I've asked the others and we all agree... they're almost within grasp. Almost.

And sometimes – when Doctor Hasturn has cots brought into the mindhouse, to conduct sleep-studies on us there – sometimes the dreams become much more than dreams. Much *other* than dreams.

Once...

I won't say it was a vision, because that *would* be insane. But it *was* very vivid, the most vivid dream I've ever experienced. Tangible. Tactile. Each sensation true to my senses, so real in its unreality, so unreal in its reality.

I heard the chimes, ringing and clinking, pure as glass, dull as bones. Papery reeds, thin as spider-legs, hissed a susurration in a hot and airless breeze. I felt the dry, pebbled ground beneath my bare feet, my steps kicking up gritty puffs of yellow dust. It smelled sour. Sour and yellow and old. Tickling my nose. The taste of it settling, dry, so dry, on my tongue. The screaming stars wheeled above me, unfamiliar and hideous constellations viewed through a murky-green veil of sky like dead sea-water. What passed for a sun hung bloated and pustulant above an endless horizon, silhouetting the corroded ruins of some ancient city.

Or palace.

Or temple.

Or tomb.

Doctor Hasturn questioned me extensively when I awoke. Had I seen anyone? Spoken to anyone? Were there landmarks I could name? Had there been any living thing besides the papery reeds? Could I plot a star-chart of those strange constellations?

I later learned from Nathan that I was not the first to have such a dream. In his, there'd been a road, cart-tracks having worn ruts in the dirt, and a pile of stacked stones like a mile-marker. Some of the others had glimpsed sticklike figures moving in the distance, wearing tattered garments of coarse brown cloth.

It doesn't *mean* anything, of course. They weren't actual visions of an actual, real place. Let's not go nuts, here. Subliminal suggestion, mass hallucination, any of that's unsettling enough without...

Though, now that I think about it, Doctor Hasturn did start questioning me even before I'd really begun describing my dream. Pressing for specific details about things I don't remember mentioning. Asking if I'd noticed marks on my skin, for instance, painted symbols, or designs like henna tattoos.

If dreams *are* messages...

And messages have to come from *somewhere*...

If the mindhouse is the focal channeling point of a psychic vortex, as Doctor Hasturn says, then what is on the other side?

On the *outside*?

Outside of ourselves, outside of everything?

What else might be there?

What... entities?

What feeds upon our mental chaos?

Nothing good, I can tell you that much.

Dark forces? Evil powers? Otherworldly elder beings who will one day shatter the dimensional barriers, enslaving or destroying us all?

Whatever happens, it'll take far longer than our meager human lifetimes to reach the tipping point. Therefore it isn't *our* problem, right? Because we're such small and insignificant portions of the greater scheme of things. From the big-picture perspective, I mean.

From our individual, personal perspectives...

It takes away our madness. We have our own minds again, our own thoughts and lives and souls and selves.

Yet we're helping to empower and strengthen something. Something dangerous. Destructive. Something *other*. Something *Outside*. Each contribution, however slight, pushes this world toward the brink. The clearer we get, the closer we all come... the closer to crossing that threshold.

Save our sanity, doom humanity.

Kind of catchy.

If horrible.

I know how this sounds. How crazy it all sounds. But I'm not crazy. Not now. Not anymore. My symptoms haven't just been managed with medication or suppressed by behavioral tricks. They're gone. *Gone.*

I'm not expecting you to believe me. I'm not asking for your forgiveness.

I just want someone to know. To understand why we do this. Why we want, and *need*, the mindhouse.

Besides, it's not like there aren't others. Other mindhouses, situated at key points around the globe. A dozen more, at least.

It's still not enough, though. When I think of all the people out there, suffering like I did... when I think of the families torn apart like ours was... when I think of all that pain, all that torment...

Wouldn't it be wonderful to be able to help them?

To restore their sanity? To heal them? To spare anyone else from having to go through what I've endured? I know I'd want to do what I could. I'm sure you would, too.

The thing is, *you* could. If you wanted to.

Doctor Hasturn showed me the articles you've written, the papers you've had published in the leading journals. You're about to embark upon a brilliant international career, sure to make a lasting and memorable mark.

They're calling you a prodigy, you know. The most innovative, intuitive and accomplished young architect of our time.

You should definitely come to Evergate for a visit. I'd love to see you again. I'm so proud. And, who knows? Maybe you'll pick up a few new ideas.

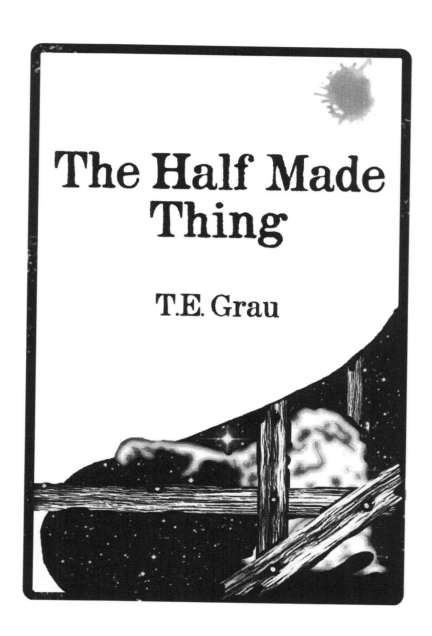

The Half Made Thing

T.E. Grau

THE HALF MADE THING
By T. E. Grau

"Let us sing, let us sing,
Of the Half Made Thing."

Miles of rolling green rose and fell under a tight vest of mist that almost seemed alive with the way it clung with purpose to the low parts of each valley, every creek bed, and sudden crevasse marked by dead Roman wall. These were clouds jealous of the earth, who came to dwell amongst man in this lonely part of Northumberland, and were therefore assigned living qualities. Moods, quarrels, secret pacts. You could tell the weather by the fog, the locals said, and sometimes the future. Today the mists said nothing.

Through this veil of milky white burst a pair of muscled mares, froth flecking the rounds of their massive jawlines. Mudded haunches churned like pistons as they careened down a winding country road first hewn by occupying Norsemen that could accommodate only one vehicle at a time, which presently was a dark green carriage, accented in gold and piloted by a cloaked figure leaning expertly into his task.

Up ahead, a herd of sheep trundled from the fog and crossed the path, bumping into each other and mewling softly. The horses didn't slow a step as they charged into the flock, which parted like a woolen sea of terrified sideways pupils and bleating tongues. One goat emerged from the group and stared defiantly at the carriage as it sped by.

Horseshoes forged from Birmingham iron clattered upon worn, black flagstones. Plumes of steam shot from the horse's nostrils as the carriage came to a stop in front of a towering English mansion. Built a millennium past, it was more castle than home, covered in browning, ill-tended ivy and shrouded by that dank mist which remained unmoved by the cold North Sea wind blowing in from the coast.

The carriage door banged open, and from it emerged Thomas Nevill, a once handsome man worn to sinew and worry by years of backbreaking labor in East London mills. He chafed inside his velvet waistcoat and baggy breeches, scratching at the lank, bone-colored wig that topped his high forehead, as if still adjusting to the stiffness of finery. The costume of a dandy.

His shiny buckled shoes slipped on the damp stone as he eagerly lowered the carriage stair, and with a dangerous creak to the axles, out stepped Marsila, Nevill's short, stout, shockingly ugly new bride. Not even a thick layer of white pancake makeup could cover the pits and moles that assaulted her distended face, punctured by a pair of close-set yellow eyes that added a piggish quality to the horsiness of her appearance. She adjusted her towering, pink-tinged wig, looked at the mansion with her deep set eyes and grinned, exposing a tiny row of rotted teeth. A fly buzzed around her mouth.

Nevill offered an arm to his wife, and they walked toward the house without a glance behind them, as Elias, a lean, eleven year old boy, hopped down from the carriage and gazed up at the towering manse with large brown eyes. He obviously resembled his mother... a mother lost far to the south.

Elias looked back at the carriage driver, who watched him beneath the folds of his cloak, only the tip of his long nose providing evidence of a face underneath. After several moments of nothing passing between the two, Elias shoved his hands deep into his pockets and trudged away, veering away from the door and heading toward the back garden. Behind him, the horses stamped their hooves on the flagstones, the impact ringing like gunshots sucked into the gloom that hid the Sun above.

The tall grass snaked against Elias' feet, soaking his trousers and tripping him up. He stepped high and pushed through, inspecting the overgrown grounds along the side of the house. The trees looked too large, and not native to the British Isles, propped up on bloated tubers that gathered above the ground, providing hiding places within the tangle of roots. Great explosions of unruly shrubbery stood uncut for what must have been decades, and seemed to take the shape of monstrous, unformed creatures.

Suddenly feeling exposed, Elias moved closer to the house, running his hand along the greenish stone textured with the play of ancient lichens. Coming upon a salt frosted window, he peered inside, framing his eyes with his hands to block out the murky, diffused sunlight smeared gray by the fog. He saw nothing on the other side of the pane. Just a greasy darkness, veined with the swirl of memories that had nothing to do with him or his father.

In the sprawling back garden, accented by randomly placed trees and weathered statuary, Elias crunched through a dead flowerbed and stubbed his toe on a stone half buried in the sandy soil. Angry, he tore the stone from the ground and heaved it at a window on the second floor, puncturing the glass in a perfect silhouette of the rock, but not shattering the window. Nevill's frowning face appeared above the hole, his expression cold. Elias looked down at the buckles on his wet shoes, a matching pair to Nevill's, purchased by another family's money. The boy remembered when his father would have thrashed him for such a transgression. Since the wedding, he only received that same, hollow look. Elias peered up at the window, but his father was gone. The boy searched for another rock.

Elias moved from room to dusty room, each one darkened by thick, pea green curtains drawn across the windows. All the furniture was covered by white sheets, like the lumpen mummies of fallen Titans. Each room, all the same. All furnished with the belongings of strangers. All covered in funeral shrouds.

Upstairs, he stood in the doorway of a cramped bedroom, smaller than the rest of the rooms. Servants' quarters, most likely. The shattered hole in the window let in a breeze, which set the sheets flapping and undulating like white tentacles of jellyfish. There was other movement, too, but they were vague, only detected from the corner of his eye. Anything regarded directly was still. Elias smiled and dropped his bag next to the rock on the floor, surrounded by broken glass. This would be his bedroom, marked as it was. Elias believed in such signs, things that weren't taught in mass. The way he saw it, one didn't argue with the destiny of stone.

Lying on the floor of the second story hallway, Elias bounced a canvas ball off of the fresco painted on the paneled wall across from him, aiming for the comically large codpiece of a hulking jester set amid an odd Renaissance party scene populated by forest creatures dancing with their human companions. The clown's four-pointed belled hat rose like sweeping horns above his head, a forked tongue lolling from his grinning mouth. Elias threw the ball at the wall, finding its mark, and the ball bounced back into his hand each time. He did this over and over, the dual thud of the ball finding a measured rhythm.

"Boy!" his father's voice shouted from somewhere lower in the house.

Elias caught the ball and held his breath, waiting for an admonishment, but none came. In the silence, the thud of the ball echoed back at him. Two beats at a time. Like a sluggish heartbeat.

Half tempted to toss the ball again to arouse his father's once-famous temper, Elias instead rolled the ball down the long hallway leading to the other end of the house, lit by a series of thin, ineffectual windows that fought to keep out slivers of pale light. The ball rolled along quickly, moving in and out of the rays of white, then suddenly stopped, half illuminated, half in the dark. Elias found this curious.

He got to his feet, walked to the ball on damp socks and picked it up. It felt suddenly heavier, like a cannon ball, and he struggled to bring it to his chest. He looked it over, and found it no different than when he had tossed it moments before. Readjusting his feet under the weight, the floor underneath him gave a little. He poked it with his toe, and found the boards pliable, soft. Elias dropped the ball, and it buried itself an inch into the wood. There was a shift behind him, and he shot a look back at the fresco on the wall, and found that the painting had changed, as it now showed the animals tossing the humans into a hole in the ground. And still the horned jester danced and grinned, his tongue wagging at the horrified faces of the figures falling into the earth. Before he could inspect this, a shadow passed across the slatted windows. He walked to one of the openings, turned his head to the side, and looked outside.

It was a view of the back estate grounds, but from a higher vantage point than he had earlier. The expanse of garden dotted with carved figures stretched to a foreboding stand of forest about quarter mile from the house. Something large jutted up from the ground in the middle, like a pointing fist. Beyond that, at the forest's edge, a stone and plank gristmill crumbled on the shores of a sludgy, nearly dead stream. Its ancient wheel, draped in algae, turned slowly.

In the dining room later that night, a brightly colored pinwheel spun in Elias' hand, reflecting as identical spirals in his brown eyes. His mother had bought it for him in Brighton when he was just a wee lad. Half the size he was now, and smaller still by four. Elias blew on it, watching it spin, finding something in the whirling, almost smelling the perfume of his mother's hair in the feeble breeze it provided.

"Boy!" Nevill barked.

Jarred from his reverie, Elias peered down to the far end of a ridiculously long table, where his father glowered at him, embarrassed. He was always embarrassed these days, ashamed of himself and his son and his dead wife and everything the three of them had been before meeting the woman who had asked him to marry her after knowing him for two months. Elias put the pinwheel down. Marsila was seated at the head of the table. Nevill was to her right, more handmaiden than husband.

"I asked you to thank your mum for..." Nevill looked at Marsila for prompting, and she mouthed the words to him. "Our lovely new home," Nevill finished, grinning with the accomplishment of a dimwit successfully reciting a nursery rhyme.

"Thank you," Elias said.

"Mum," Nevill said, finishing a sentence Elias would never, ever think, let alone say.

Elias looked at his father, who gripped his fork in a shaking hand, then at Marsila, who watched him with a curious expression. Finally, Elias sighed. "Mum."

Nevill nodded and tucked into his meal, sawing at the slab of meat on his oversize plate. Marsila continued to watch Elias, draining a goblet of dark wine, sediments cascading down the side of the garish blue glass. The trio looked tiny at the enormous table, which in turn looked miniscule set amid this sprawling dining chamber, its vaulted ceiling stretching two stories above them. Murals of naked humans frolicking with leering, piping satyrs covered the frescoed panels between massive wooden beams. The domestic help, silent and expressionless, deposited food and drink, and at an imperious wave from Marsila disappeared into the darkness of the house. Elias tried to learn their faces, and hopefully their names, but he found that as soon as they left his vision, they also left his mind, and he couldn't remember nor distinguish between any of them.

Elias picked up a fork, and looked down at the whole fish staring up at him from his plate. Nothing had been removed prior to cooking, nor afterwards, and aside from the boiled smell, Elias half-expected the gawking creature to leap from the plate and flop its way toward the nearby sea. Hacking loudly and sucking a collection of mucous down her throat, Marsila stuffed a napkin into the front of her many layered dress and tore into her roasted game hen, chewing through bone and gristle and dangerously undercooked meat. Nevill dabbed at the marrow and juices that dribbled down her chin as Marsila grunted at him with pleasure, like a sow at the trough.

"Father," Elias said, trying to distract himself, or them, or everyone at once. "I saw a curious building at the edge of the forest."

"How's that?" Nevill muttered, not looking down the table at his son.

"I said," Elias called, cupping his hands around his mouth, "I saw an old building in the far grounds, by the forest. It had a big wheel."

Nevill tried to feed Marsila a boiled carrot, but she slapped it from his hand. "The old gristmill," she said, stuffing her mouth full of fowl. "Put up before my family took over this land."

"Bloody Vikings, I reckon," Nevill said.

Marsila snorted. "Norsemen couldn't properly wipe their arses, let alone build something like that. The mill be Pictish made."

"It looked quite interesting, father, and I was thinking it would be—"

"—Stay away from it, boy," Marsila said, spitting out a splinter of bone. "The planks are old and rotten. You could fall through and end up God knows where."

"But—" Elias began.

"—You heard your mother, boy!" Nevill snapped.

Elias hadn't heard his mother. He hadn't heard her voice in a long, long time, and realized with a pang of sadness that he had forgotten the sound of it, just remembering the music. The pitch and cadence, the rich and slightly sad laughter, that was unlike any other voice on Earth. It was a beautiful sound, like a violin played in a minor key. He closed his eyes and started to hum, as Marsila watched Elias with a strange, decayed grin. He looked down at his fish, which was now on the tablecloth, several feet away. A zigzagging trail of slime led from the plate.

Elias got up from the table. He'd go to bed hungry that night, even if the breach in etiquette earned him the belt. He'd welcome it at this point, if it meant a return to the old days. The familiar comfort of paternal attention. Nevill didn't notice him leaving the room.

Elias lay in bed, continuing to hum tunelessly while staring at the wood grain on the ceiling, lit by a blue moon outside that had somehow wormed its way through the mist that seemed to shrink away from the sky at night, as if it knew it wasn't needed then. He stopped humming as the patterns of the wood began to quiver, then morph into something more than just striations in dead trees. He shrank into the heavy covers while the figures above grew into a canopy of beasts and winged demons, dancing, clutching at each other, copulating. Eating each other and giving birth to something new and then eating what was born.

Elias tore his eyes away and stared at his bedpost, counting backwards from 100, as his mother had always taught him during thunderstorms. A strange, geometric pattern had been carved deep into the chestnut. Elias traced it with his fingers, the disjointed melody inside his head beginning to find their notes.

Dawn crept hesitantly over the land, fighting in vain through the briny mist that had arisen with the Sun. Groups of sheep huddled on the damp hills, moving away from the mansion that bled smoke into the sky from only one of its many chimneys.

Under this smokestack, in the master bedroom, a rail of low flames played over a stack of damp logs that smoldered and spit in the massive fireplace, as if the wood repelled the heat. On the four post bed big enough to sleep a family of Irish, Marsila roughly pushed Nevill off of her with a wail and a burst of surprising strength.

"Stop pawing at me!" she said, her skin now greenish and loose under the ever-present pancake makeup in the strange morning light. Her stumpy shape was almost swallowed up by the swirl of her poofy nightgown.

Nevill bounced off the bed and landed heavily on the floor, his sleeping robe billowing around him. "But lovie, we're married now."

"But lovie, we're married now," she whined, mocking his voice. "Stop sniveling, you worm."

"Aren't we..." he began, losing his nerve as she fixed him with a withering glare from deep inside her face. He lowered his voice. "Aren't we going to... consummate?"

Marsila laughed, a phlegmy, guttural sound. Nevill's head drooped. She continued to laugh, covering her mouth, when she abruptly went silent, jerking her head to the bedroom door. Elias stood in the doorway, watching them. Marsila raised a finger and pointed at the boy, her eyes narrowing to slits, nearly buried inside the folds of made-up skin. "Sneak."

Nevill ran to Elias, gesticulating awkwardly. "Get outside!" he roared, slamming the door in his son's face. Elias smiled.

Elias walked with purpose through the back garden grounds, putting distance between himself and the house. He had a satchel lashed across his back, stuffed with a candle, matches, a notebook and pencil, two butter sandwiches, a butter smeared table knife, and a jar of milk. These were his expedition supplies, and the mill would be his Everest. At least for today.

As he marched through the tall grass, feeling every bit the junior naturalist in this exotic new land that was now his home, he made brief note of the insects, the pairing of birds, the scuttle of unseen creatures hidden beneath the brome. Mostly, he marveled at the menagerie of weird statuary that dotted the grounds, appearing in strange places and reposing at odd angles. All were built by uncut yet precisely stacked black obsidian stones, veined with green and gold. The figures were shaped in fantastic, half human configurations. Bare breasted women with the heads of jackals. A hunched man with spiders for hands. Octopi that walked on two legs. A circus of freakishness set in arranged, foreign stone, trussed tight with layers of dead vines that seemed to restrain them as much as hold them to the ground.

Past the collection of statues, the front prow of an ancient ship jutted up from the ground, as if jammed backwards into the earth in the planet's early days. The ship had a primitive, boxy construction, obviously from an antediluvian era long forgotten in the civilized world. Either this structure was the work of some mad Northumbrian eccentric or was an important archeological find laid bare by the elements. Whatever it was, it was most certainly abandoned to the weeds and insects of this untended estate.

At the furthest end of the property, marked by a low wall of smooth stones, Elias forded a marshy gully, then climbed a hillock covered in miniature while lilies. Cresting the hilltop, he looked down at the decaying watermill, backed by a forest of sagging trees that seemed to be curling in on themselves. The structure was built on rough-cut castle stones, topped by gray wood planks on which grass had grown on the dust and desiccated wood that had built up into a proper layer of soil over the generations. The stream under the notched waterwheel was brackish, choked with an unnatural abundance of reeds and soupy green algae.

Nothing moved. This was a dead machine.

Although the watermill was unremarkable in general appearance, looking like any of the thousands of mills anywhere in the English countryside, there was a feeling of foreboding emanating from the whole, leaking through the knot holes and gaping windows, slithering out through the foundation and poisoning the stream with overgrown fertility. It seemed somehow unholy, this collection of sawed wood and iron, which only quickened Elias' pace in time with his heart.

He climbed the limestone slab stairs and stopped at the oaken door that didn't seem as old or decayed as the rest of the building. Arcane carvings covered the door, which was fastened to the frame by two-inch thick iron hinges, girded by a system of locks and deadbolts. Weathered and worn smooth by a thousand generations of hands, it looked like it hasn't been opened in centuries. Elias tried the handle, and to his surprise, it opened easily with an audible pop, releasing a waft pungent, moist air tinged with smells of the earth and rot and vermin feces. The boy stepped inside.

His eyes adjusted slowly in the muted light that cut in from outside, cutting the darkness like pinhole spotlights from tiny perforations in the roof and walls. The room was mostly empty, cluttered here and there with the remains of rusted out, primitive equipment and broken tools. The drive shaft, as big around as a tree trunk, had been snapped in half and lay next to a ruined lantern gear, dissolved on one side, the metal dripping down onto the floor and through it like melted wax. One of the enormous flat millstones, as perfectly round as a biscuit, was snapped in half and tossed into the corner of the room. The other had cut a perfectly round hole through the floorboards, and must have come to rest in a level below. Elias took a step toward the aperture, amazed by the clean lines of its circumference, when the boards beneath his feet creaked and bowed, sinking his feet into the wood. Just like in the house. He was now the ball, stitched canvas, stuffed with all manner of spongy material. Elias froze - not from the sensation of sinking into mostly solid wood, but because he had looked up and saw the same dizzying spiral patterns that were carved into his bedpost, decorating the roof with a burst of beautifully bizarre geometry set incongruently in this roughhewn building.

Elias' head bent backwards on a jellied neck and his mouth parted as he lost touch with his body. He felt himself unraveling with the pattern from his marrow outward, swirling into it like a cloud of unstrung particles. Sand through a pinwheel. He reached up, wanting to touch it, this terrible dance of shape and angle, when the floor gave way under his feet and he fell into the darkness below.

After what seemed like an eternity spent drifting in between shadowy places he didn't know existed and certainly were neither heaven nor hell, Elias jerked back into his body and sat up slowly, realizing that he had been knocked unconscious and was now partially cocooned in thick cobwebs. The pack had broken his fall, and he, in turn, had broken everything inside of it, as evidenced by the circle of milk that had spread out behind him on the dirt floor like a pool of ivory blood. Embarrassment hit him before the pain, but both combined to produce a groan as he slowly rose to his feet, coughing and pulling off the webbing and wiping the dust from his eyes. He blinked up at the break in the floor above him, and began figuring the odds that a ladder was stashed somewhere in this dank basement when a sound stopped him cold... A choking gurgle, a scratching from somewhere in the darkness ahead of him. Seeing nothing, Elias felt the weight of a presence leaden the air, tightening the blackness around the boy, sucking the breath from his lungs as the hair on his neck prickled.

Elias squinted with one eye into the darkness and saw... something. A squat, quivering shape, huddled in the corner of the basement, slavering wetly and shifting its amorphous bulk. In the dim light, it was hard to make out details, but it seemed to be a large lump of flesh gathered together in a vaguely human configuration. A torso set on flipper-like feet. A knotted appendage - a sort of unformed arm - reached out to Elias, with two droopy fingers flexing and grasping.

Elias fell backwards, scrambling over gnawed animal bones and bits of dried fur toward the wall built of bricks as tall as a man. There was no way out. He was stuck down here, with... it.

The fleshy hump waddled forward, as a moan shook free from the thing. An opening appeared on the top part of the shape. Inside writhed a thick, fleshy worm... Not a worm - a tongue, surrounded by rows of cut ribs that formed three rows of teeth. An utterance bubbled from within it: an unpracticed voice, muffled and wet, drowning inside itself. "Wwwww....iiiill..?" the thing gurgled.

Elias covered his ears. The sound was too terrible to hear.

"Wiiill... yooou...?" it continued, battling through malformed flesh and fluid to form recognizable words.

Elias removed his hands from the sides of his head, curious by what had become recognizable human speech.

"Will you... siiing...?"

Elias was terrified, confused, but also captivated, for before him squatted something out of books, nightmares. "W-W-What?" he stammered.

"Will you... sing?" The creature's voice became stronger, better defined. "Will you sing?" The thing shambled forward one step, its topside mouth firming around the words, body quivering with anticipation. "Of the... Half Made Thing?"

"I... don't..." Elias whispered, unable to put into words what was happening in his brain, as his perception of what was reality and what was fairy tale suddenly inverted.

"I... do," the thing said.

Elias found himself moving toward the creature, his heels carving grooves into the dirt. Nearing it, he reached out a hand and touched the thing, resting a palm on the sticky skin. A painful burst of images tunneled their way into Elias' already swirling head. Impressions etched in secreted years flashed behind Elias' eyes, branding those corners of the mind that transcended sight and dwelt in the halls of memory: The stink of noxious chemicals. Bubbling decanters. Jars of powder, ash, salts. Chants of necromancy. Inexplicable equations written in blood. An invitation screamed out into the void. The rending of matter, tearing of dream. A roar, a roar, a chorus of roars. Alchemy of the flesh. A consciousness sucked back into the light from the screaming abyss...

All at once, Elias knew how and why this thing came to be, and why it remained yet undone. Elias' legs failed him and crumpled back onto the floor, his eyes wide, brain now teeming with arcane knowledge born in darker days of a blasphemous past erased from the visible libraries of the world. He wanted to tear at his hair, peel off his skin. Instead, he just wept, without knowing exactly why. For the loss of innocence, perhaps, or of sanity. Everything had been a lie, and he was ashamed at his ignorance.

"Will you... help me?" it said. A bloodshot eyeball emerged from the mass of slimy flesh. Elias turned his head to face the thing. The cyclopean eye stared directly into the hollow place that once housed Elias' naïve soul, but was now bared to the elements like an open wound. "Will you... finish me?"

Tears streaming down his face, Elias nodded.

The thing shuddered, paused, and exhaled from somewhere deep inside the mass of twisted bone and musculature. Gathering itself, it shuffled over to the wall and threw its bulk against it with surprising strength. The huge bricks shattered and crumbled to the floor, revealing an alcove behind the wall, framed by tree roots leeching down from the forest above them. Elias joined it at the wall and pulled out the broken brickwork, glancing at the patches of hair and pustules covering the back of the thing next to him. Clearing away the last of the masonry from the opening, Elias reached inside and removed an ancient book, perfectly preserved and without a streak of dust marring the dark brown leather covering its front and back. Elias looked at the thing, which seemed to nod without the ability to do so. With shaking hands, Elias carefully opened the book and turned the brittle pages, finding cryptic diagrams, blasphemous images, and unreadable text written in a spidery language. Elias shook his head. "I-I... can't. I... don't..." Words failed him again. This was all too much for a young boy to deal with. For anyone. The thing quivered expectantly. "I will teach you." A grin crept across Elias' face.

Days passed. Leaves on the towering larch and yew trees skipped the color change for the first time in decades and simply browned and fell dead to the earth. The mists outside the house increased, hailing the changing of the season from autumn to winter, which always seemed just due East of the North England coast, held at bay by Saxon magic against the Frost Giants of the great Northern Lands.

Elias spent his days with his personal tutor, a doddering old Scotsman who seemed terrified to contradict the boy or upset him in any way, either by order from the mistress of the house, or out of the reputation her family held in these parts, which Elias quickly learned lay somewhere between grudging respect and visceral horror. Either way, no one came to visit, and his father was constantly traveling with Marsila, or tending to her every ridiculous whim when they were home, leaving Elias hours per day, and every night after dinner, to spend in the mill with his new companion, unloading his satchel with household chemicals, simple tools, and various bits of food scrounged from the rubbish bin.

And the boy used every second to gain his true education, quickly forgetting everything taught to him by the house tutor aside from those slices of arithmetic, physics, Latin, and folklore that he could use to augment what he learned while sitting at the feet of the Half Made Thing, which began to change from useless flippers to nearly full functioning paws that began to look more human by the day, by the lesson, as Elias memorized and recited various incantations. They were having an effect to the point where, one night, as Elias arrived with ever more specific supplies pilfered from the house attic and extorted from his tutor, that which could only be found in the nearby town, the Half Made Thing rose on a pair of rudimentary knee joints. The thing was becoming a man, or something very close to it. The heaving figure that bled mucous and blood from many of its unfinished portions, finally cracked a smile from the middle of an onion-like protrusion, and what passed for a laugh of triumph. The sound chilled Elias, excited him, filling him with a weird sort of pride that he thought must resemble what a father feels when looking at his child. He wondered if his father had ever felt this way about him, and didn't need to wait for the answer.

The following night, the servants solemnly arranged a line of hollowed out turnips carved with fierce expressions on the front landing of the house, placing lit candles inside each one. It was All Hallows Eve, and every good Christian soul across the darkening countryside hurried back to their homes and living quarters and locked their doors tight.

Inside the house, Elias clutched candles of his own and a shaving razor as he crept down the second floor hallway with a full bag of supplies stolen from the local university archives slung over his shoulder. He carried a second, lighter bag in his free hand. He stopped at a sliver of light that cut into the hallway from inside the master bedroom. Strange noises came from within. Growling and barking, interspersed with the shrill, discordant sounds of a shepherd's pipe. Elias moved to the crack in the door and looked inside.

Two women frolicked on the bed. One was obviously Marsila, as evidenced by the full treatment of thick makeup and towering wig cackling from a mound of pillows. The other woman giggled and hopped out of bed, turning toward the door and revealing herself to be Auntie Drearia, explained to a barely listening Elias months ago while going through a book of portraits as Marsila's sister who had taken up residence as a Duchess of some sprawling mountain fiefdom in the Balkans. She was stark naked and pale as a corpse, contrasting starkly with the black hair covering her head and pubic region. Elias felt his face burn, which quickly deepened when his father danced into view. He was dressed as a tart, in full, dramatic makeup and bawdy ball costume. He twirled and blew into a bone flute, browned from age, unleashing a discordant flurry of unrelated notes. It was the song of madness. Marsila sat up and clapped along, as if he was executing the tune exactly as taught. Abruptly, she slapped the flute away and punched him in the mouth. Nevill squealed with ecstasy, picked up his instrument with a bark, and then began playing again, dancing gaily around the room.

In the crack of light, out in the hallway, Elias was gone.

In the back grounds, Elias ran though the statuary, each piece looming high in his path, ready to devour him. He stumbled to his knees and vomited.

He raised his face, wiped away tears from his eyes and flecks of dinner from his lips, and set his jaw. He got to his feet, adjusted his satchel, and walked with purpose toward the hill overlooking the old mill. Elias' shadow loomed large behind him by the light of the full moon beaming from the blackness of a rare, crystal clear night sky.

A match struck and moved to each candle that flared to life in turn, illuminating the floor, where strange, geometric patterns inscribed with grainy chemicals circled both Elias, who was covered by a black robe and cowl, and the Half Made Thing, who sat across from each other.

213

Elias removed the hood of his robe, revealing his shaved head and face, absent hair, lashes, and eyebrows. Without these accents marking his smooth face, he seemed to have no expression at all, and devolved into a wormlike appearance when he closed his eyes and lowered his chin. In a clear voice much stronger than his own, he spoke practiced phrases in a queer, forgotten language, watched by the Thing through two offset eyes bulging from that inverted teardrop protrusion that resembled a head.

"Th'sash nefmus, borelus klaav!" Elias intoned. "Nog ph'shagg, ph'shogg, ph'shugg soth pnokintanus!"

The candles flickered with a sudden breeze, then flared hotly, changing color, casting the room in various hues of blue, green, and finally a sickly yellow and seeped into every nook of the mill basement like a creeping mold.

Elias reached out both hands, adorned with strange, malevolent glyphs, and placed them on the top of the Half Made Thing.

"Ia! Nog gnaiish, 'fhalma, og ftaghu!!"

A rumbling from deep underground shook the foundation of the structure, sending ruined timber raining down from above, bouncing off the protective field erected around the two unhallowed circles.

"Ia! Goka gotha! Nog vulgtm, bug uaah yihah!!"

The jaundiced air shimmered, bent like water. The stone walls slowly heaved outward without cracking, then violently sucked inward, imploding into a black abyss under the ground, clouded with huge, swirling shapes, all watching with an infinite number of eyes...

Elias writhed, as the Half Made Thing bubbled. One crumbled as the other rose. The walls returned to stone. The outside was once again the inside. The candles guttered, sucking the light from the room and downing everything in a smothering darkness.

After several moments, the candles returned to life, casting normal light. The two figures had changed places in stature, as Elias was a quivering blob of flesh, his clothes shredded to rags, while the Half Made Thing towered above him, chest heaving, sucking in air, smelling, tasting the very atoms of this place and time...

The fully formed Thing was terrible and beautiful in its nakedness. A hulking, massive torso covered in mottled skin, powerful limbs, flexing hands. Its face was goatish, but also humanly handsome, its head topped with a crest of flowing tentacles, sweeping up like a mane of horns.

The Thing was fully made. Elias was now unmade by half. A Half Made Thing, to take the place of the other.

The newly made Thing looked down at the Half Made Elias, and cracked a cruel grin, exposing long, sharpened teeth. "It is done."

The Thing stalked from the room, climbing a hidden stairway of stone worn smooth ten thousand years ago, walking upwards, bursting a buried doorway and bursting into the night air. Behind him, in the dank basement, the Half-Made Elias shook and gibbered out of a slimy mouth on the side of his bulbous, unctuous shape. Tears of oily blood streaked from one, lone, horrified eye.

The Thing stalked past the statuary, bowing slightly to each of the creatures depicted in arranged stone. He pushed over a particular statue - one that looked exactly like him. The stones toppled into a mound as he strode onward, its hot breath steaming into the night air like a furnace vent.

In the study, Marsila sat with a drink in her hand, staring into the murky brown liquid, looking spent. Suddenly, she sat up straight and cocked her head to the side, her piggish eyes widening. After a moment, she turned to Nevill.

"What is it, dearie?" he said.

"There's something outside."

The back door creaked open. Nevill, holding a flintlock rifle in one hand and a lantern in the other, crept outside and squinted into the blackness. A rustling of grass came from outside the circle of light. He raised his lantern. "Who goes there?"

The silhouette of the Thing emerged from the veil of night and stood in front of Nevill.

"It is I."

Nevill's jaw dropped, as did the lantern. Before it had even landed on the wet turf, the Thing was on top of him, ripping off his limbs, eating flesh. Marsila stood in the doorway, a stout shadow against the inside light.

The Thing, finished with Nevill and drenched in gore, stalked toward the woman and grabbed her. Marsila screamed. The Thing snatched the wig from her head, exposing two tiny goat-like horns sprouting from amid her nest of tangled, greasy black hair. The Thing wrapped its clawed hands around her neck and brought her face to its mouth. She screamed again, cut off by its mouth over hers, kissing her roughly, blood smearing away the thick makeup, exposing the seams of a fleshy mask that began to loosen over her actual skin, which was mottled and scaly underneath.

In the pre-dawn gloom, the front door opened slowly on its own, and two heavily robed figures, one stumpy and round, the other towering and thick, emerged from the house, knocking over the turnip jack o' lanterns as they passed. The dark green carriage waited for them, and the two massive mares stamped their feet on the cobblestones dampened by the dank mist that had returned, pushed into the land from the frigid North Sea.

The mismatched pair entered the carriage, closed the door, and drew the curtains tight. The hooded driver grinned under his cowl, cracked the reigns, and piloted the carriage up the driveway.

It turned onto the lone dirt road, heading North as it wound up into the fog-shrouded hills, where the sheep huddled, far away from the road and the house and the mill and the Half Made Thing dwelling in the basement, waiting for the Sun that promised never to come.

I.

Let us sing, let us sing
Of the Half Made Thing,
Driven mad from its half birth.
Through enchantment twas born
In half-human form
A creature not fit for this earth.

Pulled from the gloom,
And locked in a room,
The Half Made Thing did wait.
Feasting on rats
Horseflies and bats
His hunger would never abate.

For it longed to taste flesh
Spoiled rotten or fresh
Hewn from the bones of a man.
So whisper it would
Like Elder Things could
And formulated its nefarious plan.

II.

One day, says a legend
Came a boy, aged eleven
Newly arrived from the city.
He crept over hill
Found the old mill
And discovered something not pretty.

He spied a chewed bone
And heard a low moan
Whilst boyish heart raced with fright.
And there in the corner
Huddled a shape quite abnormal
That made truly a horrible sight.

The boy almost screamed
But the thing suddenly leaned
Toward the newly arrived lad by the door.
Then the boy surely knew
That nightmares were true
And was curious to learn so much more.

For this boy was a dreamer
A high thinking schemer
And knew he found something quite grand.
As this was a creature
Not a dime novel feature
But alive and sniffing his hand.

The Half Made thing snuffled
Twisted and shuffled,
As it tried to move on unfinished pegs
But the wizard that made it
Beat, slashed and flayed it
And only half made it down to its legs.

Its skin was half on
Its organs half gone
Its mouth only opening to one side
Teeth framed a snout
And fluids drained out
Yet the thing had only half died.

The boy at the time
Paid it no mind
That the Half Made Thing seemed to know him
For how could he guess
That this creature, this mess
Was one of his own creations so grim.

Now this wretched beast
Only lived on to feast
But of this boy it made not a snack.
As somewhere in deep
A feeling did creep
That a new master had finally come back.

The boy became mage
And so turned a page
As sanity started to flee.
Because in the end
Enemy becomes friend
For the wizard is actually me.

III.
So now I do sing
Of this once Half Made Thing
Fully formed into a whole.
And learned once did I
That mouth, teeth, and eye
Don't mean a thing possesses a soul.

ABOUT THE AUTHORS

William Meikle is a Scottish writer, now living in Canada, with twenty novels published in the genre press and over 300 short story credits in thirteen countries. His work has appeared in a number of professional anthologies and magazines with recent sales to NATURE Futures, Penumbra and Buzzy Mag among others. He lives in Newfoundland with whales, bald eagles and icebergs for company. When he's not writing he plays guitar, drinks beer, and dreams of fortune and glory.

T.E. Grau is an author of dark fiction whose work has appeared in numerous anthologies, including *Tales of Jack the Ripper*, *The Best of The Horror Society 2013*, *Dark Fusions: Where Monsters Lurk*, *World War Cthulhu*, *Suction Cup Dreams: An Octopus Anthology*, *Dead But Dreaming 2*, *The Aklonomicon*, *Urban Cthulhu: Nightmare Cities*, and *Horror for the Holidays*, among others; and such magazines and literary journals as *LA Weekly*, *The Fog Horn*, *Eschatology Journal*, and *Lovecraft eZine*. His two chapbooks, *The Mission* and *The Lost Aklo Stories*, will be published in early 2014 by Dunhams Manor Press. In the editorial realm, he currently serves as Fiction Editor of *Strange Aeons* magazine. T.E. Grau lives in Los Angeles with his wife and daughter, and can be found in the ether at *The Cosmicomicon* - cosmicomicon.blogspot.com

Christine Morgan works the overnight shift in a psychiatric facility, which plays havoc with her sleep schedule but allows her a lot of writing time. A lifelong reader, she also reviews, beta-reads, occasionally edits and dabbles in self-publishing. Her other interests include gaming, history, superheroes, crafts, cheesy disaster movies and training to be a crazy cat lady. She can be found online at www.christine-morgan.org

Josh Reynolds is a professional freelance writer of moderate skill and exceptional confidence. His work has appeared in anthologies such as Miskatonic River Press' Horror for the Holidays, and in places such as Innsmouth Magazine and Lovecraft eZine. In addition to his own work, he has written for several tie-in franchises, including Gold Eagle's Executioner line and Black Library's Warhammer Fantasy and Warhammer 40,000 lines. Feel free to stop by his blog, http://joshuamreynolds.wordpress.com/ to tell him he's wrong about whatever it is you disagree with him about.

Edward M. Erdelac is the author of the acclaimed Judeocentric weird western series Merkabah Rider and the novels Terovolas, Buff Tea, and Coyote's Trail. His work appears in over a dozen anthologies and periodicals including most recently Steampunk Cthulhu, Swords And Mythos, World War Cthulhu, After Death, and Star Wars Insider Magazine. Born in Indiana, educated in Chicago, he now lives in the Los Angeles area with his wife and a bona fide slew of kids and cats. News of his work can be found at http://emerdelac.wordpress.com

John Goodrich endures the horror of retail work, then take his day out on fictional characters. Despite this, he loves life in Vermont, the last haunted bastion of Lovecraft's New England. His weird tales have appeared in *Dead but Dreaming II, Undead & Unbound, Anthology II Inner Demons Out*, the Lovecraft E-Zine, and *Steampunk Cthulhu*. Sample his madness and some free fiction at qusoor.com.

Jeffrey Thomas is an American author of weird fiction, the creator of the acclaimed milieu Punktown. Books in the Punktown universe include the short story collections *Punktown, Voices from Punktown, Punktown: Shades of Gray* (with his brother, Scott Thomas), and *Ghosts of Punktown*. Novels in that setting include *Deadstock, Blue War, Monstrocity, Health Agent, Everybody Scream!* and *Red Cells*. Thomas's other short story collections include *Worship the Night, Thirteen Specimens, Nocturnal Emissions, Doomsdays, Terror Incognita, Unholy Dimensions, AAAIIIEEE!!!, Honey is Sweeter than Blood,* and *Encounters with Enoch Coffin* (with W. H. Pugmire). His other novels include *Letters from Hades, The Fall of Hades, Beautiful Hell, Boneland, Beyond the Door, Thought Forms, Subject 11, Lost in Darkness, The Sea of Flesh and Ash* (with his brother, Scott Thomas), *Blood Society, and A Nightmare on Elm Street: The Dream Dealers*. Thomas lives in Massachusetts.

Scott T. Goudsward is a New England writer, focusing on the horror genre. He began writing, seriously, in 1992. The first short story sale came in 1996 from the vampire anthology *The Darkest Thirst*. His first novel sale based on the short story *Trailer Trash* and was published by Dark Heart Press. Since then Scott has co-authored two non-fiction horror books with his brother, David, edited three anthologies and has had numerous short stories published. Scott is looking forward to many releases due out in 2014, including *Horror Guide to Massachusetts* from Post Mortem Press, *Once Upon an Apocalypse* from Chaosium and several anthologies with his work in them.

Pete Rawlik has been collecting Lovecraftian fiction for forty years. In 2011 he decided to take his hobby of writing more seriously. He has since published more than twenty-five Lovecraftian stories and the novel *Reanimators*, a labor of love about life, death and the undead in Arkham during the early twentieth century. A sequel, *The Weird Company* will be released in the Fall of 2014. He lives in Royal Palm Beach, Florida, with his wife and three children. Despite the rumors he is not now and never has been a member of the Soviet Politburo.

Glynn Barrass lives in the North East of England and has been writing since late 2006. He has written over a hundred short stories, most of which have been published in the UK, USA, France, and Japan. He also co-edits anthologies for Chaosium's *Call of Cthulhu* fiction line, also writing material for their flagship roleplaying game.

Tom Lynch is a longtime devotee of the art of the terrifying tale. He is descended from a line of family that enjoys a good nightmare, so is it any wonder he writes stories with a darker twist? Tom's first fiction appeared in *Horror for the Holidays* from Miskatonic River Press, and he has since appeared in the ever-eldritch *Lovecraft eZine, Tales of the Talisman Volume 8, Issue 4, Undead and Unbound*, and *Eldritch Chrome*. As of this moment, future appearances include *When Darkness Calls, Dark Rites of Cthulhu, Atomic Age Cthulhu: Terrifying Tales of the Cthulhu Mythos,* and a special Carcosa-themed edition of the *Lovecraft eZine*. There are others, but the ink is not yet dry enough to divulge details.

By day, Tom is an elementary school teacher, looking to expand young minds and spends the rest of his spare time hunched over his keyboard writing scary stories.

Brian M. Sammons has been writing reviews on all things horror for more years than he'd care to admit. Wanting to give other critics the chance to ravage his work for a change, he has penned a few short stories that have appeared in such anthologies as *Arkham Tales, Horrors Beyond, Monstrous, Dead but Dreaming 2, Horror for the Holidays, Twisted Legends, Mountains of Madness, Deepest, Darkest Eden* and others. He has edited the anthologies; *Cthulhu Unbound 3, Undead & Unbound, Eldritch Chrome, Edge of Sundown, Steampunk Cthulhu, World War Cthulhu,* and *Dark Rites of Cthulhu*. He is currently far too busy for any sane man. For more about this guy that neighbors describe as "such a nice, quiet man" you can check out his very infrequently updated webpage here: brian_sammons.webs.com and you can follow him on Twitter @BrianMSammons.

Don Webb teaches SF writing for UCLA Extension and has over 70 stories on "Best of" lists since 1986. He has books from St, Martins, Inner Traditions and Wildside Press. He lives in Austin, TX with video artist Guiniviere Webb and two tuxedo cats. Drop him a note at writebydonwebb@gmail.com

Sam Stone is the award-winning author of The Vampire Gene Series. Her latest works include a horror novel, *The Darkness Within*, two Steampunk short novels - *Zombies At Tiffany's, Kat On A Hot Tin Airship* - and a Doctor Who spin off screenplay called *White Witch of Devil's End*.

A prolific and eclectic genre writer, Sam's short fiction has appeared in many collections and anthologies as well as her own collection *Zombies in New York and Other Bloody Jottings*. She is currently working on the second book of a post-apocalyptic trilogy, a modern day crime novel and a Victorian supernatural thriller.

Sam lives in North Wales in a vampire lair under Rhuddlan Castle with her partner David, her daughter Linzi and a Renfield called Frazer.

www.sam-stone.com

CJ Henderson's second published novel was a mythos novel and it seems he never looked back. Creator of supernatural investigators Teddy London and Piers Knight, reviver of Inspector Legrasse and Carl Kolchak, he has had scores more books published as well as hundreds and hundreds of short stories, with many more mythos outings taking place all along the way. He is also the author of *Baby's First Mythos*, an act which was condemned vehemently by more than one aspiring televangelist, but which got a big thumbs up from Jesus the Nazarene, so we think it balances out.

Robert M. Price (Selma, NC), professor of scriptural studies at the Johnnie Colemon Theological Seminary, is the editor (with Jeffery Jay Lowder) of *The Empty Tomb: Jesus Beyond the Grave* and the *Journal of Higher Criticism*. He is also the author of *Top Secret: The Truth Behind Today's Pop Mysticisms; The Paperback Apocalypse: How the Christian Church Was Left Behind; The Reason-Driven Life: What Am I Here on Earth For?* and many other works.

Dr. Price is an editor of Lovecraftian stories, articles/criticism, and introductions, in magazines like the entertaining and essential *"Crypt of Cthulhu"*, and his short stories appear in many volumes of Lovecraftian fiction.